WOLVES' PAWN

P.J. MacLayne

Wolves' Pawn

Copyright © 2014 by P.J. MacLayne

ISBN-13: 978-0-9985014-0-6

Published in the United States of America.

Dedication

To my beloved husband Al, who has to put up with me.

I love you.

ACKNOWLEDGMENTS

Thanks to the many people who helped me
turn my dream into a reality.

To Shanneen, Maggie, and Cornelia Amiri
for your invaluable assistance with grammar,
punctuation, and the story line.

To K.M. Guth for the cover and graphics,
and for putting up with my frequent requests
to experiment with minor details.

To Natalia and Ketty for the insights
you shared in your critiques.

WOLVES' PAWN

Prologue

The spring rain had left puddles in the dirt road but she no longer tried to avoid them. Under other circumstances this would have been a pretty ride. The young pale green leaves not yet entirely covering the branches she brushed by glittered in the sun that had finally chased away the storm clouds. Even the fresh scent of the earth moistened by water was unable to mask the smell of the hot motor between her legs. She didn't know how much longer the bike would last the way she was pushing the engine.

She was being herded; the one corner of her mind not busy trying to figure out how to escape was occupied with analyzing the situation. Her little 250cc Honda motorcycle was no match for the two brutes chasing her, and she had an occasional glimpse through the trees of a third bike traveling parallel to her. It must be one of those dual purpose bikes, because surely no street motorcycle could handle those conditions.

"Escape!" her instincts screamed. But escape—to where? If she ditched the bike and ran, her pursuers would catch up to her in a flash. So hide! But hide where? She anticipated no possibility of a hero coming to her rescue in these remote woods. The dirt road was not much more than a path now and she didn't have any idea how much farther it went.

A sharp curve to the right and an opportunity presented itself. She was momentarily out of sight, so she dropped the bike and rolled into a hollow in the ground covered by a dead tree trunk. It made the barest of shelters, but would have to do. She doubted any of her followers had any skill in tracking, and she hoped none of them carried a gun.

"She's got to be here somewhere," the skinny one shouted as he guided his motorcycle onto the path. "The bike is here, but I don't see her."

"Double back and hunt for her along the road. And look harder," the one with a beard ordered. After the chase, the beard was unkempt, and appeared as if it had been attacked by a flock of birds searching for twigs to build their nests. "She can't have gone far."

"What's the boss want her for anyway?"

"Don't know and don't care. Our orders were to grab her and bring her back...unharmed if possible, and that's all I know."

The lone woman, still sitting on her bike, chimed in, whining. "He said this would be easy. I didn't expect to spend my entire afternoon tramping through the woods trying to find some cunt."

"Shut up and stop complaining," the bearded one snarled. "He's paying us plenty for this job. I don't like it any more than you do, but the sooner we find her the sooner we can get back to the bar." He circled the area, kicking random rocks and tree stumps, while the other man walked back down the road.

Two orange-yellow eyes followed his movements

from behind a thick clump of bushes. Silently, edging one paw forward at a time, the gray wolf moved into position and waited for its chance. The hunters had become the hunted, but they didn't know it yet. The bearded one stood about three feet away, turning in circles and scratching his head when the wolf determined the time was right. In a flash, it struck the man's chest, knocking him to the ground. The wolf ignored the unguarded throat and swiped at the man's face, leaving a trail of bloody claw marks in the right cheek. The man screamed—a high-pitched, little girl sound, and passed out. The woman turned at the yell to see the wolf sitting unconcerned on its victim's chest, licking its paw. It looked right at her and winked. Without a second thought for her companion, she started her engine, turned the motorcycle around, and headed back the way they had come.

"I'm going to have to trade up one of these days," Dot thought as she rode away. She would have to ditch this bike soon, before it got reported as stolen, but that seemed such a shame. For now, she would enjoy the ride, with the wind against her face, and making as much time and distance as she dared.

She needed to get away from West Virginia and into the mountains of Pennsylvania. That was her home turf, and she would hole up there and try to again figure out why she was being chased. She owned nothing of value to be stolen, only her clothes and her ring, and her clothes needed to be washed. Tonight she'd make camp by a creek and rinse them out. Luckily, her ponytail had stayed in its wrappings, so her hair wasn't too much of a mess. Raiding the bearded one's wallet had supplied her with enough cash for gas and a little extra. To go back to her old campsite for the rest of her meager belongings presented too big of a risk.

The biggest problem as always was food. Changing used a lot of energy, and between shifting and the chase she had used up most of her reserves. It was too early in the year for berries, and she had no time to set snares for rabbits or squirrels. No, she would just have to do with whatever she bought from a convenience store. She longed for a rare steak to satisfy the blood lust licking her paw had awakened, but she hadn't found a gas station yet selling them. She sighed. Beef jerky would be on the menu.

Sitting by the barest of fires after dark, she decided the time had come to change her human appearance. Cut her hair short, maybe dye it red. She wondered how that would affect her wolf aspect. She could see the tabloid headlines now. "Rare red wolf spotted in the Allegheny Mountains" and underneath the article would begin "Hunters are requested not to try and capture this animal, but to report its location to the Game and Fish Commission." Then a paragraph speculating on some Native American prophecy. She laughed, a lonely sound in the night woods, leaned against a handy tree, and fell asleep.

ONE

"Order up, Dot." Billy leaned on the counter as the slender young waitress picked up the dishes and arranged them on her arms. Dorothy McKenzie had been working for him for three months now, and had turned into a damn good waitress. The only reason none of the other restaurants in the area had hired her out from under him was her appearance. With her red and yellow streaked hair, she looked more like a punk rocker than the down-home girls they favored. But Billy figured she was only twenty-five and she deserved to have a little fun. As long as the customers didn't mind, he didn't either. And under all the heavy makeup, she was really pretty.

"You okay?" he asked in a much quieter voice as she glanced nervously towards her current customers. It was mid-afternoon, and the three men were the only ones in the diner, except for a couple of truckers sitting at the counter drinking coffee.

"I don't know why, but there is something about them that makes me nervous." Dot shook her head causing the red skull earrings she wore to chatter. They matched the henna design on the back of her hand. "They haven't said or done anything wrong, but I don't like their vibes."

"Their vibes, huh?" Billy grinned and flexed his arm muscles. The dragon tattoos he had gotten during his time in the Navy rippled with the movement. "They give you any trouble and I will show them some vibes."

"Don't worry about it. I'm probably just tired. Didn't sleep good last night." Dot turned away from the kitchen and made her way towards the table balancing the full plates with ease. Giving the men an artificial smile, she leaned over and set their food down. "You gents need anything else?" she asked. "More coffee?"

"Not right now," said the tallest one. Although all three men were dressed in T-shirts and jeans, Dot had pegged the one speaking as being in charge the minute they walked in the door. The other two had deferred to him in choosing a table, and waited until he ordered before placing their own. "Are you from around here?" he asked before she walked away.

"Close enough to count." Dot knew how to get around sharing personal information without being rude. "Why?"

"We heard stories about wolf sightings in the area. We came to investigate."

She cocked her head at him, and, comforted by the chattering sound of her earrings, asked "You guys reporters?"

"No, scientists. Why?"

"We had a reporter in here a week ago. Wanted to write a story for one of those trashy tabloids." She called back to the kitchen. "Billy, you still have Dale's card back there?" she turned back to the men. "Dale is the game warden—excuse me, the Wildlife Conservation Officer in these parts," she said and giggled. "He'll tell you that there hasn't been a wolf in the entire state for over 100 years."

Billy joined her by the table with a business card in his hand. "Coyotes, here and there, but wolves, no," he said. "Don't know where those stories came from, but you aren't the first to get suckered into someone's practical joke." He laid the card down on the table. "Like Dot said, give Dale a call. He'll set you straight."

As they walked away from the customers, Dot laid her hand on Billy's arm. "I'm going to take a quick break. Be right back."

"You okay? Those guys didn't give you a hard time, did they?"

"Heck no. Like I said, I'm just tired. It's a good thing I have the next couple of days off." She headed towards the ladies room, closing and locking the door behind her. She took a deep breath to calm her shaky nerves, leaned on the sink, and stared into the hazy mirror. The face that stared back was familiar, but changed from a few months ago. The hollows in her cheeks had filled out now that she ate regularly, the makeup she wore made her eyes appear bigger, and the spiked hairdo bore no resemblance to the long brown hair she favored. But this was the third group in the past month attracted by rumors of a wolf in the area. It was time to move on. Good thing she got paid yesterday and today's tips promised to be better than average.

She washed her hands and glanced into the mirror again, double checking her appearance. Even in the harsh fluorescent lighting, the brown-colored contacts hid the yellowish tint of her eyes. All elements of her disguise were still in place. She fought down the instinct that screamed "Run!" Once her shift got done, she would load up her meager belongings and disappear. Again.

"So you have big plans for the weekend?" one of the regulars, a trucker, asked as Dot refilled his coffee cup.

She glanced at the table of the three men. Although they had long ago finished the meals, they still sat there, deep in discussion. The prickly feeling at the base of her neck told her they were keeping an eye on her, but she had been unable to catch them staring at her. Every time she walked over to check if they wanted more coffee, the discussion halted abruptly. "Yeah, big plans," she replied. "Wash clothes, catch a movie, paint my toenails." She grinned at the trucker. "Sounds exciting, doesn't it?"

He groaned and took another swallow of his coffee. "You sound like my kid sister."

Good, she thought, if that means I sound younger than I really am. One more thing to throw off the hounds. She put the coffee pot back on its burner, untied her apron as she walked through the swinging door, and then looped it on a hook in the kitchen. "I'm out of here, Billy. Have a good weekend."

"Yep. You too." He glanced out into the dining room. "If those guys leave a tip when they go, it will be waiting for you on Monday."

"Thanks. I'm not counting on it being a big one anyway." She resisted the urge to kiss him on the cheek. He had taken a big risk hiring her and she wouldn't ever be able to thank him properly. At least she wouldn't be leaving him in the lurch...the new girl wanted more hours. "Don't work too hard."

Dot's saddlebags were filled with as many clothes as she could stuff into them, her sleeping bag rolled up and strapped to the sissy bar, and her tank bag held a few other essentials. Her room had been rented by the week, and the note she had slipped into the mail slot of the office would let the landlord know she was gone for good. Her hand beaded medicine bag on its leather strap was safely tucked inside her blouse, nestled between her breasts. Now all she needed to do was gas up the bike. She liked traveling at night because there was less traffic to fight on the roads.

The gas station was busy with people filling up their cars before the weekend. Dot left her helmet on but flipped up the face shield before she started the pump. Pumping the first gallon was easy, but she kept a close eye on the tank after that. She wanted to squeeze as much gas into the bike as possible but hated allowing it to run over. She had seen more than one fancy paint job ruined that way.

Not on this bike. An old Honda 450, it sported a basic black paint job. Nothing fancy, but all she could afford on the little she earned as a waitress. Paid for in cash, the only paper trail was the registration and plates.

She felt eyes on her again as she hung up the hose. "Nice bike." The deep voice seemed sincere enough.

"She's okay." She glanced over at the man pumping

gas into a jeep across from her, and grinned. He was all alpha male. The short buzz cut made it hard to tell, but she thought his hair was brown to match his eyes. His broad shoulders strained the seams of the tailored light blue cotton shirt he wore, and his chest appeared to be all muscle, no fat. He had a strong face, and stubble on his chin. She avoided the urge to scan the rest of his body. Dot caught a glimpse of a second man, almost as good-looking, seated in the passenger's side of the jeep. Another day, another time she might flirt with the guys, but not today, not now. Instead, she headed inside to the convenience store to pay and pick up a few last minute items. She had taken off her helmet and was using it to carry two bottles of water while she perused the selection of jerky when her shopping got interrupted.

"If it isn't our little waitress. You going somewhere, sweetie?"

She turned and saw one of the men from the diner. He had struck her as a potential troublemaker, but behaved himself while they ate. A time or two he had started to say something to her, but a glare from the one she designated as the boss man shut him up each time. He moved closer and put one arm on the shelving behind her. The coolers blocked the other side. He was a tall man, but she hadn't realized how tall while he sat, and the way he towered over her now sent shivers down her spine. She tried to find a way past him, but he blocked not only her view but any path of escape.

"Since you don't have any big plans for the weekend, maybe you and me could have a little fun?" When he leaned over her, his breath smelled like the fries the diner served. Too close.

"Not interested. I have to leave now." She tried to push his arm away but he was too strong and it didn't budge.

He laughed at her attempt. The sound gave her goose bumps, but, luckily, the sleeves of her jacket covered her arms. "Why in such a hurry?" he asked, leering at her. "You seemed real friendly earlier."

"I said, I'm not interested." She moved to duck under his arm, but he laughed again and lowered it, blocking her path. He moved in even closer, so close they practically touched.

"You're not going anywhere except with me. My friend out in the car wants to talk to you."

"Leave me alone." She could smell her own scent of fear, but worked to keep her voice calm, so he wouldn't sense it. The young man working the register wasn't going to be much help, but hopefully he would see what was going on and call the police. She tried to push the man away, but he just laughed.

"She said, leave her alone."

Dot looked up to see a muscular arm wrap around the shoulders of her tormentor and pull him away. Before she turned and ran, she noticed her rescuer's brown eyes had a yellowish tint, much like her own.

Two

Gavin Fairwood stared out of the window of his motel room. The parking lot didn't provide much of a view, but he hoped to catch sight of a certain motorcycle and rider on the street beyond. "She was kin, I tell you." It was not how he'd anticipated ending a week-long road trip to visit old friends.

"You said that before." His friend, Dmitri, lounged on one of the beds, flipping through TV channels. "But you still haven't convinced me. Granted, I didn't see much of her, so I have nothing to go on, but you don't either."

Gavin grunted as he abandoned his post and sat in the single easy chair. "You're right, between the helmet and bulky jacket, I didn't get a good look. I might not even recognize her if someone showed me her picture. But I felt her, I tell you." He drummed his fingers on the arm of the chair. "And in the store, I smelled her fear. She was trying to hide it, but the odor was there."

"In the situation you described I would have been afraid too, if I was her. The guy you dragged out of the gas station was no pushover. His two friends were no wimps either. We might have had a real challenge on our hands if the cops didn't show up when they did."

"I enjoyed that more than I should have." Gavin chuckled at the memory as he examined the shirt he had taken off. He had ripped the shoulder seam on one of the sleeves. "I really wanted to punch him, but once the cops arrived I couldn't." He flexed his bare arms. "He'll be sore for a day or two anyway. Maybe he'll think twice before he pushes a woman around again."

Dmitri swung his feet over the edge of his bed and reached for another piece of the pepperoni pizza. "So you still haven't told me why you think she is kin."

"Her odor. That wasn't purely human fear I caught. It held a hint of animal fear too—specifically, wolf."

It had taken Dot two days to get here, using back roads and traveling as much as possible after sundown. A few times during the trip she had thought she was being followed, and found a place to hide until the feeling left.

Now she brought her bike to a stop at the top of the low hill and killed the engine. This spot gave her a clear view of the pasture below and the deserted farmhouse in the middle. The two story building had been vacant since the game commission bought the property to add to the land preserves back in the 1970's. It was holding up reasonably well considering no one took care of it. The roof leaked in a few spots and the basement floor was covered in a thin layer of water after a rain. Still, her plan was to hole up here for a few weeks while she plotted her next move. She was running out of options.

She kicked at the layer of leaves and uncovered bare ground. Cautiously, Dot lowered the kickstand to make sure it wasn't going to sink into the soil before getting off the motorcycle. Crouching down, she concentrated on her *other* senses. She had learned a few years ago, by accident, how to call up her wolf senses of sight and smell without actually transforming.

Moving along the ridge, she used those senses to study the house below. She was not the only one who knew of its existence, but no one else was using it now. The scent markings she left after her last visit would keep away most rodents and small animals, so it should be safe enough for her to use as shelter again. She would have to watch out for the odd snake or two, but that wasn't a problem.

She guided the bike into an outbuilding halfway down the hillside. She thought it used to be a well house, but now it was empty and starting to fall apart. Still, it worked as place to stash the bike. After removing her sleeping bag and a few supplies Dot carefully pulled the door closed as far as possible. Even if someone discovered her hiding place in the house, chances were slim they would find her motorcycle, giving her a better chance of escape. She gathered a few herbs as she walked down the hill, stuffing them in her pockets. Sage would have been better for what she had planned, but these would have to do.

The old ceramic flower pot still sat in its place outside the back door. It took some effort, but she managed to pry the nearby kitchen window open. It got harder to do each trip, but it was her way into the house since the doors were padlocked. For now, it would let some fresh air in while she worked outside. She filled the pot with dried pine needles, dead leaves, and the plants from her pockets. The peppermint, a local plant, would provide extra protection. Before entering the house, she set the pot back down and headed for the meadow.

She sat in the center of the clearing, her face raised to the sun. After several deep breaths, she adjusted her position on the ground and started again. She was out of practice. More deep breaths, and she felt strength of nature relaxing her, making her whole. She reached deep inside, faltered, and let go. Once more she searched her innermost self, acknowledging her dual nature, and found her center. With an easy grace, she rose, and returned to the house.

Using a cigarette lighter from her supplies, Dot lit the contents of the pot, and crawled through the window into the house. Once smoke started rising from the pot, she waved it around her head, around the front of her body, and then around to her back. She vaguely remembered her mother doing the same actions when they had moved into a new house. Something about cleansing the self before a ceremony. Dot didn't recall the words her mother had chanted, so she chose to remain silent as she lifted the pot high, down to the floor, and finally waved the smoke in each direction. Next, she walked through the rest of the house, sending the smoke into every corner. The last step was to set the pot down in the middle of the kitchen, and let the pot continue to smoke until it burned itself out. That would drive out many of the insects.

Supper was half of a sandwich left from her lunch. The spring near the house still ran clear, and Dot drank deeply from it before filling her canteen. With only a few clouds in the sky at sunset, she decided to spend the night in the meadow. It had been a long time since she'd slept under the stars, and autumn was not far off. These last few weeks of summer were hers to enjoy here in her sanctuary.

"I only got a partial plate, but do you think your connections can track it down, Elder?" Gavin always found it awkward to call his father "Elder" instead of "Dad" but times like this called for formality. This was business and had a chance of affecting the pack as a whole.

"Since you have the model and approximate year of the motorcycle, I think it will be enough. The model is old enough to be fairly unique." Henry Fairwood studied his son across the large wooden desk that had served the pack leader for many generations. No one seeing the two men would have any doubt of their relationship. Even though the older Fairwood was going gray, he kept himself in good physical condition. One day, he would step aside and allow Gavin to take over the position, but not yet. "Why is this girl so important to you?"

"She is in trouble. I don't know why, but I feel like it is my duty to help her."

"Did she ask for your help?"

"No. She said maybe two words to me." Gavin had gone over their limited interaction several times in his mind, hoping for a clue to her identity, and found none. He ran his fingers across the top of his head, a habit from the days when he grew his hair long. "Perhaps it was just coincidence that had me in the right spot at the right time, and maybe it was more than that."

"That may be truer than you know. I had a call from Damyon Choate this morning."

"Oh?" Damyon Choate was the leader of a rival pack. The two groups had a provisional truce and tried to avoid each other. Both packs had suffered great losses in previous years when they raided each other on a regular basis, and many members of the pack carried scars from their battles.

"Yes. He complained you interfered with one of their hunts." Henry held up one hand. "I told him you did no such thing and that he needed to check and make sure his sources weren't covering up their own failings. He didn't take too kindly to my advice."

"I was unaware that the hunt rules cover using non-pack members to track prey in public places. Besides, I wasn't in their territory."

"They don't." The older Fairwood leaned back in his plush leather chair. "So maybe this girl ran away from his pack and they are chasing her, or perhaps she was never part of his pack and they want her for some other reason. Either way, my feelings won't be hurt if you find her first. Unfortunately, I can only help you out on an unofficial basis."

"Understood, Elder." Gavin said as he rose to go.

"One more thing, son."

"Yes, Dad?" The implication was clear. This was off the record.

"Good hunting."

Dot sat in the shade of an old apple tree at the edge of the meadow meditating. This morning, she had stalked a young whitetail buck rooting under the same tree, hunting for leftovers from last year's apples, or perhaps hoping for an early fruit from this year's crop. In wolf form, she had crept within striking distance before he had sensed her and dashed away. Not that she wanted to kill it; her sole intent was to practice stalking.

A faint trace of deer scent invaded her thoughts and distracted her. She adjusted her position and tried to concentrate. Two weeks had flown by, and she was no closer to a solution. She needed to find a more permanent shelter soon, before summer was over. Florida was an option. She was sure she could get some kind of job there, and the local red wolves would be no threat to her in her gray wolf form. But Florida was flat, and her spirit cried out for the rolling hills she loved.

She had considered moving to the western part of the country, but the native species of wolves still roamed there and were no longer protected. The last thing Dot wanted was to be a fair target for some angry rancher. With little human population, it would be easier for her to find places to roam in her wolf form, but harder to hide her dual nature. And the Indians who lived there considered her kind to be evil.

She didn't think she was evil, but she remembered the stories her mother told. Stories of men turning into wolves so they could sneak into camp and kill their rivals. Stories about women turning into wolves so they could snatch babies. Stories of men with no loyalty to their friends who would turn into wolves and kill horses and cattle belonging to other members of the tribe. Dot had cried for days after the first time she had shifted at age eighteen. If her mother hadn't been a shifter, that meant her father must have been one. She didn't even know her biological father's name. Bruce McKenzie had raised her, she had loved him as a father and taken his name, but he was not a shifter. Was her father evil? Was that why her mother hated shifters so much? Dot would never know. When her mother and Bruce had died in the auto accident when she was sixteen, her chance to find out had died as well.

A crow cawed overhead, breaking into her musings. It was good timing—or maybe a warning. The sound of a motor broke the silence. It could be a group of picnickers, it might be the local game commissioner doing a routine check, or...Dot quickly headed for the hillside, staying in the cover of trees and heavy brush. She had put her sleeping bag in its hiding spot when she left this morning and all her garbage had been disposed of properly, so there should be no trace of her in the house.

From a limb high in a tree on the hill, she watched as two carloads of teenagers unloaded tents and coolers from their vehicles. She'd be spending the night in the woods. Or perhaps not—the dye in her hair was growing out, and she needed to refresh it. Tonight would be a good night to spend in a motel room, take a hot shower, and re-color her hair. It was also time to call a few friends and assure them she was all right. Her pay-as-you-go cell phone still had minutes left. She tried to remember the hours the town's little library was open. She missed reading.

THREE

"He did what?" Dot grinned as her Aunt Mary recounted the antics of her little boy, Andy. Andy was what…five years old now?—and getting into trouble constantly. Three years had gone by since Dot had last seen her aunt or her cousin, so all she knew about him was what she learned in her rare phone calls. She'd lived with Aunt Mary for a few years after the accident, but she had a reason for leaving and not going back. "Poor cat, is it going to be all right?" she asked. Andy had decided that the cat's hair was too long and needed to be cut. Aunt Mary had caught him with the shaver in one hand and the cat tucked under his arm.

She adjusted the towel around her hair. It was old and the motel was probably ready to throw it away, so she wasn't worried if some of the hair dye soaked into it. She had decided to go jet black this time. It had been a couple of years since she'd used this color, and with the tan she'd acquired the last couple of weeks she could pass as Hispanic. She had checked into the motel using the name Maria, and when she walked out in the morning she would hardly resemble the Dot of a few weeks ago.

"I promise you, everything is going all right." Aunt Mary believed that she lived in Cleveland and worked as a secretary. "I'm sorry I haven't called for so long. I will try to call you next week. Love you too."

After she ended the call, Dot turned off the phone. Even though it was supposed to be untraceable, she didn't trust technology. She readjusted the pillows and picked up the book she had borrowed from the front desk clerk. As much as she enjoyed the freedom of living in nature, sometimes she missed the simple pleasures of civilization.

"So I was able to find out her name, that she was a really good waitress and that her old boss misses her and wishes she'd come back." Gavin took another bite of his rare steak and chewed on it reflectively. His father waited. "I even got my hands on a hairbrush she left behind at the diner, so I can track her by scent now. But I didn't find out anything else—she didn't have any friends in the area, she never talked about her past with her coworkers, and I still have no idea why the Choate pack is interested in her. Anything she left behind in the room she rented got thrown out already."

"No one you talked to knew of her ability?" Henry asked.

"I don't think so. At least, not that they would admit. The folks at the restaurant are convinced that the whole wolf sighting thing is just an effort by the local chamber of commerce to attract more tourists to the area."

"I wonder if she had anything to do with that theory."

"I hadn't thought about that. It makes sense though."

"I've been doing a little research of my own." Henry picked up his wine glass and sniffed the Merlot he had chosen to go with his sirloin. "I put out some feelers to a contact in the Choate clan."

Gavin leaned forward. "I always suspected you had a spy there."

"I wouldn't call her a spy." The older man smiled. "She is an old friend. I will share her name with you another time. I do not like to impose on our relationship. If word ever got out that she knew me, it could be hazardous for her."

"So what did your old friend have to say?"

"She knows nothing about a special call to hunt in the pack. A few females left recently, but none matched this girl's description. The ones who left were mostly older women who are already past child-bearing age. There are rumors that Damyon Choate is getting ready to retire though, and there's no clear contender for the pack leader position. He has no surviving sons, and his daughters mated outside the pack."

"Leaving them in a bad position—the leader will be declared by who survives in one-on-one combat." The younger Fairwood absentmindedly ran his hand across the top of his head. "The results can either strengthen or weaken the pack depending upon who wins."

"Exactly."

"But that still doesn't explain why they are chasing this girl."

"No, it doesn't." Henry sighed. "Do you still feel the need to search for her?"

"Yes. I can't explain why, but I do." Gavin tossed his napkin on the table. "But I'm out of ideas. I don't know where she might have gone."

"We can check to see if she has a bank account anywhere, although if she is smart she pays cash for everything. It might be interesting to see if we can locate a birth certificate or Social Security number for her."

"You said 'we'," Gavin said, a slow smile spreading across his face. "Are you in this officially, or is this personal?"

"A chance to be a thorn in the side of Damyon Choate? This is all personal," Henry replied, with a smile to match his son's. He reached into his pocket and pulled out his cell phone. When Gavin stood up to go, his father shook his head. "Wait. Read this."

The message was simple. "Subject's bike spotted in Ulysses, PA."

"You have eyes everywhere, don't you?' Gavin asked as he returned the phone.

"Not everywhere. How soon will you be leaving?"

"As soon as I can throw a few clothes in a bag and grab Dmitri."

The campers were gone, but Dot hesitated at the top of the hillside. The birds were hushed, their silence unnatural. She reached out with her *other* senses but found nothing unusual. As noiselessly as possible in her human form, she moved across the top of the ridge, the breeze blowing softly across her face.

The faint scent of a campfire remained in the air, but not enough to worry her. No smoke rose from the campfire pit and that was the important thing. The grass was pushed down where the tents used to be, but would spring back in a few days. The garbage had apparently been packed out as she saw none around the meadow.

Still, she delayed going to the house. A large crow landed near her and cocked its head, staring at her. She wondered what message it carried. As the bird flapped its wings and flew off, she detected the sound of a motor coming down the road. She listened, puzzled—were the campers coming back? Why had they taken down their tents if they had planned to return?

Now the sound grew more distinct. It was not one motor, but several. Four men on motorcycles pulled into the clearing and parked a little way away from the house, talking loudly amongst themselves. Three forced their way into the house while one stood outside, scanning the meadow. Finally, the three came back outside. The conversation came to her in snatches;

"Others...here, but...recently."

"Fresh scent."

"No...tracks."

The fourth man stood still, scanning the area. His gaze moved towards the trees beyond the clearing and Dot hugged the ground. She prayed the wind would not change directions. She dared not back away from her vantage point, fearing the noise of crackling leaves and breaking twigs would be enough for them to hear.

"Spread out...the woods."

Her choices were limited. She needed to get back to her bike and leave. The only thing in the house was her sleeping bag and it could be replaced. Before she could move, she saw the fourth man go to the fire pit and grab the firewood the campers had left. He stacked it against the house, then grabbed a can from the saddlebag of his bike and poured some sort of liquid over the wood. Her *other* sight showed her the malicious grin on his face and her *other* smell caught a strong odor of kerosene. He pulled a pack of cigarettes from his pocket and lit one. Carelessly, he tossed it on top of the stack and watched as the stack lit, catching the dried wood of the old house on fire as well.

The rush of emotions caught Dot by surprise. Anger, sadness, and fear warred for her attention. Instinct took over and she started to run away, but hit an unexpected obstacle. The largest gray wolf she'd ever seen blocked her path, its yellow-brown eyes staring into hers.

"Follow me." The words echoed in the back of her skull. She looked wildly around, trying to figure out who had spoken.

"No time to explain." The wolf stepped away. *"Follow me."*

Still she hesitated. The wolf moved behind her and pushed her with its nose. *"Quickly, unless you want those men to catch you."*

She stumbled, almost fell, but caught herself. The wolf moved in front of her, guiding her away from the road. "My bike!" she said, stopping.

"A friend will take care of it. We need to get you out of here. Follow!" She heard voices yelling nearby. The wolf moved off at a quick lope and she had to run to keep up with it. Its path wound between trees and

large stones before it scrambled effortlessly up a rocky slope. It stopped at the top and waited for her to catch up. She was out of breath and paused to rest.

"Not yet. Hurry!" The wolf moved away again, leading her down the other side of the ridge. It splashed into a small creek as it headed downstream. She tried to follow along the creek bank, but there was too much brush and she was forced to move into the water. She thought she knew these woods, but the wolf led her into unfamiliar territory.

The wolf slowed as they entered a cluster of old pines. Its paws made no sound as it padded across a thick layer of pine needles. *"Almost there,"* its voice encouraged her. Dot hoped so. Her T-shirt was soaked in sweat, her legs were rubbery and close to giving out, and her pulse raced. She didn't know how much farther she could go. The wolf stopped. *"Wait here."*

Her muscles collapsed and she sank to the ground, exhausted. The wolf moved off and she quickly lost sight of it. She closed her eyes and tried to remember the Zen breathing exercises Aunt Mary had taught her. What kind of crazy dream was this anyway?

"We're clear. The Jeep is only a little further and no one else is in the area." The voice wasn't in her head anymore. The Jeep? She opened her eyes, expecting to see the wolf. Instead, a familiar man stood in front of her. Her imagination must have been playing tricks on her, because he was her hero from the gas station.

FOUR

Dot waited for instinct to scream at her, but it stayed silent. She didn't have the energy to run any more anyway. He held out his hand to help her up. "The Jeep is just on the other side of the hill. Do you think you can make it or do you need to rest more? We're good for now, but I still want to get out of here as soon as possible."

She grasped his hand and pulled herself up. He gently put his arm around her waist to support her while she found her balance. His nearness proved comforting and disturbing at the same time, but her legs were still rubbery and she clung to him. "Do you want me to carry you?" he asked.

She studied him. With his build, he probably could carry her without a problem. Suddenly shy, she pulled away from him. "Give me a minute. I will be all right."

"We have water in the Jeep and a blanket. It's getting late, and I don't want you to get a chill. We'll head down the road and meet up with Dmitri and take you someplace safe."

Things were happening too fast. If she closed her eyes and shut him out she might be able to think clearly. "Who are you, and why should I go with you?"

"Sorry, we haven't been officially introduced." She opened her eyes to a sparkling smile. The self-control she was fighting for rushed away again. "I'm Gavin Fairwood and if I'm correct you're Dot McKenzie. The rest we can talk about later."

The hot shower hadn't done it, or the cocoa, and even the blanket wrapped around her as she sat on the bed wasn't warming her up totally. She was in over her head and scared. The connecting door to the adjoining motel room was open a crack and she could hear Gavin talking to someone. She wasn't sure if it was tiredness or fear that made her reluctant to open up her *other* senses to listen to the conversation.

The knock on her door startled her. She must have dozed off—she hadn't meant to. Gavin strolled in, carrying her saddlebags, followed by another man with her helmet. She clutched the blanket closer.

"Thought you might want to change into fresh clothes before we go out for supper," Gavin said. "Dmitri parked your bike out back where it can't be seen from the road." He sat her bags down on the dresser. "If you need anything else, just knock on the door and let us know."

"Answers," Dot muttered softly. She didn't expect a response, but Gavin nodded.

"Soon," he told her. "Food first, and then you'll get your answers. We may not have all of them, but hopefully we can clear up a few things for you."

The other man pushed around him and held out his

hand. "I'm Dmitri Gromav, by the way. I apologize for Gavin's lack of social skills, but I'm his best friend and I'm used to it. I like your bike. She has a few new scratches on her, but I think I can buff them out."

She studied him closely as she shook his hand. He was not as tall as Gavin, or as broad shouldered, but still muscular. His eyes had the same yellowish tint as his friend's. His hair was as black as hers and long enough to touch his collar. She'd remembered to put her contacts back in, hadn't she? She saw dried blood on Dmitri's cheek. "I'm sorry if you got hurt on my account."

"This? This will heal up in a few days," he reassured her, touching his cheek and laughing. "Until then, it's a reminder to duck when going under low branches. Your helmet was too small for me."

Gavin coughed. "I don't know about you two, but I'm hungry. We'll get out of here so you can change, Dot." He paused at the doorway. "You're not a captive. You are free to leave any time you want." He nodded towards the exterior door. "Nothing and no one will stop you from going. But I hope you will stay long enough for us to explain things."

Dot made sure both doors were locked before she pulled fresh clothes out of her saddlebags. While she was at it, she did a quick check of their contents. Everything seemed to be there, including the banker's bag that held her remaining cash. Dmitri had put the keys to her bike on the dresser next to her helmet. She dressed quickly, still uneasy, and ran her comb through her hair. She hesitated as she pulled out fresh socks—her boots were still wet from running through the stream, but she didn't own a second pair of shoes. They would have to do for now.

She caught a glimpse of herself in the full-length mirror and sighed. Sometimes she didn't remember what she looked like without a disguise. She could make it through supper, get her answers, and if she needed to, disappear in the morning. She couldn't trust anyone, she reminded herself, and hadn't trusted anyone since the first time she shifted.

So why did she want to trust these two men so badly?

Gavin and Dmitri sprawled out on one of the beds watching the news while Dot sat uncomfortably in the desk chair. She'd chosen it specifically to keep herself alert. The easy talk and laughter at supper had lulled her into a state of relaxation. She needed to be careful.

As if he sensed her thoughts, Gavin turned the TV off and swiveled to face her. "Ready to ask your questions now? I can't guarantee we'll have the answers for everything, but we'll tell you what we can."

Always a catch, she thought. "Just who are you guys? And why were you following me?"

Gavin sighed. "Second question first. We weren't following you until that day when I stopped the guy hassling you at the gas station. We just happened to be in the right place at the right time. After that, I figured you were in trouble, so I tried to find you to see if I could help. As for today, well," he shrugged, "it was another case of being in the right place at the right time."

"Right, and you have a pet wolf trained to show up at just the right time. By the way, where is it?"

"Pet wolf?" Gavin asked, sitting up.

"Yeah, the one who is wired to project your voice.

That was your voice I was hearing in the woods, wasn't it?"

"I don't have a pet wolf, Dot. Did the voice is your head sound like this?" She shivered as the sound switched from her ears and echoed in the back of her skull.

"Don't do that!" she exclaimed as she covered her ears.

"It won't make any difference."

Gavin got off the bed and walked over to her, kneeling in front of her. Gently he forced her hands away from her head and held her wrists as he stared into her eyes. *"You can still hear me."*

"Get out of my head!" She tried to pull free, but he continued to hold her wrists.

"Has no one ever talked to you this way before?" he asked. He continued to kneel in front of her but switched to normal speech. "Not even your mother or father?"

"No," she whispered.

He let go of her, stood, and thought for a moment. "I am the wolf, Dot. Dmitri and I are both wolves. We are your kin."

"No, this can't be right. And unless you guys spiked my tea at supper you're going to have a hard time making me believe you."

"It is right." He pulled off his shirt and tossed it on the closest bed. Her eyes widened as he slipped off his pants as well, but left his briefs on. If she hadn't been so shocked, she might have enjoyed the sight. The muscles in his chest rippled with the smallest movement. "Sorry," he said, with a glance at her face. "I should have warned you, but I didn't bring enough spare clothes packed to waste these." Dot's vision blurred momentarily. When her vision cleared, a large gray wolf filled the space in front of her. She stuffed her fist in her mouth to stop her scream, jumped out of the chair, rolled across the bed, and dashed to her own room, closing and locking the door behind her.

So that's what it looks like when I change into a wolf, Dot thought. She didn't understand why she stayed, why she hadn't walked out the door. Her bags were repacked and she had the keys for her motorcycle in her hand. She moved to the bed and stared at the ceiling wondering what she had gotten herself into when she heard the soft knock on the door between the rooms. "Dot, can I come in please?" Dmitri asked.

She dragged her unwilling legs off the bed and turned the lock, opening the door a crack. "Only you," she hissed.

Over his shoulder, he glanced back into the other room and shrugged. She opened the door far enough for him to squeeze through, then closed and locked it again. "We're sorry, Dot," he said. "We thought you knew."

"Knew what?"

"About shifting. You are a shifter, aren't you?"

"You talk like it's a normal thing."

"It is."

"You call what happened in there normal? If I told anyone about it, they would lock me up in a psychiatric ward and pump me full of drugs." Dot examined the picture of sailboats on the wall. She was afraid that if she glanced at his bewildered face, the hysterical laughter she kept pushing down would break free. She felt his hand on her shoulder.

"Good gods, Dot, you don't know, do you? Haven't you ever been part of a pack?"

"There is a pack of you guys?" She spun to face him. "I am crazy, aren't I? What is this, some kind of elaborate joke?"

He stared at her and took her by the hand. "We need Gavin. I can't do this by myself." She allowed him to lead her back into their room, but sat as far away as she could from Gavin, who was back in human form and dressed. Gavin moved as if to come to her, but she shook her head and he stopped.

"I overheard the conversation. I apologize for mishandling this situation. I made some assumptions I shouldn't have," he said. "Let me start over. First of all, I need to know—are you a shifter?"

"I can't be." Her answer came out as a sob. "I'm not anything like the stories."

"What stories, Dot? I wasn't aware of the Irish having any oral traditions about shifters. Werewolves, maybe, but not shifters."

"I'm not Irish. McKenzie was my stepfather's name."

"How about your mother?"

"She was part Navajo. They were her stories." She picked up a pillow from the bed and clutched it to her chest.

Gavin growled. "We are nothing like the Navajo traditional myths. We are not Skinwalkers, Dot, you have to believe that."

"Why should I?"

She didn't see him move, but he was in front of her. "Look at me." She shivered but forced her eyes to meet his. "Are you a bad person? Have you ever hurt anyone just because you could?"

"No!" She hesitated and added, "Sometimes I want to, but I never have."

"But you can shift?'

She caught her breath and stared at the floor.

"Tell me, one way or the other, so I know how to help you," he demanded. "Can you shift?"

"Yes," Dot whispered.

Nothing in Gavin's background had prepared him for her reaction as she seemed to crumble before his eyes. If this had been one of his Marine buddies they would go out to a bar and get drunk together. Awkwardly, he sat on the bed beside her and put one arm around her to comfort her. She stiffened, but didn't push him away.

"It's going to be all right," he murmured. "We'll take care of you." He hoped she wouldn't start crying. When she started shaking, he wrapped his other arm around her to steady her. Dmitri grabbed a spare blanket out of the closet and draped it around her shoulders, and Gavin loosened his hold long enough to wrap it around her. The two men exchanged worried glances behind her back.

"*What now?*" Gavin sent.

Dmitri shrugged his shoulders. "*She's not fighting you. I guess that's a good sign.*"

About the time Gavin's arms started to fall asleep, Dot suddenly pushed his arms away and stood up. She took a hesitant step and almost fell, but Gavin caught her.

"Are you all right?" he asked.

She shook her head. "I don't know that I'll ever be all right. But maybe I'll be able to deal with it in the morning. Right now, I just want to go to bed and forget about it."

Gavin scooped her up in his arms and carried her to her room, gently setting her down beside her bed. "We'll be next door if you need us," he said. He paused for a moment before closing the door.

He stayed awake a long time, using his *other* senses, to listen to her even breathing while she slept. Something about the way she had felt in his arms made him want to hold her again.

She woke slowly; the bed was the most comfortable place she had slept in a long time. As Dot stretched she overheard male voices close by and sat up, remembering. Quietly, she got out of bed and made her way to the door, opening it silently. Someone appeared to have gone to the breakfast area off the main lobby and brought back an assortment of items, and Dmitri was placing them on the small table by the window. Gavin was busy brewing coffee. She stood and watched them for a few minutes before knocking on the wall. "Any left for me?" she asked.

Dmitri jumped, startled, turned and smiled. "Plenty. I didn't know what you liked, so I brought all kinds of stuff." He pulled the chair out from the desk in the room and held it for her. "Coffee, tea, juice?"

"Juice, I think. Anything will do. There have been a lot of mornings when I didn't get any breakfast." She sat in the chair backwards to create a barrier between the two men and herself. "Sorry about last night. I don't usually over-react that way."

"I don't imagine you have many days like yesterday," Dmitri smiled.

"More than I like to think about," was her quiet answer. She took a swig from her bottle of orange juice before continuing. "I try to concentrate on the normal days and forget the weird ones."

Dmitri carried a chocolate-covered doughnut and a bowl of cereal over to her. "Eat first. Then we can talk."

"We tried that last night and things didn't go so well." She grimaced as she set the food on the desk. "So are you a shifter too, Dmitri?"

"Yes. I grew up in a different pack than Gavin, but we served in the Marines together, and I joined his pack when we were discharged."

She coughed to loosen the bite of doughnut that had gotten caught in the back of her throat. "There is more than one pack?"

"There are several scattered throughout North America," he told her.

"I think I need some of that coffee," she muttered. "What I really need is a drink, and it's way too early for that."

Dmitri poured her a cup and brought it to her. She set it down and grabbed his wrist. "Look at me," she said. "I want to see your eyes." He gazed at her unblinking, until she nodded and let him go. She turned to Gavin, who had been sitting silently on the bed, watching her. "Yours are the same."

"It's a common trait for wolf shifters," he said. "Other shifters have different colors of eyes. Yours are not typical though."

She grinned, and sipped her coffee. "Contacts," she said finally. "These are brown. I used to have a green pair. Tried blue once, but they looked unnatural. All part of the disguise." She put down the coffee cup, and carefully touched her index finger to each eye in turn, taking the contacts out, putting them on her napkin. She blinked rapidly several times. "Without them, my eyes are like yours."

Dmitri smiled, but Gavin stared at her intently. "How long have you been running, Dot?"

FIVE

"Too long, and not long enough." Dot went over to stare out the window. "It's been more than five years, and I should be on the road now. I normally travel at night."

"I said it yesterday, and I meant it. You're not a prisoner. If you really want to, you can walk out of here right now and go wherever you need to go. But I'm hoping you'll stay." Gavin walked over and put his hand on her shoulder. "I don't think you are ready to go yet."

"You're right," she said. "I still have too many questions, and you deserve some answers too." She drew a long, shuddering breath. "Where to start?"

She sat on one bed, and sipped her coffee while the two men sat opposite of her on the other. "First time I shifted I was eighteen. I was running away from my aunt's house for reasons I won't get into. I thought I got a bad cramp, and found myself running faster and easier than I ever thought possible. When I finally got tired, I laid down under a tree to rest. Woke up in the morning miles from home, cold and completely naked. I stole some clothes from a farmhouse to wear home. Had no idea what happened. Thought I was hallucinating or something. Wondered if I should check myself in to a mental health facility.

"The next time it happened, I was being hassled by some guys when I was walking home after work one night. Got that cramping again as I tried to fight them off, next thing I knew they were running away. Went to look at myself in a store window and saw a wolf." She smiled. "Freaked me out. When I realized the wolf was me, freaked me out even more. My clothes were in shreds on the sidewalk, but I figured it didn't matter. Got my house keys out of my pocket with my mouth and trotted all the way home. Hoped people would think I was just a big dog. Seemed to work too. Fell asleep in the yard of my aunt's house, and in the morning, when I had changed back to human form, snuck in and got dressed without ever being missed.

"After a couple more incidents, I realized I had to learn to control the changing before I hurt someone. Plus, I think someone was watching me even back then. So I left my aunt's and set off on my own. Took a lot of work, but I have it mostly under control. Now if I could just figure out who is chasing me and why."

Gavin and Dmitri sat motionless during her recital. Gavin reached over and put his hand on her knee when she finished. "We think we know the who, but not the why."

Dot sat quietly while Gavin explained about the Choate pack and their ongoing rivalry. "The men in the gas station were not from that pack," he explained. "But at least one of the men in the woods yesterday was, maybe two. I didn't get a good whiff of their scents."

"So what do they want with me?"

"I hoped you could tell us." He straightened and pulled his hand from her knee. She surprised herself, wishing he had left it there.

"I've been asking myself that question for five years now," she said. "I thought they were government agents chasing me because I could change form, but that doesn't make sense anymore. Not when there are lots of other shifters." She stopped. "If there are so many of us, why didn't I hear about this before?"

"What was your reaction last night when I changed?"

"Oh. Yes."

"What I want to find out," Dmitri said. "Is where you got your ability. Usually it's inherited. Both of my parents were shifters."

"My mother didn't shift," Dot said. "I don't know who my father was."

"Isn't he listed on your birth certificate?" Dmitri asked.

"I don't know. I've never seen it."

"Then I think that's our next step," Gavin said thoughtfully. "One of the Elder's hobbies is genealogy. Perhaps she can help."

"Elders?"

"The Elders are part of the leadership of the pack. Usually they are older members selected for their experience," Dmitri explained.

"It's time." Dot stood up and stretched.

Dmitri and Gavin exchanged puzzled glances.

"Time for what?" Dmitri asked.

"Time for you to take me to this pack of yours."

"I wish you'd ride in the Jeep with me and let Dmitri take the motorcycle," Gavin said over lunch.

"My helmet doesn't fit him." Dmitri pretended to try to put it on and she giggled. "His head is too big."

"I'm hurt," Dmitri said, setting the helmet down and putting his hand over his heart.

She chuckled. "Don't worry." She pointed at Gavin. "His is bigger than yours."

"Too true." Dmitri grinned. "In more ways than one."

Gavin frowned and tossed a crumpled up straw wrapper at Dmitri. "I thought you were my friend."

"You know me; I'm a sucker for a pretty girl."

She blew a kiss at Dmitri. "You say the nicest things."

He grinned. "Nothing but the truth."

"It's getting deep in here." She laughed, then pushed her chair away from the table. "And before things get any deeper, I'm going to step away for a minute." She put her napkin on the table. "I'll be right back."

Gavin's eyes followed her as she threaded her way between the tables and headed towards the restroom. "I'd feel better if she rode with me. Maybe we should stop somewhere and buy a helmet."

"I don't think she would like that. You can't smother her."

"I'm just trying to protect her."

"She's been doing okay so far without our help."

"You're right." Gavin sighed. "And she had a good idea. I'll be right back."

Those hand dryers never get your hands dry, Gavin thought as he pushed through the restroom door, wiping his hands on his jeans. You think they could make a better system. He headed towards their table where he could see Dmitri, but didn't spot Dot. He hoped she was all right—it seemed like she had been in the restroom too long.

"Let go of me!" echoed in his head. *"Leave me alone!"*

Dot! But where was she? He scanned the restaurant searching for her. He turned sharply, and pushed open the woman's room door. "Sorry," he mumbled to the sole woman inside, busy applying fresh lipstick. Swinging back around, he saw Dmitri charging out the exterior door. He forced his way past a waiter with a loaded cart, and followed his friend.

By the time he got outside, Dmitri had one man on the ground, but another was dragging Dot towards the parking lot. As he ran in her direction, she landed a series of kicks on her attacker's legs, staggering him, but he didn't release her. Gavin reached them before the man could recover, and threw a hard punch, sending the assailant to the ground.

Dot tumbled to the ground as well, but rolled away. Free, she stood up and kicked her attacker in the side before backing away and standing by Gavin. He put his arm firmly around her waist. "The lady is with me," he said.

The other man stood, rubbing his chin where

Gavin's punch had landed. "You're interfering with a lawful hunt," he growled.

"I see nothing lawful about it." He tightened his hold on Dot. "Take it to the Council."

Dmitri stood, brushing off his jeans. "Are you all right?" he asked Dot when Gavin led her over. When she nodded, he reached out and wiped a tear from her cheek "Change of plans. I'm taking the bike."

"We'll be there in a half hour, Elder." Gavin told his father, the phone in one hand and the steering wheel in the other. "I don't think she's hurt, but I would like Dr. Tracy to check."

He glanced at her sitting rigidly in the passenger seat. "I hope she'll stay for a while, but that's up to her."

"He's right behind us on her motorcycle."

"I'm sure he will be glad to join us for supper."

"See you then."

He flipped his cell phone closed and slid it into his shirt pocket. "You doing okay?" he asked.

"Not really." Dot chewed on her bottom lip. "I'm sorry for being such trouble."

He concentrated on steering through a series of sharp curves on the narrow two-lane road. He was exceeding the speed limit but didn't care. He knew this road well, and the edge of the pack's territory and its relative safety was only a few miles ahead. When they reached a straightaway, he pushed harder on the gas pedal, Dmitri sticking close behind. The car following them about half a mile back bothered him. As they passed the unmarked boundary, he felt the knot between his shoulders release, and he eased off the gas.

"My older sister Raven offered to let you stay in her guest room," he said. "If you can put up with my niece Dawn, who turned three a few weeks ago and never seems to stop talking except when she is asleep." He watched in the rear-view mirror as Dmitri stopped the motorcycle and several wolves came out of the woods. The wolves nosed the gates shut. They were in the clear now. "I can only stand to talk about the Disney princesses for so long."

"Does she make you drink out of tiny teacups too?"

"Yes." He groaned. "Sitting at a little table I can't fit my legs under, with her favorite stuffed animals in the other chairs."

He pulled his eyes away from the road long enough to see the smile on her face. "I can't wait to see that."

"You may have a few bruises tomorrow, but I can't find any major damage." Dr. Tracy pulled off her sterile gloves and tossed them in the garbage. "Take a couple of ibuprofen tonight if you need to, but I think a hot shower will do as much good."

Dot slid off the table and buttoned up her blouse. "I hate taking pills. They don't seem to work for me anyway,"

The doctor nodded. "Let me know if you need something else. Sometimes herbal remedies work better for us."

"Us?"

"I'm a shifter too. Most of us here are. My form is a panther, though, not a wolf."

"I still can't get my mind wrapped around the concept," Dot admitted. "I thought I was the only one."

"That must have been hard. While you're here, I would like to give you a more thorough check-up." Dr. Tracy said as she walked Dot to the door of the office. "Run some blood work, etc. I have the feeling it's been a while since you've seen a doctor. Just drop by when you have time."

"I don't have much money," Dot admitted hesitantly.

"The pack pays me a retainer. You're a guest, and there won't be any charge. Do you know where you're going?"

Gavin strolled up. He'd been sitting on a nearby bench, waiting. "I'll take it from here. The Elders are anxious to talk to her."

Six

"They can't wait until tomorrow?" the doctor asked.

Gavin grimaced. "Not my decision."

She muttered something that Dot didn't catch. "Are you going to stay with her?"

"I don't know if I'll be allowed to."

"Then I better make a phone call." Dr. Tracy put her hand on Dot's shoulder. "Don't let them push you too hard. If you get tired, tell them you have had enough. I know our Elders, and as much as I admire their commitment, sometimes they have a one-track mind."

"Are they really that bad?" Dot worried as they walked towards a large office building. The trees surrounding it reflected in the many glass windows, helping it to blend into the nearby woods.

"The Elders?" Gavin shook his head. "I don't think so. Granted, if one of us mess up, they call us on it, and they are tough but fair. You don't have anything to worry about." He had been called in front of the group several times as a teenager, and a couple of the Elders would never let him forget it.

"I wish you could be there with me."

He squeezed her hand. "You'll do fine."

This wasn't what she expected. Although Dot wasn't really sure what she'd expected but it was certainly not this group of five men and three women in business suits sitting in plush leather chairs around a large wooden table. They reminded her more of corporate raiders than wolves. She was unable to imagine any of them in their other forms as wolves, except for the man seated at the end of the table, farthest from her. He sat silently with a scowl on his face, while the others talked among themselves, occasionally directing a question to her. She sensed he could be very, very dangerous.

According to Gavin, Elder was the honorary title these pack members held, and it had nothing to do with their chronological age. At least she didn't have to try and remember their names—she could just call them Elder and be polite.

She shifted in the chair. It was comfortable, but she wasn't used to sitting for long periods of time. She snuck a glance at the clock and restrained a sigh. No wonder she was getting tired—she'd been there two hours already. A minute later, the Elder at the end of the table cleared his throat. "I think we have imposed on our guest long enough," he said. "Ms. McKenzie, I apologize we did not have the luxury of letting you get settled in before putting you through this questioning. I hope you will not hold it against us."

"Of course not, Elder. I feel like I should be the one apologizing. I don't want to impose upon the pack."

"Nonsense. We may want to talk to you again in a day or two, but in the meantime, please make yourself at home here. You have two excellent tour guides in Gavin and Dmitri."

"Thank you."

"As a matter of fact," and his face went blank for a moment, "They are on their way now." As she stood up to leave, he added. "See you at supper tonight."

Dot recounted the story of the meeting as the three of them walked, linked arm-to-arm-to arm, to the home where she would be staying. Dmitri had parked her bike there and had already hauled her saddlebags to the guest room while she was busy with the Elders. Dot surreptitiously studied her surroundings as they strolled down the street.

She wondered how old the houses were. Most of them seemed to run on the small side, were painted in a variety of pastel colors, and they reminded her of the Victorian cottages she had seen along the shores of Lake Erie. It looked like a scene from a Thomas Kinkade painting. With the office building and clinic out of sight behind rows of trees, there was nothing to show that the village was anything more than a well-kept remnant of a different time.

"So does the pack eat together or something?" she asked.

"No, not normally. On a special occasion we might have a group meal, but we have our own homes and families. We do maintain dorms for single men and women who don't want to live at home any longer. Why?" Gavin asked.

"One of the Elders said something about seeing me at supper." Dmitri laughed, and to her surprise, Gavin blushed. "What? Did I say something funny?"

"Big guy?" Dmitri asked. "Older but still athletic? Rather imposing, sat at the end of the table? Seemed to be in charge?"

"Yes. He seemed familiar, but I couldn't figure out why."

"That's our pack leader and CEO." Dmitri grinned. "We're having supper with him tonight because he happens to be Gavin's father. I guess Gavin forgot to mention that fact."

The stars blinked in the darkened skies, and the quarter moon hung low on the horizon. Gavin and Dot sat on the porch steps, listening to the calls of the night birds and the chirping of the crickets. Dmitri had gone home, and Henry—he had insisted Dot call him that—was in the house watching the news.

"This is nice," she said. "I'm glad I came."

"I'm glad you did too." For more reasons than one, Gavin thought, studying her profile. At supper, once she had finally relaxed and started laughing at the stories his father was telling, he had seen for the first time how beautiful she was. "I wish I could spend tomorrow with you, but I really need to go into the office."

"What exactly do you do?"

"I'm the director of the procurement division for the pack. I'm responsible for working with our vendors, scouting out new suppliers, and overall inventory."

"Director, huh?" She studied him in the dim light. "That makes you a big shot, doesn't it? I'm honored that you deign to spend your time with me."

He sighed. "I'm supposed to be learning

management from the ground up. Dad would really like me to get an MBA, but it's hard enough for me to sit in an office a couple days a week and I can't imagine sitting in a classroom too. This job makes me appear like I'm trying without totally tying me down."

"You don't seem the MBA type."

"What's that supposed to mean?" he asked, raising one eyebrow.

"You have muscles. And you know how to use them for something besides carrying a briefcase."

He grinned and flexed his biceps. "I did a lot of weight training in the Marines," he told her. "Kept me busy and out of trouble."

She stiffened as a shadow slipped by at the edge of the yard. "Did you see that?" she asked in a whisper.

"One of the sentries. We keep guards on duty all the time. Old precautions from when we had an active feud with another pack. We take turns and pair older members with younger members. Helps to keep the pack strong."

"Oh." Dot reached down and plucked a leaf from a bush at the edge of the steps and tore it in bits. "I am safe here, aren't I? I don't need to be watching over my shoulder all the time anymore?"

"Safe? I don't know, the way I saw some of the guys eying you earlier today, I think there might be a big bad wolf or two after you." He grinned, and she punched him in the arm. "Ow, that hurt!"

"Yeah, right. You want me to kiss it and make it better?"

A kiss sounded good. Really good. Without thinking about it, he leaned over and pressed his lips against hers. He meant to barely touch her lips, but a shockwave ran straight from his mouth to his chest and his heart stopped. He pulled back so he could look into her eyes, and was lost. With a soft growl, he wrapped one arm around her, pulled her close and kissed her again.

A need for air finally made him pull away. "All better now?" she asked. She didn't push away from him, or try to get loose from his grasp.

"Not yet." He shook his head. "I could use some more of that medicine."

"Now who's the big bad wolf?" she laughed. But she stopped laughing when he leaned in for another kiss.

"So what are your plans for tomorrow?" Gavin asked as he walked Dot back to his sister's home. His arm was draped around her shoulders because he didn't trust himself to touch her anywhere else.

"Elder Blackhaw wants me to come talk to her about my mother's family, Dr. Tracy mentioned something about getting a full physical, and Dmitri wants to work on my bike. He said he heard it missing when he geared down."

"Sounds like a full day. Think you can save some time for me?"

"What did you have in mind?"

"Supper." They had reached the door of Raven's house, but he was reluctant to say goodnight just yet. "And then maybe watch a movie or go for a walk or something."

"Are you asking me for a date?" Dot grinned.

He smiled and lightly stroked her cheek. "I guess I am."

"Do you know how long it's been since I've been on a date? I think I was seventeen the last time a guy asked me out. Other than truckers wanting a one night stand." She wrinkled her nose. "They don't count, do they?"

"Absolutely not."

"Good. Because I turned them all down."

He bent to kiss her again when the door opened. "I thought I heard voices out here," Raven, a tall, brown haired woman, said, "Say goodnight, Gavin. Dot has had a long day."

"You sound like Dad," Gavin grumbled, but he smiled at his sister. "Goodnight, Dot." He placed a soft kiss on her forehead. "Sleep well." Before he could change his mind, he turned and strode away into the darkness.

It wasn't like she had much to choose from, thought Dot as she stared at the five shirts hanging in the closet. One of them had a rip in the armpit she hadn't gotten fixed yet, and another had a hole from when a spark from her campfire had landed on it. Her choice of jeans was just as slim. So much for dressing up for their date.

"Are you going to be here for supper tonight?" Raven called from the kitchen.

"No, Gavin is taking me out." Dot closed the closet door. Not that she knew where he was taking her— hopefully no place fancy. He was a good guy, but she had the feeling that he wanted more than friendship, and she wasn't sure she was ready for that. She needed to keep her guard up. She had enjoyed the kissing last night, but needed to be careful.

She walked into the kitchen and asked, "Can I help you with something?"

"No, I have it under control. At least until Dawn wakes up from her nap." Dot grinned. Gavin was right—the little girl did talk non-stop. "Is that what you're going to wear?" Raven asked, stepping away from the stove.

"It's the best I have. I only have room for the necessities in my saddlebags."

"You're about my size. Maybe I have something you can borrow."

"You look pretty," Dawn said solemnly from the bed, where she was supervising Dot's preparations.

"Thank you, sweetie." Dot pushed an errant lock of hair into place. Her hair hung at an awkward length, and she needed to either get it cut or put up with it while it grew out.

"Me help." The little girl bounced off the bed and ran out of the room, but was back in a minute, clutching something in her hand. "Here." She crawled onto the bed and opened her hand to reveal several small plastic barrettes. "Me do it."

"Okay." Dot grinned and sat down so Dawn could reach the top of her head. She waited patiently as the barrettes were snapped into her hair, taken back out, and rearranged.

"All done!" Dawn announced.

Dot liked what she saw in the mirror. She had borrowed a deep blue, knee length dress from Raven, and a matching pair of heels as well. The shoes were a little too small, but Dot figured they would do for the evening. The heavy boots she wore for riding went with jeans, but not this dress. The barrettes added a whimsical touch. The cord to her medicine bag was hidden by the collar of the dress, and the bag itself hung safely in its normal spot.

She heard voices coming from the living room, and Dawn dashed out of the room, squealing, "Uncie Gav!"

Gavin picked up his niece and laughed as he twirled her in the air. Dot stopped in the hallway to watch. Dawn spotted her first. "See!" she said, pointing. "Me helped. Fixed her hair."

Gavin's eyes followed the little finger, and he sucked in his breath at the sight of Dot standing there. He carefully lowered the little girl to the floor. "You did a good job." Suddenly, he was like a teenager on his first date. "You look great," he said, not moving, but staring at Dot.

"Kith her, Uncie Gav," Dawn ordered, grabbing his hand and pulling him towards the hall.

"I think I will." And he did just that.

"Where are you two going?" Raven asked, interrupting.

"Well, I had planned on taking Dot down to The Pub for pizza, but now I think I will just have one delivered." Gavin grinned. "I don't want to share her with anyone else."

"Don't you dare," Raven scolded. "She spent the last hour getting ready, and you'd better show her off."

As he helped Dot into the Jeep, he asked anxiously, "Is pizza all right? I should have asked first."

"Pizza sounds wonderful. I don't get it very often."

"Good." He climbed into the driver's seat and waited until she had her seat belt fastened before he started the engine. "You really do look great. Every other man is going to be jealous of me."

"Flattery will get you everywhere." She put her hand on his knee and he covered it with his own. His pulse quickened as he felt her warmth. "You're not too bad either," she added. He wore a pale green dress shirt and a pair of tan dress pants. "Quite the young executive."

"Dad is always after me to wear a business suit," he explained. "He thinks it would make me appear in charge. And I would rather wear jeans every day. This is our compromise."

Dot sipped on her cola and watched as he chatted with yet another couple who had come over to the table to greet him. He seemed to know everyone in the bar, and they all seemed to like him. With their smiles and easy conversation, they made her feel welcome too. She was enjoying herself. Maybe she would stay with the pack for a little while. Maybe she could get a job close by.

The bar wasn't technically within the boundaries of the pack territory, Gavin had explained, but a good many of its customers were pack members. As he exchanged pleasantries with the couple, she occupied herself with trying to figure out who was a shifter and who wasn't. The two men approaching now were, but they gave her the shivers. They were rougher in appearance than the other men in the restaurant. She took a bite of her slice of cheese pizza to avoid their glances but she saw Gavin tense when they stopped at the table.

"We're here for the girl," the taller one said.

SEVEN

"I don't think so," Gavin said, tossing his napkin down on the table. "She's with me, and I don't believe she wants to go anywhere."

The other man stepped behind Dot's chair. He poked something hard and round into her neck. "She doesn't get a choice," he snarled.

Dot remembered to slip off Raven's shoes before taking a deep breath to cleanse her spirit. She reached up with one hand to grab the man's arm, and used it to propel herself out of her chair. With a move she had practiced mentally, Dot swung around and wrenched his arm behind his back, forcing him to drop the gun. She kicked it away. "There's always a choice," she said. Even though her heart was racing, she thought she sounded calm. "And you made a bad one tonight."

Using both hands, she forced his arm higher, until he grunted from the pain, then kicked his feet apart before checking her surroundings. Most of the customers were on their feet, and three or four wolves paced towards their table. Gavin had the first man in a sleeper hold.

"We'll take it from here." Dot remembered the

speaker as an off-duty state trooper Gavin had introduced her to earlier. The pack worked closely with the local office, and their special skills were often put to work on search and rescue operations. He pulled a set of handcuffs out of his jacket pocket. "I assume you want to press charges."

"Yes." She stepped away as the trooper snapped cuffs on her attacker's wrists. Sirens wailed outside, and other troopers streamed into the building. One trooper pulled her aside to question her, and she lost track of Gavin in the confusion. She watched as her attackers were hustled out of the building, but the sense of panic building inside of her did not end. Her instincts screamed "RUN!" but she was stuck here without her motorcycle and having no real idea of where to run to. She always made plans for escape, but in the space of two days she had been lulled into an artificial sense of safety and regretted it.

The bar was clearing out, and she slipped outside behind some other patrons. Shadows moved among the cars in the dimly lit parking lot and she recognized them as being created by wolves—so much for finding an unlocked car with the keys left inside. If she worked her way unseen into the nearby woods, she could shift and have a chance of getting away. She edged towards the end of the building, careful of where she placed her bare feet. Once she shifted, she could move faster.

"Don't go." The deep voice rumbled from behind her stopping her as she started to move. His approach had been silent. She twirled around, trembling.

"What, are you reading my mind now?"

"No, your body language." Gavin took a step closer and she took two steps away.

"I can't do this." She turned to face the hoped-for safety of the woods.

"Do what?" She felt his warm breath on the back of her neck, but he didn't touch her.

"Every time I think I find a shelter, they take it away from me." Tears hovered close to the surface, but she fought them back. No one was allowed to see her cry. "You told me I was safe here, and see what happened? I figured out a long time ago that they want me alive so they won't hurt me, not bad anyway, but they could have killed you. I can't do this anymore."

He twisted her around and pulled her into his chest. "I'm not going to let you leave. I just found you, and I can't let you go. Promise you'll stay and we'll beat them together."

"I can't promise you anything." She tried to pull herself free, but he didn't let go of her.

"One week. Promise me one week to figure something out. You can promise me a week."

It had been a long time since anyone had done so much for her without expecting anything in return. She owed him. At least, that's what she told herself. "One week. I will give you one week." With his big arms wrapped around her, and his lips suddenly pressed to hers, she wanted to give him more.

Gavin carried her to the Jeep. "Raven is going to be mad at me for losing her shoes," Dot said. The shoes had disappeared in the confusion inside the restaurant..

"I'll buy her new ones. I'll buy her ten pairs of new ones if that's what she wants. And I'll buy you even more so you won't ever have to borrow hers again." He used more force than necessary shifting into first gear and pulled out of the parking space. Dot spotted the shadows following them.

"I can't go back to her house, Gavin."

"Why not?" He glanced at her as he waited for an opening to pull onto the main road.

She didn't answer until he had joined the flow of traffic headed north. Many of the other customers were calling an end to the night as well. "I can't put her and Dawn in danger," she said, "As long as I am in the house, they are at risk. I can't put them in that position." She sighed, and it turned into a moan. "You too. We can't be friends anymore." She buried her face in her hands.

He abruptly braked and pulled the Jeep to the side of the road. "Don't you think that's a decision I can make for myself?" he asked, his voice harsh. "I will do whatever it takes to get you through this. I've been in worse spots before."

"I can't risk something happening to you," she said in a tone so faint he had to strain to hear her. "It'll be easier to give you up now than later."

He slammed the parking brake on and undid his seat belt. "It's not going to happen, Dot. You promised me a week, remember? I'm going to hold you to your promise. There are other ways we can tackle this without you running away. Trust me."

"I want to, but it's hard. I don't know if I know how to trust anymore."

"*Everything okay, Gavin?*" asked a voice in his head. Two wolves trotted out of the woods and stood by the side of the Jeep.

"Is the road clear up ahead?"

"Yes and your father asks that you two go directly to the board room when you arrive."

"We will. And pass the message that I want all of Dot's belongings moved to the guest room of our place."

"It will be taken care of. Drive safely, Gavin."

"Good hunting."

A sentry at the entrance to the village waved Gavin down. "The Elders are waiting for you," the man told them. "We've doubled the number of guards and are calling all pack members who live away to tell them to stay vigilant. Some of them are on their way here, so we will have more help soon." Gavin nodded. The sentry smiled at Dot, and tapped the cell phone in his pocket. "The story of how you disarmed your attacker got here before you did. Elder Fenner, who is in charge of security wishes to congratulate you, and hopes you will consent to join his detail when the crisis is over."

"Jumping the gun a little," Gavin said between clenched teeth as he drove down the main street to the pack's headquarters. "But that was an impressive move." He squealed the tires as he stopped the Jeep in front of the building. Others, both human and wolves, rushed in and out of the brightly-lit building. He hurried around to the passenger side and opened the door. "Want me to carry you inside?"

"I can walk." She ignored the hand he held out to her, and stepped onto the sidewalk. Without waiting for him, she walked as fast as possible into the pack's building. A guard at the entrance led her to the boardroom, Gavin taking the role of rear guard.

"It seems you have brought some excitement to our lives, Ms. McKenzie," Henry said from his spot at the head of the table. She and Gavin were seated side by side at the other end.

"My apologies, Elder," she said calmly. "It was never my intention." No emotions would break through the shell she had erected around herself.

"We're aware of that. We are also aware you did nothing to bring this on yourself. However, according to our contacts with the state troopers, they have been unable to extract any information from the guilty parties as to their motivation in this attack."

"Unfortunately, I'm not surprised, Elder. I've never been able to establish a reason or pattern to the attacks."

"So what do you intend to do?"

"My instinct is to leave so I don't put the pack at risk. The members have been nothing but kind to me and it makes me unhappy I'm putting it in danger." She was speaking only to the man opposite her, ignoring the others around the table, and especially ignoring the man at her side. By focusing on the older Fairwood—Henry, she might be able to keep her composure. "However, in a moment of weakness, your son managed to extract a promise from me to give him a week to come up with another solution. With your permission, I will honor that promise." She fervently hoped she would not regret the decision.

"Granted. I will ask you do not leave the pack territory in that time, so we can better protect you." At her nod, he sighed. "It isn't our intention to confine you, but I will insist you be accompanied by a member of the pack at all times. Elder Fenner is assembling a team of females for that duty."

Gavin interrupted. "I can handle the job, Elder."

"I'm sure you can but I need you for other things. Additional supplies will need to be stockpiled, and you are the best informed on what we have and what must be acquired. Besides, this will be a good opportunity for Ms. McKenzie to learn more about how the pack works, and it would be best for her to learn from other females."

"But..."

"The Elders have spoken." Henry's frown grew deeper.

"Yes, Elder." Dot wanted to let Gavin know it would be okay, but she dared not to look at him. Her shell had to remain intact.

"In the meantime, I have sent a message to the head of the Council, requesting an emergency session. I have also requested a council-wide moratorium on any efforts to capture Ms. McKenzie. I don't anticipate a response tonight however, so our sentries will remain on high alert."

"I apologize, Elder, but I don't understand. What is the Council?" Dot asked.

"I keep forgetting you know nothing of our ways. Until a few years ago, the various packs resorted to raiding each other's territories to establish dominance, resulting in many injuries and deaths." Henry rolled up one sleeve to reveal an ugly scar running up his forearm. "I have more, and everyone seated at the table has their own collection." He rolled his sleeve down and continued. "A number of elders realized the fighting made us weak, not strong, and as a result, the council was formed. It has a representative from each pack, and they are responsible for settling disputes between packs that can't be settled in other, non-violent ways. If the Council votes to put you under their protection, a pack defying the order risks not only censure from the Council, but destruction. It may seem a harsh punishment, but it is necessary."

It was war, Dot realized. He was referring to an all-out war between packs. Over her. She couldn't allow that to happen. She had promised Gavin a week, and he would get it. The time would give her a chance to make plans of her own.

Outside the conference room, a number of men and women with guns stood at alert in the hallways. Dot shivered at the sight, and Gavin placed a comforting hand on the small of her back. One of the women, a tall blonde with two guns strapped across her back, a pistol stuck in the waistband of her pants, and a nasty looking knife strapped to her thigh, jumped out of the chair she'd been sitting in, and approached them.

"Hey, Gavin," she said with a grin as she pulled one of the guns over her head and handed it to him. "The arms master sends his regards—said he remembered this was your favorite model rifle." Nodding, he hefted the AK-47 then slung the band on his shoulder. She handed him a magazine. "He said to see him if you want more ammo," she added. She turned to Dot and extended her hand. "I'm Tasha. One of your bodyguards for the night. Tanya will be the other one. She's my twin sister. You won't see much of her, she'll be taking outside duty."

"Is this really necessary?" Dot asked. Bruce had not been a hunter, and guns made her uncomfortable.

"The Elders seem to think so," Tasha answered. "But we can't stand around here talking—we need to get moving. Slip on these shoes, Ms. McKenzie, Raven thinks they will fit. Tanya reports the way to your house is clear, Gavin. You take the lead and I will bring up the rear."

The street that had seemed so comfortable to Dot the night before now bristled with activity. It felt as if all eyes were on her as the three of them walked the short distance to the house Gavin and his father shared. In the light streaming through the windows, she spotted several wolves patrolling the yard. One paced up to Gavin and they stared at each other silently for a moment.

"We're clear to go in," Gavin said out loud. They made their way up the stairs, Gavin nodding at the guards before they entered the house.

Tasha closed and locked the door behind them, then went around the room closing the curtains and turning off most of the lights. "If you'll wait here for a moment," she said to Dot, "I'll go check your room one more time."

Gavin adjusted the weight of the gun on his shoulder as he scanned the room. "Is this the way it's going to be?" Dot asked. "Always being watched, never alone, worrying every time a door opens, jumping at every little sound?" Her shell was gone now, and her eyes reflected the fear that had taken hold.

"We may be overreacting a little bit," he said, putting his arms around her waist and kissing the top of her head. "But it's good practice. I overheard Elder Fenner complaining a few weeks ago about how the youngsters think sentry duty is a big game and don't take it seriously. And it's just until we hear from the Council." He pulled her a little closer. "Besides, things were getting boring around here, and a lot of us were getting restless. You've given us something to do besides play video games."

She didn't pull away, but she didn't snuggle into his chest the way he hoped she would. "I don't like it, Gavin, and I won't I pretend I do."

"Will you at least cooperate with us?"

"For now. As long as I can stand it." Dot finally gave in and leaned against him, putting her arms around his neck. He tightened his hold on her. "But I reserve the right to complain to you as much as I want."

"If you can put up with us, I guess I can deal with that." He sighed, but then grinned. "At least if you're complaining, you're still talking to me."

Tasha came back into the front room. "The rest of the house is clear. I suggest you turn in, miss, they have an early day planned for you tomorrow. I believe you are scheduled to meet with our trainers. They want to see if there is anything they can do to clean up your method of shifting. It shouldn't hurt."

"Give us a minute alone, will you, Tasha?" Gavin asked.

"Sure, I need to get a drink of water from the kitchen anyway." She grinned. "Don't take too long."

He waited until Tasha was out of sight and then brushed his lips against Dot's. "If I had my way, I'd be sleeping on the floor next to your bed," he whispered. "But since they won't let me do that, I'll stay awake all night long worrying about you."

"Don't. Tell you what, I will give you something to hold you until tomorrow." She put her hands on his broad shoulders and pulled herself up until she was on her tiptoes. The kiss she gave him sent his pulse racing and he longed for more, but she broke away. "Sleep well, Gavin," she said with a wicked smile as Tasha came back out of the kitchen. She winked at him before she followed her minder to her room.

Gavin's dreams were of her; but they kept him half-awake most of the night. He dreamt of her being chased and caught and crying. In his dreams he was unable to reach her and rescue her. When he finally had a dream that started with kissing her, his alarm went off as their lips touched. Groaning, he tossed back his covers and rolled out of bed.

She was gone already. He'd missed her. His father sat in the kitchen having breakfast.

"You look like hell," Henry commented.

"Gee, thanks," he said with a grimace. "Didn't sleep well."

"Too much excitement?"

Gavin plopped into a chair and poured himself a bowl of cereal. "No, too many nightmares." He reached for the milk and almost knocked over the pitcher. "Heck, I've slept better in the back of a Humvee than I did last night."

His father brought him a cup of coffee. "I need you wide awake today. Drink that, and get another one before you come into the office. The Elders are preparing lists of things they need or want. You have a lot of work to do."

It was late by the time Gavin got home. He'd eaten both lunch and supper at his desk, going through lists, figuring out what they already had on hand, what they really needed, and trying to work out what budget they could pull the money from to buy everything. The AK-47 slung over the back of his chair reminded him of why he needed to concentrate on the task. When he walked in the house, Dot, Tasha—or was it Tanya tonight—and his father were sitting in the living room watching TV. Dot moved over and made room on the couch for him. He sat beside her, and as he slid his arm over her shoulders, she leaned against him. Something inside him stirred as he realized how happy touching her made him.

"How did your day go?" he asked.

"Pretty good. Worked on my shifting and the trainers started helping me with my mental voice."

"Any luck with getting the pain to stop?"

"Not really." She sighed. "Elder Lockhart's theory is that it's a psychological reaction to my original belief of changing being evil. She says my overall form is fine." He moved his hand to play with her hair. "She would like to work with me more later this week."

"Sounds like a good idea. What's on the agenda for tomorrow?"

"I'm going to attend a woman's circle." Dot said with a wide smile. "And that's all I am going to tell you. I'm sworn to secrecy on the details."

"Is that a good idea?" Gavin asked Tasha-Tanya. He still hadn't figured out which twin it was tonight. They even smelled the same. He didn't know exactly what happened at the circles—men weren't allowed to attend—but the rumors spoke of deep meditation and nudity. Either would leave her vulnerable.

"She will be well protected," the bodyguard assured him. "A number of us have opted out of the ceremony to act as guardians."

"I'm supposed to go to bed early tonight to prepare." As she straightened up, his hand brushed a leather strap around her neck.

"What's this?" he asked, his fingers following where it led.

She hesitated before answering. "It's a medicine bag."

"I've heard of them. Traditional Indian belief, right?"

"Yes."

"I've always wondered what was in them."

"It varies from person to person." She gently moved his hand to her shoulder. "And no, I'm not going to tell you what's in mine."

"Maybe you can help me make one someday. There's supposed to be some Seneca Indian blood in the family tree."

"I don't know the Seneca traditions, but I don't think your ancestors would be offended if I helped you." Dot stood up. "I should go to bed now."

Tasha-Tanya jumped to her feet before Gavin could pull himself off the couch. "Let me go clear the area first."

Gavin was painfully aware of his father's presence. Tradition demanded that he consult with the pack leader before selecting a mate, and he wasn't ready to have that discussion yet. It was far too soon. "Supper tomorrow night?" he asked her.

"Probably." Dot must have sensed his discomfort, because she gave him a swift hug but no kiss, waved goodnight to Henry and then followed her bodyguard out of the room. Gavin sat back on the couch and tried to concentrate on the show on the TV, grateful for his father's characteristic silence.

Dot was gone again when Gavin got up the following morning. His father had left as well, but a quick glance out the window told him he wasn't alone. He spotted two sentries outside in easy sight, and a shadow he caught in his peripheral vision made him suspect the presence of a third. He decided to skip breakfast, but grabbed a cup of coffee as he headed out the door. It wasn't as warm as he liked it—the warmer plate on the coffee maker must have turned off a while ago, but the microwave in his office would fix that..

EIGHT

The late arrival of a semi-truck loaded with supplies thwarted Gavin's plans to get home in time for supper with Dot. The shipping foreman had already gone home, so he supervised the unloading and check in process himself.

When he walked in the front door, he immediately noticed the absence of both Dot and her bodyguard.

"So where are the ladies tonight?" he turned and asked the sentry at the front door with a casualness he didn't feel.

"Moved to an undisclosed location," the man grunted. "Purely as a precautionary measure, not based on any active threat."

"Good tactic." Gavin muttered, hiding his true feelings. All day he'd been waiting to see Dot, and it annoyed him that she was gone.

Inside, his father bore the brunt of Gavin's anger.

"Who made the decision to move her and why wasn't I consulted?" he asked, without even saying hi. He shrugged the rifle off his shoulder and leaned it against the kitchen table, where his father sat, working on his laptop.

"Elder Fenner is responsible and I was not aware he needed to clear his decisions with you," Henry answered. The disapproval evident is his voice brought Gavin up short. It was his choice to allow his father to remain pack leader and until he was ready to take over the job his father was in charge. He hid his irritation.

"Sorry," he all but mumbled. "But I feel personally accountable for her safety. I'm the one who brought her here after all."

"Yes, and I'm sure she appreciates it." Now Henry was talking as his father again. Gavin learned young to recognize the difference. "However, you are letting your feelings for her get in the way of your training as a warrior." He arched one eyebrow. "And don't try to tell me you don't have feelings for her. They are written all over your face every time you look at her."

Gavin slid into the chair opposite of his father. He put his elbows on the table, and rested his chin on his entwined hands. "I think I've fallen in love with her. Crazy, isn't it? I've only known her a couple of days, but I'd do anything for her."

"I suspected as much." With a sigh, Henry closed the lid of the laptop. "Have you considered how this will affect the pack?"

"I'm not sure what you mean."

"One day you will be pack leader. I appreciate that you're not in a hurry to push me out, but for the pack to stay strong, that will happen, perhaps sooner than you want it to. You're twenty-seven, you'll need to take a mate soon, and there are eligible females in the pack who would love to fill the position. I understand a few have turned down proposals from other men in the hopes of being picked by you. If you can't choose one of them, you should consider mating with a female from a pack we need to strengthen ties with."

"I've dated most of the single women in the pack and none of them appeal to me like Dot does." Gavin leaned back and crossed his arms. "I want her."

"Does she want you?"

The younger man sighed. "I think so, but I haven't asked her. I didn't think it would be fair to her until we figure out what's going on. She's under enough stress already."

Henry nodded. "So let her have this time for herself. You do realize that Elder Fenner is doing you a favor, right?"

"Keeping her away from me? I don't see that as a good thing."

"But it is. She's staying in the single woman's dorm. This is her chance to make friends with other female members of the pack. Then, if you decide to choose her, there will be less resentment of your selection and the chances for a challenge go down."

Gavin stood and stretched, then picked up his gun. "I've spent too much time behind a desk the last couple of days," he said. "I think I'll go for a walk."

"Double patrols have been posted around the building," his father chuckled, reopening the laptop. "And the tree branches within reach of the balconies were trimmed back. If you find another security hole, let Raven know. She's in charge of the detail tonight."

"You're no help." Gavin paused by the front door. "I'll tell Raven you said hi."

Gavin set down the heavy box to wipe off the sweat

rolling off his forehead. Between the extra shipments coming in and the number of crew members who were pulling night duties as sentries, inventory was piling up on the dock. He needed the exercise anyway—he was spending too much time shuffling papers. The workout would help relieve the frustration of not seeing her for two days. He missed her smile.

"Call for you, boss," one of the crew called from the office. He waved in acknowledgment and moved the box into its proper position before heading in that direction.

"Gavin here...Right now? Can I cleanup first?...Be right there."

"The Elders call," he said to the dock foreman as he left, grabbing his rifle. "So I'll be out of your way for a while."

"You'll be in the small conference room," his father's secretary intercepted him as he reached the executive level. She handed him a bottle of water and he wiped it across his head before unscrewing the lid and guzzling down half of it. "Elder Fenner and your father are waiting for you. They have sent for Ms. McKenzie."

"The Council has reached a decision?"

"I can't say." She smiled, winked at him and nodded her head. "You can leave your gun in the corner over there."

"Elder Fenner, Elder Fairwood," he said formally, nodding to each man as he entered the conference room. He noticed another man on the TV screen at the end of the table, and the green light on the webcam. "Counselor," he added nodding towards the screen.

The insignia on the man's collar was a clear indication of his rank.

"This is my son Gavin," Henry explained.

"He takes after you."

The older Fairwood smiled. "I've been told that many times."

"Are we ready to get started then?" asked the man on the screen. Gavin didn't recognize him, but he hadn't met all the members of the Council. He must have been a newer member of the group. Gavin had heard several packs had recently elected different representatives, and the previous chair had retired.

"In a moment. I asked the young lady in question to come as well, but she was on the far side of the village. It may take her a minute to arrive."

A soft knock on the door, and Dot entered. Her face was flushed, and her hair rumpled, with flecks of green paint scattered among the black strands. More paint streaked down one cheek, and her shirt and pants showed additional signs of the same activity. Gavin thought he had never seen her so stress-free.

"Apologies for my appearance, Elders," she said. "I was helping to paint one of the schoolrooms, and the message I got was that this was urgent and I shouldn't take time to make myself presentable."

"We've been including Ms. McKenzie in all normal pack activities." Henry explained to the counselor. "It seemed the best way to help her understand how the pack functions." He turned to Dot. "Please, have a seat."

"Thank you, Elder." She slid into the empty chair next to Gavin. Under the table, she placed her hand on his knee. Avoiding her eyes, he took a drink of his water, and after setting down the bottle, put his own hand on top of hers.

"The Council has been having phone conferences in this matter," the Council chairman said. "And they asked me to convey our decision. Unfortunately, we were not able to reach a unanimous vote, and we will hold a full council meeting in two weeks' time to discuss the issue in person. In the meantime, a majority of the counselors agreed to offer Ms. McKenzie the Council's pledge of protection, and the decision is binding for all packs under our rules."

"Thank you," Henry said. Gavin managed to restrain a sigh of relief.

"We request that you make yourself available to the Council for the duration of the meeting, Ms. McKenzie. We will send detailed information for you through Elder Fairwood."

"Of course," she said demurely.

"Goodbye," said the man on the screen, and the connection was abruptly cut. Gavin leaned back in his chair and rotated his shoulders to ease the tension in his neck.

"So does this mean I'm safe?" Dot asked. "And everything here can go back to normal?"

"Not yet." Elder Fenner shook his head. "It will take a few days until the ruling can be passed down through the ranks. Until the actual Council meeting, I want to maintain our current level of security."

Dot chewed on her bottom lip. "I still have to have bodyguards?"

"Getting tired of the company?" Henry asked her.

"I don't want to seem ungrateful, but yes. I've spent much of the last five years alone, and being followed around all day and all night makes me nervous."

"Any chance we can ease up on the bodyguards?" the older Fairwood asked his security chief.

"As long as she's accompanied by a pack member, I think we can pull the guards during the day."

"In that case, maybe you'd like to join me for lunch in my office?" Gavin said to her with a smile.

She squeezed his leg, where her hand was still resting. "I'd like that."

"You'll need to take her back to the school afterward to rejoin her work group," Elder Fenner said. "I'll go update her current guards."

Henry waited until he was gone. "You're responsible for her now, son. Remember that."

"Yes, Dad." Gavin grinned. Sometimes his father forgot he was a man and not a little boy.

"What have you got up your sleeve?" Gavin asked her as he escorted her back to the school after lunch.

Dot smiled. "Why, what do you mean?"

"You're up to something." He stopped and grabbed her arm. "Call it instinct, but it worries me."

"Maybe I'm just enjoying being part of the pack."

I don't believe it for a second, he thought. But when she pulled him behind a building and pulled his head down to hers, he didn't think about it anymore. The kiss was light at first, but when her tongue traced the edges of his mouth, he couldn't stand it and he pulled her closer and increased the pressure. He wanted more, so much more, but he limited himself to making love to her mouth for now.

"Where do you think you're going?" Tasha asked, leaning casually against the wall of the woman's dorm. Dot was walking out the back door with her helmet in one hand, and carrying her saddlebags in the other.

"Dmitri got done with my bike. I thought I'd take it for a test drive around the village." Dot avoided her bodyguard's eyes and kept walking.

"In the dark? And you need your clothes in your saddlebags to do that?" Tasha stepped in front of Dot to stop her.

"I promised Gavin one week and I gave it to him," Dot said, stepping to one side to go around Tasha, but Tasha moved with her.

"So now you're going to run away?"

Dot quickly considered her options. Tasha was stronger, faster, and armed. "I'm not running away. I have a plan."

"Why don't you tell me about it?"

"I'm going to my see my aunt. I suspect all of this is tied to my father, whoever he is. I'm hoping she can tell me why."

"Where does she live?"

"If you don't know, you can't tell anyone else, and I can't be tracked there." Dot turned to Tasha with tears in her eyes. Crying was an effective tool to use against men, she wondered if Tasha would fall for the ploy as well. "I need to do this, Tasha, please don't stop me. I will be back in time to go to the Council meeting."

"The sentries will stop you before you ever get out of pack territory. I can get you out, but I will help you on one condition." Tasha grinned. "Did you know I have a motorcycle too? I'm going with you."

Nine

"I thought Dot was going to join you for lunch?" Henry asked from the door of Gavin's office.

"Is it that time already?" Gavin pulled his attention away from the computer screen and looked up at the clock. "I wonder where she is. Do you know what her schedule is today?"

"She's with a group doing cleanup on the road south of the village. We thought it would be a nice break for her to get out in nature for a little while." The older Fairwood pulled a cell phone out of his pocket. "Maybe they're just running late." He scrolled through his contacts and pushed a couple of buttons. "Is the road cleanup crew back? Is Ms. McKenzie on her way here?"

"What do you mean, she wasn't with them?"

"When was the last time anyone saw her?"

"Last night? With Tasha?"

"I want the sentries responsible in my office in the next five minutes." Henry growled. "Drag them out of bed if you need to. I want answers now!"

He turned to his son. "She's gone. Left last night. Come to my office and we'll talk."

"We were all so concerned with someone coming in and trying to grab her that we never thought about telling the sentries she couldn't leave." Elder Fenner stood in front of his pack leader's desk with his eyes on the floor. "And the men last night knew of the Council's protection order, so they didn't think twice when Tasha said they were going for a ride."

"I've put the word out to friends to keep an eye out for her," Henry said. Gavin stared out the window of his father's office, keeping track of the conversation. "But with no idea where they were going, there's not a lot we can do except hope that Tasha keeps her out of trouble."

"She promised me she would stay," Gavin said, shoving his hands into his pockets. Punching the wall wouldn't do him any good.

"If I recall, she promised you a week. It's been eight days."

"Do you want me to pull the added sentries?" asked the security chief. "It doesn't make much sense to keep them on duty."

"No, I want security as tight as ever. No one knows she's gone, and if anyone is watching, I want to make it seem as if nothing has changed."

"I should have known she was up to something." Gavin sat heavily in one of the chairs. "She was almost too happy when we talked yesterday. I thought she was settling into pack life."

Henry walked across the room to the bar, and pulled a couple bottles of beers from the mini-fridge. Gavin heard the hiss as the lids popped off. One was shoved into his hand. "She had us both fooled," his father admitted. "Now all we can do is wait and hope one of them calls."

His alarm clock was broken; at least the red numbers glowing in the darkness of his bedroom never seemed to change no matter how long Gavin stared at it. He couldn't sleep, and every time he dozed off the dreams someone chasing her woke him again. He rolled over on one side so the moonlight streaming in his window wasn't in his eyes. He closed them, tired of staring at the clock.

The cell phone on the nightstand vibrated and the mournful jazz strain set as his ringtone startled him. He rolled over to grab it. "Hello?"

"It's Tasha. Are you alone?"

"Yes." Gavin sat up with the phone pressed to his ear and checked the clock. Two in the morning. He sat up and swung his legs over the edge of the bed. "Is Dot okay? Where are you?"

Tasha chuckled. "Yes, she's fine. And I have no idea where we are, except a little hotel between here and there. I could probably nose around and find out, but it doesn't really matter. She tells me we will get where we're going tomorrow."

"Does she know you're calling?"

"Yes, she's right here. She says to tell you this phone is untraceable, so don't even try. She has all the makings of a good spy, this girl of yours."

"Let me talk to her."

"Not yet. I'm supposed to tell you that if you need to reach us, you can call this number—she unblocked it for this call, so it should show up in your display."

Gavin checked. "It does."

"Good. We'll be keeping the phone turned off, and only turn it on to check for messages."

"I want to talk to her."

There was a muffled conference at the other end. "She's afraid you are going to yell at her."

"I won't if she'll talk to me."

A moments silence was followed by a quiet, "Hello, Gavin."

"Dot? Where are you? What do you think you're doing?" he barked.

"You promised not to yell at me."

"I'm sorry, don't hang up. I won't yell anymore. Where are you?"

"I can't tell you yet. I will when I get back." There was a long pause and Gavin wondered if the connection had dropped. "If you want me to," she added, and Gavin's breath hitched at the longing in her voice.

"Why didn't you take me with you?"

"I need to be able to think straight, and when I'm with you I can't do that."

"Yes, come back to me, Dot. Please come back to me."

"I will." He heard the phone changing hands and then Tasha came back on the line.

"We'll call you tomorrow. Dot says to tell you to get some sleep. Goodnight." The silence in his ear let him know the call had ended. He immediately dialed the number back, but the call went to voice mail.

Dot sat on the floor of the living room at her aunt's house, playing with the toy soldiers her nephew had carried out of his bedroom. He knelt next to her, lining the toys up and knocking them over randomly. "Tell me about my father," she said, glancing at her aunt as she placed a plastic horse near the pretend battlefield. Tasha had excused herself to take a walk around the neighborhood.

"Bruce? He was a good man, and so in love with your mother."

"Not Bruce," Dot interrupted her. "I remember Bruce, and I loved him too. Tell me about my birth father. Did you ever meet him?"

"Are you sure you want to hear this?"

"No, I'm not sure, but I need to, Aunt Mary." Her aunt hadn't changed much in the five years since Dot had last seen her. Her Navajo heritage showed in her high cheekbones, black hair and dark complexion. Dot remembered her mother appearing more white than Indian. "What do you know about him?"

"You're not sick or something, are you, Dot? Do you need the family medical history? I've been trying to collect it, but it's pretty sparse because the Navajo side of the family didn't keep written records, and the oral histories don't cover the topic."

"No, I'm fine. I have a new doctor, and got a checkup about a week ago. She wants me to take vitamins and eat more fruits and vegetables, but I'm fine. What do you know about my father?"

"I only met him a few times, and if first impressions count for anything, I didn't like him, but for some reason your mother loved him. She was my big sister, and when I tried to talk to her about it, she laughed at me and said I would understand when I got older. It made me mad because she always got to do things I couldn't do because she was bigger than me." Mary thought for a minute. "I remember him being a handsome man, all muscles, with wavy brown hair—men grew their hair longer back then—but something about his eyes bothered me. They were the funniest color."

Probably like mine, Dot thought. They'd been plain brown when she was a little girl, and had changed after she started shifting. Good thing she wore her contacts today.

"Your mother destroyed all the pictures she had of him after she met Bruce. I remember she made a big bonfire and burned them. Called it a cleansing ceremony."

"So what happened between them?"

Her aunt sighed. "I don't know. After she got pregnant with you, she started to dig into the old stories about tricksters and other creatures."

"She told me those stories as a child," Dot said quietly.

"I don't know what they had to do with your father, but he left before you were born and never came back. He sent flowers to your mother when you were born, and a stuffed animal for you, but she threw them out."

That was news to Dot. She had always thought her father had abandoned her mother. She would need to think about the revelation later. "Do you remember his name?"

"It was a weird one, and I was pretty young. I always called him Mike, but his name wasn't Michael, and I don't remember his last name." She stood. "I know she didn't put his name on your birth certificate. I remember she and your grandmother had a fight about that. Did you know your mother used to keep journals? I saved them for you when I cleaned out your house after she died. I have them in a box in the closet. Maybe they will tell you what you want to know."

The call came in about three o'clock in the morning. Gavin had lain awake the entire time, afraid that if he let himself fall asleep he would somehow miss it.

"Hello?"

"It's Tasha. You're alone?"

"Yes. How are you two doing?"

"Good. We'll be leaving here in the morning."

"Are you coming back?"

"Yes." She yawned. "Dot says to tell you it will probably take two days and not to worry. She is planning an indirect route so we can't be tracked."

"Can I talk to her?"

"Just a second."

The quiet voice he missed so much spoke next. "Hey, Gavin."

"Hello, Dot. How are you?"

"I'm doing all right. A little bit tired, but I've been worse."

"Did you find what you needed?"

"I'm working on it."

"The Council meeting will be in four days in Atlanta."

"We should be back in two."

He cleared his throat. "I miss you, Dot."

"I miss you too. I just hope we can still be friends."

"I hope we can be more than that."

Abruptly Tasha was back on the line. "She's crying, Gavin. What did you say to her?"

"I just told her I hoped we could be more than friends."

"You hurt her and I'll make you regret it. I don't care if you are the pack leader's son."

"Hurting her is the last thing I want to do. Bring her home safely, Tasha."

They were being followed. The four right turns they'd made proved it. One SUV, one pair of motorcyclists. She and Tasha needed to split up. Dot spotted a break in traffic, geared down, made a hard left and headed down an alley. Tasha followed her, but oncoming cars blocked their pursuers for the time being. At the end of the alley, a left-hand turn put them going the opposite way she wanted to go, but also gave them a chance to pull into the parking lot of a biker bar. She nosed her bike among the others and checked to see that Tasha did the same.

A couple of bikers stood outside smoking, and she pulled off her helmet as she walked up to them, fluffing up her hair with one hand, waiting until Tasha caught up with her. "Follow my lead," Dot said quietly. Then, fluttering her eyes and leisurely unzipping her jacket, she went up to them. "How's it going, boys?"

"Better now," grinned one. "Care for a smoke?"

Dot accepted a cigarette and let the biker light it for her, while she watched the parking lot and the street beyond. "You ever have any trouble with anyone messing with your bikes here?"

"Used to, but since the bar owner added a new security system," he poked another of the men in the ribs, "We haven't had any problems."

It must have been a long-standing joke, because both men roared with laughter. Dot grinned. "We were a little worried," she said. "We stopped at a convenience store down the road and a couple of suspicious guys were eying our bikes. We hope to have time for a beer, but are afraid to leave them for very long."

The SUV that had been following them slowly rolled down the street, and Dot felt Tasha jab her in the ribs. She barely nodded in acknowledgment. "If you ladies want a beer, we'll keep an eye on things out here for you. We're waiting for a friend anyway."

"Thanks." Dot dropped the cigarette on the ground and ground it into the dirt with the toe of her boot. "Maybe I can buy you one later."

"Well, I would like that but the old lady wouldn't and she's inside, so I'm going to have to decline the offer." He grinned. "Maybe another time."

She pouted and sighed. "Just my luck."

"*What are you doing?*" Tasha asked as they headed inside.

"Just playing the game," Dot explained in a low voice. "And I'm not done yet."

The bar wasn't crowded and Dot picked a bar stool in the middle of an unoccupied stretch, and Tasha took a seat beside her, clearly uncomfortable. "Beer," Dot told the bartender. When he moved out of earshot she explained, "My mental voice isn't focused enough yet to use in a place like this. I can't guarantee it won't be overheard."

The drinks arrived, and Dot paid for them, smiling broadly at the server. "You ladies from around here?" he asked.

"No, just in town for a few days, hoping to have some fun while we're here."

"You've come to the right place."

Tasha scanned the bar nervously. They were too close to Choate territory. When the barman moved away Dot asked "Anyone in here kin?"

"Not that I can sense."

"Good. Drink your beer now."

It didn't take long until a man slid into the barstool beside Dot. "You ladies want some company?"

"Depends on who's asking," she said, turning towards him with what she hoped was a dazzling smile.

"Care to join me and my friends?" With a jerk of his head, he indicated two men at one of the tables. They were typical bikers, big, burly men dressed in black leather jackets, jeans, with scarfs on their heads. Just what Dot was hoping for.

"Sure." She picked up her beer and slid off her seat. "I'm Maria, this is my friend Trish."

Tasha wanted to object, but Dot seemed to know what she was doing. They pulled up chairs and Tasha kept one eye on the front door while she watched Dot flirt with each man in turn. Her diligence was rewarded when two men walked in and she caught the distinct scent of wolf. She kicked Dot under the table. Dot half-turned to her and nodded.

"You want another beer?" one man asked as Dot drained her glass.

"I'd better not," she said, sounding reluctant. "I don't like to drink and drive." She glanced around the bar and faked a look of dismay. "Oh, no."

"What?" asked her new friend.

"See those two men at the bar?" Dot chewed on her lower lip. "I think those are guys who gave us a bad time earlier today."

"You sure?"

"No." She leaned forward. "Tell you what. We'll make a trip to the restroom, and you keep an eye on them. When we come back you can tell us what happens." She stood and grabbed Tasha's hand. "Come on."

When they got to the restroom, Dot checked to make sure all the stalls were empty. "Here's the plan, Tasha. We'll have the guys run interference so we can get out of here. My guess is that the others are waiting outside. Hopefully our buddies are making sure no one messes with the bikes. You still have that revolver strapped to your leg?"

"How'd you know about that?" Tasha thought she'd kept it hidden.

"Never mind. Put it in your pocket. You may need to use it."

"You want me to shoot them?"

"No. Their tires. If the SUV follows us, we'll stick together. If they follow on motorcycles, we'll have to split up. When we get back to the table, switch helmets. It might confuse them."

"Are you sure you know what you're doing?"

"You have a better idea?"

"No."

"I'm glad we filled up a few miles back. We should have enough gas to get back to the village. You know how to get there from here, right?"

"Yes." Tasha grabbed Dot's hand. "Don't take any unnecessary chances."

Dot grinned. "Depends upon your definition of unnecessary. Now my advice is to use the facilities while we're here. Then put on your sexiest smile and we'll play the rest of the game."

When they left the restroom, they had to walk past the bar. The two men blocked their way. Dot instantly noticed the yellowish tint of their eyes.

"Going somewhere?" one asked with a sneer.

A large hand was placed on his shoulder. The other man found a large arm wrapped around his neck, and the bartender casually hefted a gun he'd pulled from under the bar. "You ladies ride safe," the bartender said. Dot blew him a kiss, and she and Tasha grabbed their helmets and left.

"Nobody touched your bikes," the man Dot had been talking to outside told them as they exited. "Although a couple of guys were sniffing around them."

"Thanks." Dot stood on her toes and kissed the man on the cheek. "Appreciate the help."

Tasha sniffed the air as they approached the bike. "*Kin.*"

Dot nodded. "Stick to the plan, Tasha. I've done this before and you haven't."

"We should stick together."

"They won't hurt me, Tasha, they want me alive. You're the one in danger. I'm betting we will be followed by the motorcycles, and splitting up is the best thing. If one follows you, shoot out the tires and then get back to the village as fast as your bike will go."

Tasha put on Dot's helmet and adjusted the chin strap. She hesitated before climbing on her bike. "Good luck, Dot."

Dot grinned. "Good hunting, Tasha."

They pulled out of the parking lot and onto the street together. Dot and Tasha had gone no more than a block before two motorcycles pulled onto the street behind them. *"I'll wait until we are out of town to make my move,"* Tasha sent.

Dot nodded and switched gears. At the next intersection, she made a sharp turn to the left, and Tasha continued straight. Several miles out of town, Tasha spotted a billboard just past the crest of a hill. She pulled her bike behind it and killed the engine. Crouching low, with her revolver in her hand, she ran around the end of it and found a spot with an open view of the road. She was barely in place before her follower came over the top of rise.

Her first shot missed, but her pursuer must not have heard the sound of the revolver because he slowed down, apparently searching for her on the road ahead. A second shot found its mark, and the rider lost control. He fought the bike, but couldn't save it and went down hard with the bike halfway on top of him. Tasha waited, but he didn't get back up. Good hunting indeed, Tasha thought, as she ran towards her bike. The motor responded promptly when she turned the key, and she guided the bike back to the pavement. It was a touring bike, and not made for riding on the dirt, so she half-walked it until she got to the road. The other rider didn't move, and without another thought she shifted into second and headed home.

Sentries at the west entrance flagged her down and she gave them the barest of details. As she pulled her bike up in front of the headquarters, the front doors flung open and people boiled out of the building. She shut down the engine, lowered the kickstand, and pulled off Dot's helmet. Gavin was the first to reach her.

"Where is she?" he demanded. "Where's Dot?"

TEN

"She's on her way," Tasha said She almost stumbled as she climbed off the motorcycle. It had been a long, hard ride. "At least, I hope she is." She glanced up at Elder Fenner. "I suggest you alert the sentries at every entrance. No telling where she'll come in, or if she'll be alone."

Let's find out just how good this guy is, she thought. Dot guided her bike full speed over a series of speed bumps in the busy parking lot. She clung to the handlebars as she went airborne and landed with a heavy thud. The bike stayed upright and straight, but the man behind her wasn't so lucky. In her rearview mirror she watched as he almost lost control. One for me, she grinned.

He didn't let up. She would have been disappointed if he had given up so soon. What to do next? She didn't want to draw too much attention to the two of them. She had a plan formulating for the finale and if the cops interfered it would put an end to all her fun.

A short set of stairs leading to the sidewalk along

the road caught her eye. The heavy-duty springs Dmitri had fitted on her bike should be able to handle them. Without considering the consequences, she slowed, rose off the seat, bent her knees, and fought the bike to the bottom. The other rider stopped at the top, revved his motor, and drove off to find another way. Two.

She could duck and hide at this point, but now she wanted this over. For the first time in a long time, she had somewhere to be and hopefully, someone waiting for her. No, she couldn't think about that now. She made her way to the edge of town, her senses constantly scanning for pursuit. It wasn't long coming. Time to get serious.

She spotted a heavy stand of oak trees not far from town, but it stood too close to a small subdivision for her comfort. She needed to get farther away. She wanted no witnesses. If the size of the image in her mirror was a correct indication, her pursuer was about a half mile behind her. A bigger gap would give her more time to set her trap.

Another five miles on the smooth pavement and he remained the same distance away. She was starting to get tired of this. Time to end the game. A dirt road ahead that appeared to wind through farmland and into a forest held promise. Her smaller bike should handle the bumps and potholes better. Besides, he would be eating her dust. She grinned again. Three.

Past the tree line, she dropped the bike, killing the engine. There wasn't time to do this gracefully. A flock of crows rose from the trees, protesting her appearance. In her tank bag, she found the nylon rope she remembered stashing there several months ago. Out of sight of the oncoming rider, she tied it tightly around the trunk of an old maple, then dashed to the other side of the road and loosely wrapped the rope once around the trunk of another tree. She wished she had time to cover the line with a scattering of leaves, but the other rider was too close. She hid in the brush that lined the road and waited, her breathing no louder than the barest ruffle of leaves.

The helmetless rider drove faster than he should have, probably fearful he'd lost her. Just before he passed her on the narrow road, she pulled hard on the rope and caught the bike below the handlebars. He flew over them and fell to the ground, hard, hitting his head on a large stone embedded in the road. The bike continued a few feet before toppling. She let go of the rope and watched, but he didn't move. Her hands hurt, and she saw the rope had torn her palms open, making them bleed. She had no time to worry about them now. She ripped off her blouse, removed her shoes, and dropped her jeans. Remembering her lessons, she reached for her *other* half, ignoring the pain. A shimmering in the air, and a large gray wolf stood in her place.

The wolf paced out to the road and cautiously sniffed at the fallen rider. Definitely kin. The leather bag around the wolf's neck dragged across the man's chest as it licked his face, and he groaned, but did not open his eyes. A quick swipe of the man's cheek left streaks of blood. Four. The wolf bared its canines, howled, and licked its bloody paw.

Dressed again, Dot retrieved the rope and stuck it back into her tank bag. She might need it another time. She slipped the wallet out of his back pocket and grabbed what little cash it held. After the trip, her own supply was running low. Out of curiosity, she checked the name on the driver's license, and filed the information in her memory for later, then returned the wallet to its pocket. Taking care of one last detail, she pulled the keys out of the ignition and tossed them as far into the woods as possible.

A single headlight pierced the falling darkness and the sentry sprang to alert. The motorcycle slowed, and rolled to a stop at his post. Dot pushed the face shield up on the helmet and bucked the gear shift into neutral. She planted both feet on the ground and stretched her legs.

"Tasha make it back?"

"About an hour ago." He noticed the blood on her clothes. "You need medical attention?"

"No, my hands will take a few days to heal, but I'm all right." She'd wrapped her palms in a scarf she'd bought when she stopped to get gas a few miles back. The blood had already soaked the leather grips on the handlebars. They would be hard to get clean. "Are they mad at me?"

"I wouldn't know." He grinned, understanding immediately who "they" were. "But I do know they are waiting for you at headquarters."

She sighed. "Radio in and tell them I'm on my way. And ask if a big juicy steak could be waiting for me, preferable rare. Hunting was good, but now I'm hungry."

The steak was delicious, and even the bowl of fresh fruit Dr. Tracy placed in front of Dot enticed her. With all the gauze wrapped around her hands, it was hard to cut the steak into bite-sized pieces, but as tempted as she was, she didn't think she could get away with picking it up and tearing into it with her teeth. Not in present company anyway.

Elder Fairwood had chased away most of the people, and he and Elder Fenner were waiting impatiently for her to finish eating before throwing more questions at her. Dr. Tracy had finally stopped fussing, and Tasha was hanging out, grinning like the Cheshire cat. Tasha had already been put through the wringer, and she was having too much fun watching Dot's discomfort. From the corner of her eye, Dot saw Gavin sitting in a chair, staring at her. He had finally stopped pacing, but the frown on his face told her he wasn't happy. She finished off the bowl of fruit and pushed away from the table. Those last two bites of steak looked good, but she was full. The wolf had been fed, and now she felt human again.

"Those guys were definitely kin," she said. "Tasha and I both sensed them. So much for the order of protection from the Council. And I'm pretty sure I know the pack affiliation."

"We will bring this to the Council's attention," the pack leader said. "They will not be happy. I wish we could prove who the attackers were."

"I got a name," Dot said casually. "On the one I dropped. We might not want to reveal the information unless the Council asks for it. Wouldn't want word to get out in case he decides to file legal charges. I can always plead self-defense, but I really don't want the hassle."

"How about you give me the name later, in private," Elder Fenner suggested, then he grinned. "And we can talk about you joining my team at the same time."

"I don't know how to use a gun," she protested.

"With the way your mind works, I don't care. You can learn to shoot, but I can't teach someone to think the way you do."

"I don't think we should be making decisions about Dot's long-term role with the pack tonight." Henry put a gentle hand on her shoulder. "I'm hoping she will stay, but there is plenty of time for her to make that decision, and I suspect she is too tired to think about it right now. Besides, several other Elders have asked me if she would be available to work with them."

Gavin's father wanted her to stay? Other Elders wanted her to stay? Luckily, he moved his hand before he felt her trembling.

Henry continued. "We had your things—what little you left behind—moved back into our guest room, Dot. Tasha, will you get her saddlebags and take them to the room?"

"I'll get a few of my things as well," Tasha said. "That is, if you still want me as her bodyguard."

"You've had a long day too. I think Gavin can handle the duties tonight, as long as we have patrols outside."

The security chief nodded. "Tanya is still on duty."

"Then let's break this up and call it a night. Gavin, will you please escort Dot to the house?"

Gavin stood and adjusted the rifle on his shoulder.

"Of course, Elder," he said, avoiding Dot's gaze.

His silence as they walked outside made Dot nervous. She had expected him to yell at her, but the stillness was worse. "You're mad at me," she said about halfway to the house. He grunted, but didn't say anything. The moisture in her eyes was just because she was tired, right? She blinked to clear them. "You don't have to do this," she offered. "I'll ask your father if I can go back to the woman's dorm."

Suddenly he pushed her into a spot not illuminated by the street lights and up against a large tree trunk. The ridges of the bark imprinted themselves on the skin of her back even through her shirt. "The problem," he said in a voice was as rough as the hand grabbing her shoulder, "Is I can't decide whether to be mad at you or kiss you." He moved closer so his body pinned hers against the tree. "And the kissing part is winning out." Then his other hand slid behind her head pushing forward so when he leaned down their lips crushed together.

"You had me so scared," Gavin said, when he finally pulled away. He didn't want to, but if they didn't get to the house soon, the sentries would start to worry. "I just found you, and then you were gone."

"I'm sorry," she said running her fingers down his chest. He shivered at the touch. "But it was something I had to do."

"Where did you go?" He put his arm around her waist and they resumed walking. When the Elders had asked, she hadn't given them a straight answer.

"I visited my past. I've been avoiding it for six

years, but I think I'm closer to understanding it now."

"You could have taken me with you." He nodded to the guard that stood at the front door of the house as he opened it so Dot could enter. She plopped down on the couch, and he put the rifle on the coffee table and sat next to her. She sighed and leaned against him, and he ran his fingers through her hair.

"One day I'll take you where I went," she said. "But not yet. Not until this is over."

"Don't you trust me?"

"You I trust. But I have to protect you too. The less you know, the less of a target you are."

Gavin chuckled. "I can protect myself and you too. If I can survive a war, I can survive anything."

I've been living a war of my own for five years, one battle at a time, Dot thought, but no one seems to understand that. Sometimes, it seemed the war would never end. "Is your father on the Council?" Dot asked, switching the subject.

"No. Most of the representatives are retired pack leaders, but ours is one of the Elders. Active pack leaders are not allowed on the Council, they're welcome to attend meetings and speak, but they don't get a vote."

"Why is the meeting in Atlanta?"

"Neutral territory," Gavin told her. "There's no pack in the area, and under the rules, one can't be established there. It's nobody's turf."

"I've never been to Atlanta," she lied.

"Me neither. We can explore it together."

"Don't you have a smaller suitcase than this one, Raven? I'm only taking a couple of blouses and an extra pair of jeans."

"You're going to Atlanta! The conference will be two or three days, I'm sure Gavin will want to take you out to eat. Plus, you'll probably have to attend Council meetings so you will need more than that." Raven stopped halfway through her task of pulling luggage out of the attic and stared at Dot.

"It's all I have," Dot admitted.

"I knew you didn't have any dresses," Raven muttered. "If you can go get Dawn to put her shoes on, I'll get the car. We're going shopping."

"Try this one on too." Raven handed another outfit to Dot. She held three more.

"They're very nice, but I can't afford any of them even if they do fit."

"Not a problem." Raven eyed a selection of fancy bras. "The company is buying. I already cleared it with Dad when I told him we were coming here."

'Here' was a department store in the town closest to the village, but out of pack territory. Raven knew several of the salesladies by name. Dot suspected at least one of them was a shifter, and it made her more comfortable.

"You think Gavin will like these?" Raven handed her a lacy red bra and matching bikini panties. "I'm guessing they're your size."

Dot felt the blood rushing to her face. "I wouldn't

know," she said, leaning over and picking up a toy Dawn had dropped to cover her embarrassment. She handed it back to the little girl who was securely strapped into her stroller.

"He's taking it slow?" Raven grinned. "Good for him. He's finally learned something. I've seen him rush into relationships too many times. When he falls, he falls hard."

A wave of jealousy struck Dot. She tried to convince herself to be reasonable. They had done nothing more than share a couple of kisses. Of course he'd been with other women. He was a handsome man after all. She had no claim on him, and until she got the mess that was her life straightened out she shouldn't be making any long-range plans.

"Let's hit the dressing room." Raven had picked out two more dresses for Dot. "We can check out the jeans next."

Raven had gone off to pay for the clothes they'd selected—far too many in Dot's opinion—and she was admiring the jewelry while she waited. One particular necklace caught her eye, but it was sterling silver, and for some reason silver irritated her. Her skin itched when she wore it.

She smiled at the saleslady watching her, and moved down to the costume jewelry display. The prices for these pieces fit her limited budget better anyway. As she reached to examine a pair of star earrings, a little girl screamed. Dashing around the counter, she frantically tried to locate Raven. A flurry of activity at one of the checkouts caught her eye, and she spotted Raven chasing after two men running towards the door. Dot saw Dawn grasped in the arms of one.

Dot was closer and faster. She swerved around an old woman standing, mouth open, watching the action, and reached the exit before the men did. She had no weapons, and frantically scanned her surroundings to see what was within her reach. There is always something to use is what a friend had told her when she was living on the streets.

"Put the girl down," she ordered in the firmest voice she could muster.

"Sure, sweetie," drawled the one carrying Dawn. "Just as soon as you join us for a little walk out to our car. The four of us will drive away, and later we'll let Mommy there know where she can find the brat." Dawn screamed again as he rearranged his hold and nearly dropped her. "You don't have a choice."

ELEVEN

There's always a choice. Find it. "I'm under a protection order from the Council," Dot said. She couldn't see if either man had a gun—if she charged the one holding Dawn, she might be able to make him drop the little girl long enough for Raven to get to her.

"Don't know about no protection order or no council," the other man said. "Just know there's a nice little bounty on your head and we aim to collect the money."

Carefully, she extended her senses and sniffed. These men didn't smell like kin. That gave her a small advantage, but she didn't dare drop into wolf form. From the corner of her eye, Dot saw a man in a uniform running up behind the abductors. He wasn't wearing a police uniform, so he must be store security. She wondered if he carried a gun, but he wouldn't be able to use it if he did—not with Dawn at risk. She risked a tendril of thought aimed at Raven. Somehow, she didn't think it would matter if anyone else overheard it. *I'm going to try something. Be ready to grab Dawn.*

"What's going on here?" At the sound of the security guard's voice, the man holding Dawn turned his head for the briefest of moments. That was all Dot needed. Three swift steps and she dropped and slammed her body in his legs. He fell on top of Dot and dropped Dawn. At the same time, Dot's feet hit the shins of the second man, and he lost his balance.

Dot struggled from under the weight holding her on the floor, and, as she got to all fours, she saw Dawn in Raven's arms. The security guard restrained one man, and two male bystanders were holding down the one she'd crashed into. She noticed the gauze around her hands showed the color of fresh blood—she must have broken open the scabs when she hit the floor. Her legs shook, but she managed to stand up and walk over to Raven. "Is she all right?" she asked, her voice unsteady, as she stroked the little girl's hair. Raven had tears in her eyes, and Dot reached out and drew her and her daughter into a tight embrace.

The argument had been going on for at least an hour. Dot had stopped paying attention. The same things were repeated over and over, and she grew tired of listening. She wanted to sneak out, but Tasha and Tanya sat on either side of her, and she couldn't even go to the bathroom alone.

"Raid their holdings tonight and put an end to this."

"Council protections? What Council protections?"

"Too dangerous in Atlanta!"

"A risk to everyone else!"

"Owe her nothing."

"An asset! We need her!"

"Didn't ask for this."

If they would stop yelling, she might be able to fall asleep. She wondered if Dr. Tracy had slipped something into the bottled water she offered Dot while patching up the bleeding palms—again. She heard Tasha laugh as she leaned her head against her friend's shoulder and closed her eyes.

"Time for you to go to bed." A soft chuckle woke her.

Dot realized that she lay stretched out on the couch where the three of them had been sitting. Someone had covered her with a blanket. "I'll just stay here," she protested. She didn't want to move.

Another chuckle and then strong arms slipped under her body. "Not when there's a nice warm bed waiting for you. And we have an early morning if we want to get to Atlanta on time."

Her eyes popped open. "Atlanta?"

"Yes." Gavin easily hoisted her and placed the barest of kisses on her mouth. "We're going. Dad got the Council to agree to provide bodyguards for our entire delegation, including you. They're extremely upset that their protection order was broken, and are anxious to get to the bottom of this."

"I didn't mean to create any problems."

"We know." Much to her embarrassment she realized he was carrying her through the hallways of the headquarters.

"I can walk, Gavin. Put me down."

"That's okay, I like having you in my arms." She was too tired to come up with a smart response. Whatever Dr. Tracy had given her kicked back in, and

Dot dozed again, safe in his grasp. She awoke enough to know when Gavin put her in her bed and kissed her. But she thought she was dreaming when he whispered "Sleep well, Dot. I love you."

The hotel room was nothing like the rooms in the rundown places where Dot normally stayed. They were on the twelve floor of a downtown hotel, and from the large window she had a view of the flower-filled courtyard. She had a room to herself, big enough for a small family, but Gavin and his father shared a suite with Elder Talbot, the pack's representative to the Council. Part of the team of bodyguards who would be staying with them for the entire trip met them at the airport and brought them here in a limo. It had been the first time she'd ever ridden in a limo—even her bike had been a luxury when she bought it, old and used.

"You should move away from the window, miss." Jack was not what she imagined a bodyguard should look like, but evidently he knew his job. He was only about five and a half feet tall, and a bit on the chubby side, but the revolver he carried in a shoulder harness showed he meant business. And as he was to be her shadow sixteen hours a day for the next three or four days, that was a good thing.

She reluctantly stepped away from the view, and he closed the curtains. "Don't want people knowing which room you're in," he said. "Now I'll step out of the room if you want to get changed." Dot was puzzled, but he continued, "For the opening session of the Council meeting. That's about an hour from now. I figured you'd want to freshen up."

"So are you going to be my tour guide as well as my bodyguard?" Dot asked.

"Pretty much."

That would be all right for a day or two, but hopefully this trip would wrap up soon. She stared at the closet with all the new clothes she and Raven had bought, and wondered what she should wear.

"Most women wear a business suit." Jack grinned, one hand on the door. "But that's just my two cents worth."

"Bodyguard, tour guide, and fashion adviser? You're a good man to have around."

Dot was going to have to do something about her hair. The roots were showing, and it was time for another dye job. She wondered what Gavin would think if she went back to her red and yellow streaks. Or maybe purple and pink this time. She grinned at herself in the mirror. She could see it now—neon green hair to go with the dark blue skirt and blazer she had chosen to wear.

The knock on the door was the pattern Jack had told her he would use, but she peered out the peephole first anyway. She opened it a crack and peeked into the hallway before opening it the rest of the way. He looked her up and down approvingly, and then stepped aside to make room for her to enter the hallway.

Gavin and his father were leaving their room at the same time followed by their bodyguard. Gavin slipped his arm around Dot's waist. "Stay close to me," he whispered in her ear.

"Is there a problem?" she asked anxiously.

"No." He grinned. "I just want everyone to know that the most beautiful girl in the place is with me."

Blushing, she said, "You're pretty darn attractive yourself. Did your father talk you into wearing a suit?" The gray suit must have been custom-made to fit him, the way the jacket sat gracefully across his broad shoulders and chest, then narrowed at his trim waistline. He wore a pale green shirt underneath, and a silk tie with a pattern that reminded her of wolves. He'd shaved, and it was the first time she'd seen him without at least a day's growth of stubble.

"Suits are mandatory for today's meeting," he explained. "And for the business dinner tonight. Tomorrow we may have time to relax a little."

"I don't know if I can relax at all with our shadows around." She glanced back at Jack and his co-worker. "No offense meant, Jack. I'm not used to this."

"None taken." The serious face he wore slipped for a moment and he winked at her, then he was all business again.

Dot tried to ignore the stares directed her way and pay attention to the speaker. At this rate, she would have to resort to pinching herself to keep from yawning. She heard a lot of references to "unity" and "for the good of all kin" and "brothers under the skin." Nice phrases, but no reference to women in his speech, no women on the elevated platform where the representatives sat, and very few women in the audience. Her skin prickled even though she and Gavin sat in the back corner of the room. The eyes that roamed in their direction were more than curious.

The speaker finally wrapped up his speech with one last reference to "oneness," and earned a round of polite applause for his efforts. The audience waited until all the counselors left the dais before they stood and trickled out of the room. Jack laid a hand on Dot's shoulder as she started to stand. "Wait until the room's cleared," he said. "I don't want to try to push through a crowd."

She fidgeted in her chair, watching as others chatted with old friends. A group of three men on their way out stopped in the aisle near them. She felt Gavin stiffen beside her. The oldest of the trio stared at her for a long moment, and Dot had the impression he wanted to intimidate her. Let him try. She stared back at him with contempt. It would take more than a glare to frighten her. Finally, he nodded at her and he and his companions moved away.

Dot let out the breath she hadn't even realized she was holding, and turned to Gavin. "Let me guess," she said, hiding all emotion. "They were members of the Choate pack."

TWELVE

"Not just members," Gavin explained. "That was Elder Choate, the pack leader." They were sitting in the men's suite resting for a few minutes before dinner.

Henry grunted. "He hasn't been seen out of his territory for a couple of years now."

Dot fiddled with the bandage on her palm. "I don't think I gave him any reason to like me."

"Not every pack allows women a voice in the running of things," Gavin said. "A few only allow males in any leadership activities. I suspect the Choate pack is one of those. Even Dad didn't give in to having women as Elders until a few years ago," he said, grinning. "You probably gave Elder Choate a heart attack when you didn't back down from him. Or at least a major case of indigestion."

"Keep those comments private," Henry reminded them. "I don't want to hear them anywhere but here. He is a pack leader, and deserves respect."

"Of course," Gavin agreed, but his mouth twitched.

"It would've been better if he hadn't seen Dot

ahead of time," Henry mused, "But since he did, at least Dot knows who to avoid now."

The next morning Dot was left to entertain herself. Henry and Gavin needed to attend a part of the Council meeting she was not welcome at, and Jack didn't want her wandering through the public areas of the hotel. Gavin had promised to take her to the aquarium after lunch, so she lounged in an overstuffed easy chair reading. Jack sat in another chair, cleaning his gun, when they heard a knock on the door. "Housekeeping," a woman in the hallway said.

Jack jumped up and cracked the door slightly after peering out the peephole. "Let me see your employee badge." He nodded. "All right, come in."

Dot glanced up as the little Hispanic woman came into the room, somewhat hesitant. She barely glanced at Dot before going into the bathroom to start her cleanup. Jack re-assembled his revolver. "I'm going across the hall for a moment," he said. "I'll be right back."

As soon as the door clicked shut behind him, Dot jumped out of the chair and went to the bathroom. "Serena?" she asked.

"Si?" The maid glanced up and then looked again. "Maria? Is that really you?"

"Yes, it's me." Dot gave her a quick hug. "You don't know how glad I am to see you, but you must pretend you don't know me."

"But why?"

"I can't explain. There's not enough time. But I may need your help later." At Jack's knock on the door she put one finger on her lips. "Remember, you don't know me."

She stared in amazement as a dark form floated overhead. "This is so cool!" The long plastic tube put them in the middle of an ever-changing display of sea life.

"I haven't been to an aquarium since I was a little boy," Gavin said. "And I don't remember seeing manta rays or sharks."

"Thanks for bringing me here." Dot squeezed his hand. With Jack hanging back a few steps, she didn't feel comfortable doing anything more.

"Depending on how things go tomorrow, maybe we can go to the zoo in the afternoon."

"That sounds like fun." She studied a brightly colored fish as it sailed by. "Although I'm not looking forward to tomorrow morning." Henry had told her she would need to attend the council meeting as she would be the main topic of discussion. She dreaded it, but might finally get her answers.

Gavin pushed a lock of hair away from her face. "It'll work out," he said. "You'll see." They moved on to a display of a tropical reef. "I think the penguins are my favorite," he confessed. "I still think the way they waddle around is funny."

"Do we have time to go back?"

"Sorry, but it's time to leave," Jack said, suddenly very close to her side. "This place just got unfriendly."

"How many of them?" Gavin asked, without taking his eyes off the exhibit. He pulled Dot a little closer.

"I can only spot two, but that doesn't mean there aren't more."

"There's three of us, and one of us is armed. I don't think we need to worry. Besides," Dot said, and the determination in her expression surprised Gavin. "I won't let them ruin a perfectly good afternoon. My vote is that we stay as long as possible just to annoy them."

Jack chuckled. "It's probably not the safest move, but I like it."

Dot's mouth twitched. "What I'd like to do is flip them the bird, but there are little kids here. So let's turn around and let them see that we know they're here, then go on to the next display." She studied the leaflet in her hand. "The river, I think."

"You sure you want to do this?" Gavin asked quietly as they turned.

"No, but I'm going to do it anyway." She held her chin high, and nodded regally as she swept by their followers.

"I can't believe you let her do that," Henry said to his son as they waited for their food. They had chosen a restaurant near the hotel for supper, and surveying the room, Dot recognized others from the meeting eating there as well. Jack and the other bodyguard sat at a nearby table.

"I don't think it was a matter of letting me," Dot chuckled. "I don't think Gavin could come up with a way to stop me." She wore a low cut deep red dress Raven had picked out for her, and noticed that Gavin's eyes seemed glued to her. She caught his eye and winked. Other men seated nearby were checking her out too, and she decided to take it as a compliment and not a threat.

Henry shook his head. "Tomorrow you must be on your best behavior. The Council won't take kindly to anything that seems disrespectful."

"I understand," Dot said. "I'll try my hardest." She waited while the server put her Chicken Marsala in front of her.

"The representatives haven't ever dealt with an issue like this," he explained. "I can't even get a feel for how they are planning to approach it."

"Are they going to let Dot speak?" Gavin asked.

"I don't know." Henry took a bite of his steak and chewed it while he thought. "It's pretty rare that women are allowed to appear at Council deliberations. Of course, there are a number of new members this year, so we'll see."

They don't let women speak? What is this, the 1950's? We'll see about that, she thought, as she stabbed a piece of her chicken with more force than needed. Out of the corner of her eye, she saw Jack stand up and quickly looked up from her plate. The empty chair across from Dot was pulled out and a man sat in it.

"Pardon the intrusion, but I thought we could have a conversation before the assembly tomorrow," said Damyon Choate.

"I'm not sure we have anything to say to each other," Henry said.

"It's not you I want to speak to. It's the young lady."

Dot took her time answering, examining him. He was older than she expected, and his hair totally gray.

Had it been brown like hers when he was younger? His cheeks were sunk in, but she guessed his face had been firm and well-formed at his peak. She wondered how he managed to hold onto his position as pack leader—the only reason Henry maintained his control was because Gavin had chosen not to challenge him. What power did this man have over the younger men in his pack?

"I don't believe we have anything to talk about," she said eventually.

"I have some information I would prefer to tell you in private."

"Everything you need to say to me you can say in front of the Council," she said firmly.

He leaned across the table. "You have been lucky so far," he said. "Your luck will run out one of these days." He stood up as Jack moved in behind him. "And then you will come to me."

"What was that all about?" Gavin pushed his plate away, no longer hungry.

"I guess we'll find out tomorrow," answered Henry, but he studied the emotions flickering across Dot's face. Why did her face suddenly seem familiar?

For the last hour, the Council had argued about the lawfulness of making prey out of an unaware shifter, without referring to her directly. They hadn't even tackled the question Elder Talbot had raised about the ethics using of any human as the target of a pack hunt. Dot picked at a loose thread on the chair; she'd been seated in a corner of the closed conference room and the representatives avoided glancing her direction. At first, the plan was to deny access to Henry and Gavin, but she insisted they be able to accompany her. It was only fair because Elder Choate had two of his men with him.

It was clear to Dot that several of the representatives were getting tired of the argument. "We haven't been told yet why this girl is your target," one shouted.

The rest of the members fell silent. "Yes, tell us," said Elder Talbot calmly. "What is special about her?"

Elder Choate picked up his glass of water and took a drink, drawing out the moment. Dot thought she knew what was coming, but her hands were clenched and she could feel her fingernails digging into her sore palms. He glanced around the table. "She is my granddaughter," he announced. "And she is the prize. Whoever claims her gains pack leadership."

THIRTEEN

The Council members were on their feet. Everyone talked at the same time, and no one voice stood out. Henry and Gavin, one on either side of her, were standing as well, and Gavin's hand gripped her shoulder. Dot kept her face expressionless, but she could feel the blood trickling from the wounds in her hands. Her fingernails had broken through the tender skin.

Finally, the chairman banged his gavel on the table. "Everyone sit and be quiet," he ordered, and his voice carried above the others. Once all the men had settled back down, he turned to Elder Choate. "How can that be?" he asked. "I remember when your son died. He had not mated yet."

"Not within the pack. However, several months after his death, I found out he had been in a relationship with a woman outside the pack—a non-shifter. This girl is his daughter."

"Do you have proof?" Henry asked, striding towards the platform.

"Only what I was told. But a DNA test would prove it. Besides, where did she inherit her ability to shift?

We all know she is not a member of your pack," Elder Choate pointed out. "So what gives you the right to speak for her or protect her?"

"The right of friendship. We are her friends. The right of battle. She has fought side by side with members of my pack."

"Friendship doesn't override genealogy. I claim her by the right of blood ties. She belongs to my pack." The Choate leader smiled grimly as he met the gaze of each man around the table. "I ask the Council to order that she be turned over to me."

Chaos broke out again. Representatives were pounding on the table and yelling at each other. Elder Choate sat silent, with a grin on his face. The two men who had accompanied him slowly edged across the room towards Dot and Gavin. She'd had enough. She stood up and turned towards Gavin. "Forgive me," she said in a whisper.

Before he could stop her, she was pushing past the Choate men. She stopped for a moment where Henry was standing. "Thank you," she mouthed, and then leaped onto the raised area and stood beside the chairman. "Maybe you should let me speak," she said quietly.

Counselor Carlson studied her for a moment. "It isn't normal, but yes, perhaps we should let you speak." He banged his gavel for silence again. Dot scanned the men sitting around the table, her eyes settling on Elder Choate.

"Go ahead," the chairman encouraged her.

"You ask for the Council to turn me over to you," she said, not taking her eyes from those of her grandfather. "For what reason? So you can hold me captive until a time of your choosing, and then release me so the men of the pack can hunt me down? And what do you expect me to do once one catches me? Lie down and spread my legs willingly so he can mount me without calling it rape? And what happens next? Do you cage me up and only let me out when the new pack leader wants to impregnate me? Is that what you plan? You already know I won't stay willingly."

She ignored the stunned response of the Council representatives. "And I suppose the two men who are here with you are the best your pack has to offer? I would never consider mating with a man who I can beat in battle, and both of these men already bear my scars." She pointed to one of the men with Elder Choate. "Under his bandage, that one wears the mark of my paw on his cheek." She swung around and pointed to the other. "I could have broken his arm a few weeks ago if I had wanted to. Besides, these are the same men who betrayed the Council's wishes and violated the protection order. And you think they will make good pack leaders? The same men who would pay non-kin to capture me?"

"So you do not deny the blood bond?" the chairman asked.

"Was your son's name Merikh?" Dot asked the elder Choate.

"Yes."

"Then I do not deny blood history, although there is no bond. I have been reading my mother's journals, and it's clear your son was my biological father. I believe sperm donor is the current slang."

"She does not deny it! She is a member of my pack!" roared the Choate leader. "I see no further need for discussion."

"A member of your pack?" Dot shook her head. "I

think not. Where was the pack when my mother almost died in childbirth? Where was the pack when she went without food so that I would have enough to eat? Where was the pack when the other kids in school made fun of me because I didn't have new clothes and all my toys were given to me by charities?"

She stalked around the table and swung his chair around, leaning over so his face was only inches from hers. "Where was the pack when my parents died in a car accident when I was sixteen? Where was the pack when my aunt's boyfriend tried to rape me? Where was the pack when I first started to shift and thought I was evil and a freak of nature? I have been packless since I was born and the fact you choose to claim me now to serve your own purposes does not change who I am." She straightened up. "I didn't even know other shifters and packs existed until the Fairwoods were kind enough to let me stay with them and show me what a pack could be."

"You fool! They only did that as a way of attacking me!"

"I'm not the fool you think I am, Elder Choate." Dot looked to find Henry and Gavin and nodded at them. "I considered the possibility, and discarded it. That may have been a part of the plan in the beginning, but I believe things have changed." She allowed the barest of smiles to reach her lips. "You might learn something from them, Grandfather. If you had come to me after the accident and offered me a home and a family, I would have taken your offer. Instead, you chose to wait to find out if I had inherited the ability to shift and then made me a pawn in your game." She walked away from him and faced the chairman. "I believe my feelings are perfectly clear. What the

Council decides to do is none of my concern. As I am packless, the Council has no authority over me."

Ignoring the heated discussion that broke out, she stepped off the platform and headed out of the room, her eyes firmly on the floor. When Gavin stepped in her path to stop her, she shook her head and pushed by him. She didn't even notice when Jack fell in step behind her as she left the conference room. In her room, she quickly stripped out of the business suit she was wearing, tossing it on the bed, and switched into a blouse and comfortable pair of jeans. She opened the door without checking the peephole first. She walked into the hallway and someone grabbed her arm.

"Where do you think you're going?" growled her bodyguard.

"For a walk. I need to go for a long walk," she told him between clenched teeth.

"Not safe."

"Then take me somewhere safe. Somewhere away from here. Somewhere away from the eyes making a note every time I move. Please, Jack." The tears were close to the surface, but she didn't want to give in to them.

The Botanical Gardens was almost empty of visitors and Dot had no problem finding an unused bench bathed in sunlight. There weren't many flowers blooming this time of year, so visitors were scarce. She was cold even though the temperature of the air was pleasant, but even the sun couldn't warm her. This was going to be the hardest thing she had ever done.

She had forgotten hard-learned lessons and allowed the walls to fall, allowed herself to care again. When she slipped away, it would hurt her friends too, and she regretted that. Especially as there would be no goodbyes.

A shadow moved between her and the sun, and she shivered. "It's getting late, it's time to go back," Jack said. "Your friends are worried about you." She had forgotten about him.

"It's no good, I can't go back."

He sat on the bench beside her and patted her knee. She remembered Bruce doing that when she was a little girl. She wondered if Jack had children of his own. He might appear to be a street-tough goon on the surface, but she suspected a soft heart underneath the starched shirt. "You should at least go back and find out if the Council made a decision. Who knows, maybe they told Elder Choate to go jump in a lake."

"I'd rather see him jump in a puddle of mud—a deep one."

He grinned. "Nice picture." His phone buzzed, and he pulled it out of his pocket and tapped the screen. "He's calling again."

"Who?"

"Elder Fairwood."

"Ignore it—let him go to voicemail. Let me think for a minute."

Dot pushed the fried rice around on the plastic plate, but didn't raise the fork to her mouth. Jack knew the owners of this little Chinese restaurant, and they were in a back booth near the kitchen where they couldn't be seen from the sidewalk. She and Jack sat on one side, Gavin and his father on the other. She needed her distance from Gavin, but every time she glanced up from her plate he filled her vision and her thoughts. At least he wasn't touching her. She was keeping her feet and legs pulled up against the bench so he couldn't "accidentally" bump his legs against hers.

"The Council chairman wants to give their message to you directly," Henry said. "They made us leave before the final vote, and Elder Talbot is sworn to secrecy. He won't tell me what it was."

She pushed her plate away. Jack pulled it right back in front of her. "You need to eat."

She knew that. She might not get a chance for a meal for a day or two. She forced herself to take a bite of her sweet and sour chicken. "Where does he propose we meet?"

"He said he would be available in his room at the hotel most of the evening," Henry said.

"I don't think so. Sorry, Elder Fairwood, I don't trust anyone right now. If I go back to the hotel no telling what the Choates might try to pull. If he wants to meet with me, we can arrange for a neutral spot. I'm sure Jack can suggest someplace. Right, Jack?"

"I have an idea or two. I'd rather you went back to the hotel though," Jack said.

"You're going to have to come back sometime. Where else are you going to stay tonight?" Henry asked.

"It wouldn't be the first time I spent the night on a park bench or in a bus station," Dot told him. She pushed her food away again. She had no appetite.

Jack shook his head and put the plate back in front of her. "Eat," he growled. "If you go back to the hotel, you will have all three of us to protect you. And I will get a friend or two to help out. It will take a small army to get to you."

Dot shivered. Exactly what she wanted to avoid.

"Are you all right?" Henry asked.

"Just tired," she said. "It's been a long day."

"Finish eating and I'll go make some calls." Jack stood, pulling out his phone. "You two will keep your eyes peeled, right?"

Henry nodded. "Yes, we'll protect her."

They put Dot in the middle of a diamond. Henry and Gavin were on either side of her, Jack directly in front of her, and one of his friends walked behind them. Three more of his friends cleared the path in front of them as they paraded through the hotel lobby and hallway. Gavin tried to take her hand, but she didn't want him touching her. She needed to keep the wall up.

The three men took stations outside the door of the chairman's room, and Jack knocked. The door opened, and he went in, motioning for Dot to wait. "It's clear," he said, coming back out. "The chairman is waiting for you."

Dot entered first, with Gavin and Henry close behind. "Would you care for something to drink?" he asked and indicated the couch with a wave of his hand. "Please, have a seat."

She thought she would rather stand, but didn't

want to be rude, so she sat. Her short time with the pack had taught her much about the wolves' views on respect. "Water would be fine." She kept both eyes on him as he opened the mini-fridge and got out a bottle to hand to her. Henry closed the door and he and Gavin stood on either side of it.

"You are a rather unusual young lady," Counselor Carlson said, settling into a chair across from her. "You seem to inspire loyalty and friendship without effort. It's too bad the pack structure only allows leadership to be males. The Choate pack could use you."

"If you're going to demand that I give myself to my grandfather's pack than this conversation is over." Dot started to stand.

"No, no demands." The chairman sighed. "More of a request. We want you to be aware of the consequences if you don't go."

"So essentially, you are asking me to sacrifice my future for the stability of my grandfather's pack," Dot summed up.

"Not just his, but all the packs. When pack leadership gets thrown open, the resulting conflicts have a history of going beyond the pack in question. We wolf shifters are a bloodthirsty bunch, and although many of our young males serve in the military, it isn't enough to satisfy all of them. We have managed to keep the raiding and deaths to a minimum in the past few years, but I don't know how long we can do that."

"And if I choose to follow my heart and join the Fairwood pack, all my friends there would be targets."

"Most likely."

Dot avoided Gavin's eyes. She didn't want him to read her face. "I can't make this decision tonight. I'll let you know something tomorrow." She got up from the couch. The chairman stood as well.

"Please do not delay too long, Miss McKenzie, there is already too much tension among the representatives."

Isn't it your job to fix that? Dot thought as she left the room. Henry and Gavin fell in beside her, and Jack took the front again. A condemned prisoner on her final walk, she missed seeing the bump in the carpet and almost tripped, but Gavin caught her. The wall fell, and with a little sob, she allowed him to pull her tight against him. "Hold on," he urged, whispering in her ear. She nodded, knowing these would be the last few minutes she had with him.

"I don't know if I can do this," Dot said. She and Gavin had been left alone in her room and they stood together gazing out the window, barely touching, studying the lights of the city spread out around them. Jack and his friends were stationed outside the door. "It's not fair. I've only known about other shifters for a few weeks now, and I'm being asked to be a savior for the whole batch of you. I can't do this."

"Stay with me," Gavin urged. "We'll figure it out together."

"Do you know how I felt when I saw those men with Dawn? How can I do that to her again? How can I do that to any of my friends?"

He kissed her forehead. "We're a strong pack, and we made new friends this trip. It'll work out, you'll see."

"I shouldn't even be here with you. The Choates will never let me be with anyone but one of them."

He gently brushed her cheek. "What do you want, Dot?"

It didn't matter, because she wasn't going to get it. "Why didn't the Council ask me that?"

"I guess they aren't used to looking past the overall picture and considering the individual." Gavin wrapped one arm around her waist and pulled her close in a protective move when there was a knock on the door.

"That's Jack," she told him. "It must be time for you to go."

"In a minute," he called. "I need to do something first." he added so only she could hear him, and pulled her even closer for a kiss. She allowed herself to melt into it, and returned the kiss with all the feelings she had for him. She needed this memory. The memory was the only thing of his she would be taking with her. At a second knock, he broke away reluctantly. "Whatever you decide, remember I..."

"Don't say it," she said. "Don't make this any harder than it already is."

"I have to say it. I want you to know. I love you, Dot."

FOURTEEN

The wall was back. Dot had allowed herself to cry, but it was time. Serena had gotten her note, and the uniform hung in the closet, buried behind her other clothes. All the pieces were in place, now she had to hope her luck would hold. She set her alarm so she would not miss her opportunity. She'd asked Jack to let her sleep in, but she didn't plan on sleeping late.

Mid-morning, Gavin was startled by loud pounding. "Is she here?" he heard Jack yell.

Gavin yanked the door open. "Is who here? Dot?"

"Yes, Ms. McKenzie. Is she here?"

"No, I left her in her room last night. You saw her there."

"She's gone now. I let her sleep in and now she's not there."

Gavin shoved past Jack and ran into Dot's room. Her unmade bed was empty. He peered through the open bathroom door; empty as well. "Where did she go? Where did you let her go?" He threw open the closet and pushed the clothes aside, hoping she was playing a trick and he'd find her hiding there. His heart plummeted when there was no sign of her.

"She never left the room. Not unless she turned into a bird and flew out the window. She can't do that, can she?" Jack examined the ceiling to see if any ceiling tiles were out of place. Gavin checked too. None were.

"Not that I know of." Gavin checked the windows anyway. They were closed and locked. The fear showed in his eyes when he turned to Jack. "So where is she?"

"I never left her door," Jack insisted. "No one went in, no one left." He stopped. "Except the maids."

"Maids?"

"Yeah, two. One was new and being trained."

"There was only one in our room."

Jack let out a stream of curses. "Security tapes. There's bound to be security tapes."

They squeezed into the small office of the security manager to review the grainy footage. "There's the maid and the cart," Gavin said, squinting at the monitor.

"One maid," muttered Jack. "The same one we've had all week."

"I'll check the records and see which maid worked your floor," said the chief of security. He made a call from his desk phone.

Jack jabbed at the monitor with one finger. "And there I am, and I walk away because the boss called. Watch, one maid goes into the room."

"And the maid comes back out. Wait, what? There she is again? No, now there are two maids going into the next room." Gavin said.

Jack groaned and cursed as they watched him walk back down the hall. "And I talk to them. I didn't even pay attention. I just took for granted they were both hotel employees because of the uniforms. They looked enough alike to be sisters although the new one seemed shy. They even talked about coming back to vacuum when the lady got up." He checked the timer on the tape. "That was two hours ago. She could be anywhere now."

"She didn't take anything with her," Gavin pointed out. "No purse, no clothes. She couldn't have gone far."

"Back the tape up," Jack requested as the security chief hung up the phone. "Now stop." He tapped the screen again. "There. She threw the dirty towels into the cart. Her clothes and other belongings could be wrapped up in them."

The security chief stopped the playback. "The maid's name is Serena Montinez. She has been an employee of the hotel for over five years. She went home early today, told her supervisor she was sick."

Jack shook his head. "I thought I was good," he said. "I never expected to get fooled by a sweet young thing like Ms. McKenzie. Can we get the home address and phone number for Ms. Montinez?"

"The maid said she offered to take Ms. McKenzie home with her," Jack said. "But Ms. McKenzie turned her down. Said she didn't want to cause her any more problems." Gavin, Henry, and Jack were giving a report to Counselor Carlson. "They met a couple of years ago when Ms. McKenzie worked in the hotel for a short time. We've searched the room, and didn't turn up anything. She left most of her clothes behind, and we have gone through those too. No notes, no clues of any kind."

"From the stories she told us, she's been doing this for five years, so she has lots of experience," the older Fairwood added.

The chairman sighed. "I didn't think my proposal would drive her to this. I thought perhaps her ties to your pack would lead her to a different decision."

"I believe those ties are exactly what drove her away." Gavin fiddled with the phone she had left behind, trying to figure out a way to restore all the erased calls and contacts. "She didn't want to place the pack at any additional risk."

"I'll inform Elder Choate we have given her more time to make a decision. Perhaps she'll change her mind and come back today."

She's not coming back, Gavin thought. He gripped her phone so tightly that the case popped open. She's gone and I've lost her forever. He wanted to howl and let the world share his misery.

Even through its tinted windows, the restaurant across the street gave her a clear view of the front entrance to the hotel. Dot wasn't worried about anybody recognizing her; with her hair dyed blond and with the heavy layer of makeup and green contacts, even she didn't recognize herself in the mirror. The clothes she wore came from a thrift shop across town. The pocket money Henry gave her at the beginning of the trip would have to last her awhile, but it was enough to get her the supplies she needed to get out of the area and make a new start. With her out of the lives, her friends should be safe. It was a solid plan, anyway.

The Council members had been trickling out of the hotel all morning, but the Fairwood group hadn't left yet. The waitress came by and filled her coffee cup one more time. "I guess your friend isn't going to show up, honey," she said.

"Stood up again," Dot agreed. "If you don't mind, I'll stay for a few more minutes."

"Fine by me. We're not busy now anyway."

Dot had sensed Gavin calling to her yesterday, and ignoring him had been hard. Waiting to see him one more time was just torturing herself. She watched as the Choates left earlier, and the disappointment on their faces almost made up for the pain. She blew across the surface of the coffee before taking a sip as yet another limo pulled up to the entrance of the hotel. Jack came out and scanned the street before motioning towards the lobby. Elder Talbot appeared first, followed by Henry, and Gavin brought up the rear. He stood by the back of the car and waited while their luggage was loaded into the trunk, as if hoping she would come rushing up to him.

As he moved towards the door the driver held open, Dot sent him the tightest tendril of thought she could manage. *"I love you too, Gavin Fairwood."* She didn't wait to see his reaction. Her payment already sat on the table and she was on her way out the back door.

"We should have stayed." Gavin stared out the limo

windows, but she was nowhere to be seen. How could he find her in this city with all its streets crawling with people when she wouldn't answer his call? It was her he heard as they left, but he hadn't been able to spot her even with his *other* sight, and he hadn't been able to pick out her scent from the myriad of smells of the city. At least she was all right. Her voice hadn't conveyed any fear, only sadness.

"It would only put her at risk," Henry pointed out. "She made her choice. We need to accept it and wish her luck. I hope she can stay out of the way of the Choates."

"I didn't even get to say goodbye," Gavin muttered as he undid his tie and unbuttoned the top buttons of his shirt. "Did their entire delegation leave?" he asked, louder.

"One stayed behind, according to my sources," Jack answered. "One of the younger men. He checked out of the hotel, so we are trying to find out now where he went. When we find him, we'll keep an eye on him. And unless he is as good as Ms. McKenzie, we'll find him."

As the limo sped along its path to the airport, Gavin found no comfort in Jack's reassurance.

No motorcycle limited her options. It was surprising how quickly Dot had gotten used to having it. She wanted to avoid public transportation, so she might be resorting to the four pawed method of getting from one place to another. She studied the maps in the small branch library, debating whether to make Florida or Arizona her destination. Florida had lots of people to mix in with and hide among, and she'd always wanted to visit her ancestral home in Arizona. One of the librarians came by the table where she had several atlases open. "You finding everything you need? We have a small selection of state road maps behind the desk."

Something about her caught Dot's attention and she studied the woman's eyes. They showed the tell-tale marks but Gavin had said there were no packs in Atlanta. She opened her *other* senses the smallest bit and sniffed. Kin. "Shifter?" she asked in a level suited to a library.

The librarian nodded and sat down. Dot examined her. Except for the eyes—blue with streaks of yellow, there was nothing unique about her. Dot guessed her to be in her mid-forties, and she was of medium height and slender without being skinny. She wore her blond hair in a bun, and her wire-rim glasses helped to hide the strangeness of her eyes. "Form?" Dot asked.

"Cougar," the librarian said. She studied Dot in return. "You?"

"Wolf."

"Pack affiliation?"

"None."

"You're the one they are searching for."

Dot decided to gamble. She didn't understand what was going on but instinct told her she needed to explore it. "Yes."

"Come with me." The librarian stood and called to a co-worker. "I'm going to take a smoke break, Hannah. Be right back."

Outside, she pulled out a cigarette and offered one to Dot. Dot shook her head. "Smart. I'm Lisa, by the way. Don't give me your name yet. That way I have plausible deniability." She grinned broadly and her canines showed. "Let me tell you a story."

The apartment was small and comfortable, but Dot felt uneasy. Life had taught her that things that seemed to be good to be true usually were and this situation definitely fell into that category. "We're a little group," said Noelani, Lisa's roommate. A full-blooded Hawaiian, her form was that of a large lizard. "But we have contacts all over the place."

Lisa pulled out another cigarette and lit it. "We're mostly female. The majority of us left because we didn't like the traditional pack structure. Just because men are normally stronger in their shifter forms doesn't mean they should be in charge all the time. And a few of us traditionally run solo." She blew a circle of smoke out the opened window.

"We first started getting together because some of us who were raised in a pack had a hard time adjusting to life on our own. You could say we were a support group."

"Then one of the girls was grabbed—tracked down by her pack members and forced to return. We haven't been able to contact her since." Lisa angrily ground the remains of her half-smoked cigarette out in the nearby ashtray. "We decided to do everything we could to make sure it never happened again. In a way, we turned into an underground railroad."

"Which leads us back to you." Noelani fiddled with a strand of her long black hair. "We have a friend who works for the same security firm as your bodyguard. He heard the story and alerted us. So we were keeping an eye out for you."

"We can help you if you want us to, but it's your call."

Dot stared at the floor. "It's too dangerous. I would be putting you at risk if I stayed here. That's why I ran away in the first place."

Lisa laughed. "Your escape was a smooth move. The security firm has already put out a memo to their agents to tell them how you did it. You're a legend."

Dot bit her bottom lip. "I don't think I like that. The wolves wanted me to be some kind of savior, you're saying I'm a legend, and all I want is a chance to settle in one place and not be afraid anymore." Noelani and Lisa stared at each other, their eyes unfocused, and Dot recognized that they were communicating with unspoken words.

"You didn't say anything about being happy," Noelani said gently.

Surprised by the sudden rush of tears to her eyes, Dot couldn't answer right away. "I lost my chance for happiness. I lost it before I ever really had it."

Lisa nodded. "We'll help you. No matter what the risk."

"It's time to go, Maria," said Lisa, shaking Dot out of her sound sleep.

"Now?" Dot checked at the clock. It was two o'clock in the morning.

"We just got a call. Unfriendlies are in the neighborhood. We spotted them hanging around the apartment complex this afternoon, asking questions. It's not safe for you anymore."

"How did they find me so fast? I've only been here a week and I hardly left the building!" Staying inside that long had grated on her nerves, but Lisa kept her supplied with a steady stream of books to help break the boredom. Dot had only started to get settled in.

Lisa shrugged. "No time to figure it out. We have a friend on the way over to move you someplace safe. We'll have to find our leak after you're gone."

Dot rolled off the sleeper sofa and grabbed her clothes.

"You've got everything in the backpack, right?" Lisa asked, grabbing it from a nearby chair.

"Yes. Money, new ID, toothbrush, what few clothes I own."

"Remember you're Maria Lapahie now." It had been Dot's idea to use her grandmother's maiden name. "I slipped a cell phone in there too. It's turned off, but I programed in the library's number."

A knock on the door made Dot jump, but Lisa nodded. "There's your ride now." She handed Dot her backpack and hugged her. "You know what I hate the most?" she asked with a shaky laugh. "I hoped to pull some more ideas out of that weird brain of yours. I've never known anyone who thinks the way you do. You would have been a great addition to the group." She let go, and opened the door. "She's ready."

The man who stood in the hallway was dressed in black leather and was someone she wouldn't want to meet in a dark alley. Dot reached. "He's not..." she said.

"No. He's not a shifter. That's what makes him perfect for this. Now get out of here." Lisa gave Dot a gentle shove. "Maybe someday we'll meet under better circumstances."

"Where are we going?" Dot asked as she followed the man down the stairs.

"No talking. No names. That's part of the deal," he said. He led her to a beat up old pickup with a camper on the back, and opened the camper door. "Get in," he grunted, "And lay on the floor." He reached up and grabbed a pillow off a shelf. "It's going to get bumpy."

Dot tossed her backpack in the bed of the pickup as far as she could and pulled herself up. As he slammed the camper door behind her, she wondered if she had just been a willing participant in her own capture.

FIFTEEN

Dot lost track of time as they bumped along the roads. The ride started out fairly smooth as he drove through town, but after a while no more city lights shone through the windows and she was tossed around in the back of the truck. Thank heavens for the pillow protecting her head, but her hips and shoulders would be black and blue. She wondered if it would be safe to sit up and look for a blanket because she was cold, but decided against it. She didn't want to risk anyone seeing her outline in the flash of headlights.

The first rays of daylight drifted through the windows before the truck stopped moving, but the engine kept running. "Stay down and wait," the man ordered, and Dot listened as his door opened and then slammed shut. She needed to use the bathroom, but he had said to wait. She waited.

She tensed again when she heard voices nearing the truck. She identified them as women's voices, and relaxed a bit. The door to the camper opened. "Good morning, Maria." Two women stood outside. "You're here." A crow called as she climbed out of the camper. One woman took her backpack from her and she glanced around. A door opened and closed, and the pickup pulled away.

They stood near a log cabin in the middle of an old pine forest. Dot could see the steam rising from a lake through the trees. When she reached and identified the women as shifters, she relaxed a bit more. "So where am I?"

"About as far south as you can go in Georgia without running into Florida," one grinned. "Come on in and we'll answer your questions."

Dot huddled close to the fire crackling in the fireplace, trying to get warm after the long, cold ride. She held a cup of coffee in her hands, and the heat coming through the cup drew the ache out of her hands, still tender from the cuts from the rope. At least they didn't bleed every time she bumped something anymore.

"We refer to ourselves as Free Wolves," explained Eleanor. She was the oldest of the three shifters, all wolves, who lived in the cabin. One was currently visiting friends out of the area, and the third, Sue, was in the kitchen making pancakes. "We didn't like the sound of packless, so we made up another name. Besides, we don't have anything against packs in general, only certain ones." Sparks were sucked up the chimney as she tossed more wood on the fire. "Some of the packs are quite open to us—if we want to visit for celebrations or mating purposes, they don't mind if we drop in for a visit. Don't know about the Fairwood pack, their territory is further north than I usually go. I did run into one of their members a time or two."

Dot's head hurt. It was simply too much to take in,

especially after the long night. But Eleanor wasn't done yet.

"We're usually pretty quiet here, so we'll hear about it if any stranger wanders into the area. Course, if any of the local boys catch wind you're here, it'll be hard to keep them away. You're quite a looker."

"No one can know I'm here," Dot protested, and put down the cup, ready to run.

"Relax. Eleanor was teasing," Sue called from the kitchen. She came in wiping her hands on a towel. "You'll have to forgive her, she has a strange sense of humor. I think she's spent too much time up here by herself. Now, come and get breakfast."

The sun was setting over the lake, and the three of them sat in lawn chairs, drinking wine coolers and watching the clouds turn purple and orange. "How long have you been here?" Dot asked Eleanor.

"Close to twenty years now. Didn't like how things were done in the pack, so I left. I had a reputation as a troublemaker, so I don't think the pack minded me going. I expect to be here the rest of my life."

"I've only been here ten," Sue said. "And I don't stay all the time. All this peacefulness gets on my nerves, and I have to get away from it once in a while. But you'll only be here about a week before we send you to your destination, so it shouldn't be a problem for you."

"I'm enjoying it so far." Dot spotted the evening star flickering in the sky. "I used to have a place like this I could go to."

"What happened?" Sue asked.

"They burned down the house. I guess they wanted

to make sure I could never go back." Dot blinked rapidly, trying to keep her eyes clear. Alcohol wasn't a good idea right now.

"The Choate pack? The same ones that are chasing you now?"

"Yes. They will stop at nothing to get me."

Eleanor sighed. "I was a member of the Choate pack, so it doesn't surprise me."

"Did they tell you who I am?" Dot asked, her voice quavering.

"No, just that you are on the run from my former pack."

"I am Damyon Choate's granddaughter. We could be related."

Dot was swept into surprisingly strong arms and hugged. "Sisters. We are sisters, whether or not we share any relatives. I'm going to have a hard time letting you go."

Dot checked the loft she'd been using as a bedroom to make sure she didn't leave behind anything important. Tomorrow she'd be heading for a new life in Orlando. The free wolves already had a job lined up for her and a place to live. She turned at the sound of someone climbing the stairs, but it was only Sue.

"Eleanor and I have been talking," she said, sitting on the bed next to Dot's backpack. "And we started wondering. Have you ever gotten the opportunity to run with a pack?"

"No. I did some work with the trainers of the Fairwoods, but I've only run alone."

"Thought as much. If you want, we can go for a run tonight. This may be the last chance you have for a while, and I know it would mean a lot to Eleanor."

Three gray wolves stood at the top of a hill watching the valley below, one so gray she was almost white. *"We try not to hunt here very often"* Sue said. *"We save the game here for special occasions."*

"And this is a special occasion. I get to take my sister on her first run." voiced Eleanor.

"Stick to rabbits," Sue added. *"A fox shifter comes here once in a while to hunt. We don't mind sharing the rabbits, and don't want to hurt him by mistake."*

"It doesn't matter if we catch anything or not," Eleanor chuckled, lifting her nose to sniff the wind, and let go a howl. "It's *all in the chase. I think it's better than sex. Ready? Follow me!"*

On four legs and running against the wind, tasting all the scents of the night forest, Dot ran, unafraid and free.

She savored the moment now, as she climbed onto the bus that would take her back to the apartment she shared with three other female kin. What passed for winter in Florida was over, and based on the temperature and humidity, they'd skipped spring and gone right into summer. Sweat beaded on Dot's forehead in the few minutes she spent waiting at the bus stop. Perhaps she should cut her hair to keep it off her neck but it was finally shoulder-length again and she liked the style. A rush of cold air greeted her when the bus driver opened the doors, so the air conditioning on the bus worked today. The trip home would be bearable.

Either the Choates had given up the chase or her new identity hadn't been cracked. She hadn't shifted once in the nearly six months she'd been in Florida, and she wondered if that had anything to do with it. Or maybe her ability was masked by all the shifters around her. Sometimes, when she slipped on the bulky costume for the character she played at the theme park, she felt like she shifted as she changed her personality to fit the face the tourists saw. So far she hadn't been asked to play either a wolf or a rabbit. Playing the rabbit might have been a challenge. She remembered tearing into the one she had caught that night, and the joy of the fresh meat and blood. It didn't matter if Eleanor had driven the old jack in her direction—she'd been the one that made the kill. Maybe it was a good thing she never got asked to play the wolf on the job, she reflected with a grin.

Between work and the classes she was taking at the community college, she didn't have much free time, and the bus ride was one of the few times she got to sit and relax. Sitting on a crowded bus bothered her at first as she continually watched the passengers getting on, checking for signs of kin, but now she recognized most of the regulars. One, an older lady who worked at one of the local hotels, liked to sit next to her, talk about her grandchildren and show off the newest pictures of them. Most of the time Dot enjoyed listening to her, other days, when she realized she would never have grandchildren of her own, she would go back to her apartment, grab a beer, and sit on the balcony by herself.

Her roommates nagged her about all the time she spent alone. To get them off her back, she would occasionally accept the blind dates they set up for her. Only two of the men ever got a second date—nice enough guys, but none of them soothed the ache in her heart. She should be over Gavin by now, but she still thought about him all the time. She hoped that, with her out of the picture, he had chosen one of the females of the pack as his mate. It would be good for the strength of the pack. He and Tasha might make a good match. She was no matchmaker, but it would be easier to think of him mated with a friend than a stranger.

The bus got noisy when a group of tourists got on. That was unusual, tourists normally traveled by taxi or rental cars, so Dot studied them from behind the paperback she was reading. She sniffed. Kin. But only one. Dot was glad that one of the regulars sat beside her today. The group claimed empty seats near the front of the bus. She didn't sense a threat, but at the next stop, Dot excused herself, and slipped out the back exit. Her apartment was only a few more blocks, and she could walk the rest of the way. Better safe than sorry.

Gavin sat impatiently while Dr. Tracy cleaned and bandaged the scratch on his arm and didn't allow himself to wince when she applied the antiseptic. "That one won't leave much of a scar," she said. "But if you keep it up you might not get off so easy the next time."

"I do what I have to do," he said, ripping off the rest of his sleeve. The shirt was ruined anyway. The night's raid went off without a hitch for the most part; none of the pack came home with more than a scratch or two. The Choates, on the other hand, would be nursing their wounds for a few days.

He hadn't asked for this. After Dot disappeared, things settled down for a while. Then the raids had started. A new test to choose pack leadership, Gavin guessed, and the Fairwood pack was a logical target. A bad choice, because Elder Fenner, with his years of experience, had anticipated it, and his sentries were on full alert. The rival wolves went home with their tails between their legs.

Last night was not the first raid Gavin had led in retaliation, but it had done the most damage. At least while the raids went on, Dot would be safe. At least that's what he hoped.

He slid off the examining table. "Thanks, Doc."

"Any more?" she asked wearily.

"No, I am the last. Go get some rest." He'd made sure all the other injured wolves got treated first and sent them home after being treated. But he needed to go to the office to check on supplies. Luckily he had a fresh set of clothes in his closet. He could change, and resume being the businessman instead of the wolf. His heart wasn't into either; his heart was somewhere far away and he never expected to get it back.

His father was proud of the more active role he was taking in pack leadership, and putting the skills he had learned in the Marines to work. His dad thought he was over her, but damn, he missed Dot. At least, the additional work helped during the day. At night, images of her being held captive still haunted his dreams. When people asked, he blamed the dark circles under his eyes on the stress caused by the raids.

Dot finished washing the last of the pots and put it away before turning on the dishwasher. It was her week to do the dishes. Penny, one of the roommates, had whipped up a batch of spaghetti for supper and she and the other two girls sat in the other room watching the news.

"You guys hear about the rising tensions in the Northeast?" Penny asked during the commercials.

"What are you talking about?" Dot asked, coming out of the kitchen, a towel still slung over one arm.

"Greg told me about it at work today. You remember Greg, don't you, Maria?"

"Yeah, he's a nice guy, but there just wasn't a spark." She tried to act casual, but inside her stomach churned.

"Well, anyway, guess he has some friends up in Western New York. He says that two packs up there are going at it. No serious damage done yet, but he's talking about heading up there to join the fun."

Stay calm, Dot, she told herself, no one here knows who you are. Her roommates didn't know her history. Protection for her, protection for them. "Did he mention any pack names?"

Penny wrinkled her nose. "He might have, but I didn't pay attention." She giggled. "You know us rabbits. We don't get involved in those kinds of things. Can you imagine if I shifted in the middle of a pack of snarling wolves?"

"You familiar with any of the packs up there?" asked Crystal, curious. "I thought you were a Georgia girl." She was also a wolf in her *other* form. She considered herself one of the free wolves, so Dot had never asked about her pack history. She didn't have the appearance of a typical wolf shifter—she was tall with long blond hair and deep blue eyes. Even when she studied them, Dot had a hard time spotting the golden streaks in Crystal's eyes.

"I spent a few weeks up north," Dot said. "Made a few friends. Haven't been in touch with them forever."

"Let me call Greg and ask him." Penny pulled out her cell phone and giggled again. "He still has the hots for you, Maria. I bet this is the excuse he's been waiting for to come over."

"You should go change into something else," Crystal suggested, teasing. "A pair of sweats isn't what most guys want to see their girl in."

Dot picked up one of her throwing knives from the table and casually juggled it from hand to hand. One of the other character actors at work had been teaching her a few tricks during their breaks together. She grinned, covering her anxiety. "What you see is what you get," she said, casually tossing the knife so it stuck, quivering, in the cork board target mounted on the wall.

Greg arrived in a few minutes. "The details are kinda sketchy," he told them. "But what I'm hearing is that our favorite villains, the Choate pack, have started raiding a neighborhood clan. They claim that the Fairwood pack broke Council orders by hiding this chick they wanted to talk to." He whistled in admiration as two throwing knives left Dot's hand in quick succession and ended up side by side, handles touching, in the target. "Anyway, me and a couple of other guys are talking about heading up north to see if we can get in on the action. Prove our manhood, earn our scars, that sort of thing. We will fight on the Fairwood side of things, naturally."

"How to do you propose to get the Fairwoods to accept you?" Crystal asked. From the malicious gleam in her eyes, Dot assumed she had her own bone to pick with the Choates.

"Well, we're hoping if we show up with our own supply of weapons they will want us."

"Won't work." Crystal exhaled and stared at the floor. "Without an introduction, they won't let you in pack territory. They won't know where your loyalties lie. Besides, how are you going to get there? We can't run that far and carry weapons too."

"We?" Greg's voice almost squeaked.

"I know several of the free wolves who are going to want in on this."

Penny laughed nervously. "I'll pass."

"You can hold down the fort here and be our communications center," Crystal said. "We need everyone's help on this. Even yours, Maria."

Two knifes whistled through the air at once. "You need me more than you know. Make your phone calls and get your friends over here, Greg, Crystal. We need to start planning tonight. I can get you in."

Sixteen

"I fought side by side with the Fairwood pack. I ate with them, played with them, cried with them, participated in their Woman's Circle. They will accept me without hesitation. However, unless you agree to put me in charge, I'll go by myself."

"You? Why you?" Greg scowled. Glancing around the room, Dot could tell others were upset as well. Chips and other assorted snacks were everywhere and the gathering looked more like a come-as-you-are party rather than a council-of-war.

"Because not only have I fought with the Fairwoods, I've fought against the Choates, I know their ways. This is my battle, not yours. If you want to play, you'll have to play by my rules."

"What aren't you telling us, Maria?" Greg asked.

A knife twirled high in the air and Dot caught the handle easily on its downward arc. "I've been on the run from the Choates for the last six years. I'm the reason this conflict started. I'm the one they want. I'm the pack leader's granddaughter, and the prize in the contest for leadership."

One of the free wolves nodded. "I left the pack two

years ago. I heard about you. You're a legend among the females of the pack, and a thorn in the side of the males." She laughed. "They call you a bad influence and worse."

Dot sighed. There was that word again—legend. "I'm afraid my reputation is overblown. I've been extremely lucky and had the help of a lot of people." One at a time, she met the gaze of each person in the room. "So will you help me now?"

"Are you sure you should do this, Maria?" Crystal asked. "You'll be in more danger than any of us."

"You're right." Dot put the knives down on the table. The hardened steel blades glittered in the light of the nearby table lamp. "But I'm tired of running. It's time I make a stand. With the help of all of you, I can do that. If I win, my friends win. If I lose..." she paused. "If I lose, the war is over and my friends still win."

Crystal nodded. "I'm in."

"Me too," Greg said. "It will be different taking orders from a female, but I think I can deal with it, since it's you, Maria."

Maria. She had grown used to the name. Maybe she would keep it after all this was over.

They would leave in three days to give everyone time to make the needed preparations—arrange to take vacation, pay bills before they left, buy more supplies. Enough people in the group had cars to get everyone there. Dot only half-listened to the discussion. How would Gavin react when she showed up with her motley crew? Hopefully the fact that she was bringing willing warriors would deflect his anger at her. She was worried enough about fighting the Choates, she didn't need to fight with him as well.

Greg stayed behind after everyone else left. He sat beside her on the couch. "Why didn't you tell anyone else this before, Maria?" he asked, putting a hand on her knee. She let it stay. Greg wasn't a bad guy, he just wasn't Gavin.

"The fewer people who know, the less chance there is that someone will spill the secret."

"We're your friends, we wouldn't have told."

"I know that now. But you need to understand, for five years I had no one to depend on but me. It's a hard habit to break."

He rubbed her knee and they sat silent for a while. "Some of the guys are uncomfortable taking orders from a female," he finally blurted out.

"I guessed as much. A few of the free wolves don't want to take orders from me either. They didn't say anything, but I could tell. I am going to make you and Crystal my lieutenants. We'll strategize together, and then you two can pass on the plans to everyone else. How's that sound?"

"I like it," he grinned. "If it means I get to spend more time with you."

"We'll be spending a lot of time together for a few days, but we won't be alone."

"We're alone now," he said as he moved closer on the couch, put his arm around her waist, and leaned in for a kiss. She turned her head at just the right moment so his mouth found her cheek. She couldn't help remembering how Gavin's lips had felt against hers.

Dot slid the comb through her hair, still wet from a shower. This had been her last day at work. Her boss got upset when she didn't give him two weeks' notice, even after she explained her sister had gotten sick and she didn't have any idea when she would be back. Only partly a lie. He didn't need to know that she wasn't sure she would survive the trip. No one needed to know.

A movement reflected in the mirror caught her attention, and she noticed Penny in the hallway. "What's up?"

"I'm feeling left out," her roommate admitted. "I'm no fighter, but I don't want to miss out on all the excitement."

"The pack leader of the Fairwoods has a scar running from his elbow to his wrist," Dot said. "And others he never showed me. Is that the kind of excitement you want?"

"No. But I feel like I should be doing something besides answering the phone and passing along messages."

"I'll tell you what. I'm thinking about doing something new with my hair now it doesn't need to be plain for work. There's a challenge for you—find something different that I haven't ever done before. I warn you, I've dyed it almost every color you can think of."

Penny grinned. "Not only will I do something with your hair, I'll get you a new wardrobe too. I've always imagined you as some sci-fi character, not those silly animals you played at work."

The raid on the southern border came unexpectedly, but the Fairwood pack had been ready for it. The sentries spotted the intruders early, and reinforcements got to the area quickly, repelling the attack. But for some reason, Elder Fenner had not radioed in the report. He wanted to present it to Gavin in person. So Gavin paced in the conference room turned command center and imagined the worst. Which one of the pack members had gotten killed? Of course, the task of telling the family would be his. He hoped it would be one of the unattached young males—the pack would mourn the loss and celebrate the heroism and move on. But if an attached male with children died, the pack would feel the loss on a much deeper level.

"Gavin."

"Elder Fenner." Gavin turned and acknowledge the security chief. Tasha—or—Tanya—accompanied him. Gavin still hadn't learned to tell the twins apart. They even had the same scent. "Please, sit."

The elder took the nearest chair, pulled a cell phone out of his pocket and put it on the table. Gavin got two bottles of water from the mini-fridge and handed one to him and one to his companion. The girl was pale, but her face hard and determined. Gavin recognized her expression. He'd worn it himself after battles. "What happened?"

"It wasn't your usual attack. I'm convinced they accomplished their goal, even though we fought them off." Elder Fenner paused to take a drink. Gavin hid his impatience.

"Their goal was not to gain territory. There were enough of them that they might have been able to get in a little ways. No, that isn't why they attacked."

"So why did they attack?" Gavin asked, unwilling to wait any longer.

"They wanted a hostage, that's all. They got one and left. That's what they were after."

"Who did they take?"

"Tasha. They left her phone behind—I think on purpose. But they made off with her."

"Have you sent out a rescue squad?"

"Yes, but the raiders left in vehicles. We won't be able to catch them. We'll have to get her back another way.

Just then, the phone on the table vibrated. Gavin stared at it for a moment before picking it up. It seemed too soon for Damyon Choate to be calling with his demands. "Hello?"

Four cars parked on the street outside the apartment complex, packed and ready to leave. Greg and Crystal were busy checking off lists of supplies and fighters. The guns were neatly wrapped in blankets and placed in the trunks or tucked under the seats. No one was taking more than a small bag of personal things.

Dot, a cell phone in her hand, stood on the balcony of the apartment watching the changing colors of the sunset, knowing her lieutenants could handle things.

The plan had them finding a place to stop for the night halfway there, probably in North Carolina. They didn't need tents or sleeping bags. They would shift and sleep in their animal forms. These few moments would be the last she had alone before the trip.

It was time to make the phone call. She'd decided, and Greg and Crystal agreed, that she should call before leaving to inform the pack they were coming. Penny's phone had a Montana number and she would use it to place the call. Just another tactic to throw off anyone eavesdropping. But it wasn't Gavin she planned to call.

She dialed the number and waited. A man answered, "Hello?" he said.

Dot hesitated. "Sorry, I must have a wrong number." She swore she had dialed correctly, but perhaps Tasha had changed phone numbers.

"Wait. Who were you trying to reach?"

"My friend Tasha. Like I said, wrong number. Sorry." Why did the man at the other end sound familiar?

"This is Tasha's phone. Who is this?"

"Gavin?" The voice was strained, but she finally recognized it. The flutter in her chest was just because she was worried about Tasha, right? "What's wrong with Tasha?"

"Who is this?"

"Maria." She remembered. "Dot. What happened to Tasha?"

"The Choates grabbed her tonight. We're trying to figure out our response." His voice faltered. "Where are you Dot? Are you okay?"

"I'm fine. And I'm on my way. We'll be there tomorrow."

"We?"

"I'll explain when we get there. Goodbye, Gavin."

She turned and returned to the front room of the apartment, tossing the cell phone back to Penny. Greg and Crystal waited for her. "Change of plans," she said, plucking her backpack off the couch. "We leave now. And we don't stop until we get there."

The four car caravan that left Orlando grew to seven vehicles by the time they crossed the New York state line. The only stops they made were for quick rest breaks, gas and to change drivers. They ate sandwiches they bought from the gas stations and slept while someone else drove. As much as Dot wanted to go faster, they stayed within the speed limits, so the police would have no reason to pull them over. They made it in eighteen hours, just after nightfall

Dot was dozing in the back seat of the third car when the convoy reached the southern boundary of the Fairwood territory. "You're on," Crystal said, shaking her gently to wake her.

Dot climbed out and stretched, stiff after the long drive. Greg, who had been traveling in the lead vehicle, was already out and having an animated discussion with a man with a familiar face. A smile on her lips, she walked forward. "Hello, Dmitri. Long time no see."

After he got done hugging her, Dmitri joined Dot in the car and rode with her the rest of the way, chatting the whole time. She listened and asked questions, but gave him little in the way of information in return. Gavin deserved to hear it first. Elder Fenner stood outside, waiting, when they drove up to the brightly-lit pack headquarters "We haven't informed Gavin you are here yet," he said, after giving her a hug. "We thought you should tell him yourself." He eyed the group exiting the vehicles and gathering in the parking lot. "When you said you were bringing help, I didn't expect this!" He held her at arm's length and examined her. "You're a sight for sore eyes, Dot. Glad you're back. Go on in."

Greg and Crystal fell in beside her as she headed towards the building. Dmitri stayed behind to assist the arrivals. "Dot?" asked Crystal.

"Previous identity. Switched to Maria before I moved to Orlando. Changed last names too." They reached the door to the conference room, and an armed sentry stopped them. "We're expected," Dot said. The sentry's radio beeped, and Dot recognized Elder Fenner's voice. "You're cleared to enter," the sentry said formally, moving aside. Instinct whispered "run!" but she took a deep breath and stepped into the room.

The white board was covered with scenarios and diagrams. Henry and Gavin had explored a number of ways to try and get Tasha back. Henry thought he knew where they might be holding her, but he had been unable to reach his contact to confirm the information. They agreed a frontal assault on the Choates could result in Tasha's death, so a sneak attack would be the way to go. Gavin drew a red circle on the border of the enemy territory. "This is a weak spot our scouts identified in their defenses. We can get in there, but what we need is a diversion."

"You have it."

SEVENTEEN

Gavin turned towards the voice, and dropped the marker he held. "Dot?"

"Hello, Gavin, Elder Fairwood." Gavin couldn't believe his eyes. Her hair was bleached white, shaved on the sides, with the top about two inches long and dyed bright pink. She wore a sleeveless camo-colored T-shirt, and tribal tattoos decorated her upper right arm, while a bright pink bandanna was tied around the left one. Her cargo pants were also of camouflage material, another bright pink bandanna hung from one of its loops, and the belt she wore had a strange metallic decoration. On her hands she wore a pair of pink fingerless gloves, and on her feet, a pair of black combat boots.

Gavin wondered if her socks were bright pink too. He'd find out when he pulled them off her feet later followed by other articles of her clothing. At least that's what he hoped would happen. He took a half step towards her but stopped abruptly when he saw the expression on the face of the man who came into the room behind her.

"These are my friends Greg and Crystal," she said

in way of introduction. She turned their way. "Elder Fairwood is the pack leader and Gavin is his son."

Henry stepped forward. "You've come to help? Thank you."

Dot's mouth twitched. "Not just them. Greg and Crystal are my second-in-commands. I brought along thirty others—mostly wolves, but we ended up with a puma and a red fox as well. Elder Fenner and Dmitri are finding places for them and getting them settled. A lot of them are free wolves, and they have a bone to pick with Damyon Choate. By the way, Elder, Eleanor regrets she couldn't come along, but she sends her love."

Gavin was surprised when his father turned deep red. "How's she doing?"

"Pretty good in spite of the fact she spends so much time by herself. She said you're welcome to come by and visit her when you can get away. She'll take you for a run." The smile on Dot's face went from ear to ear. "And I don't think her definition of a run is the same as mine."

Crystal stared at the diagrams on the whiteboard. "Your map isn't right," she said. She went to the whiteboard and picked up a marker. "Things have changed." She quickly sketched out a couple of corrections. "And my information is old too. We should have Daphne take a look. She's our newest member—left only three months ago."

"We can fill in the details in the morning," Gavin said, finally finding his voice. "What did you have in mind for a diversion, Dot?"

She came and stood between him and Crystal and studied the whiteboard. The little bit of distance between them was too much for him, but he restrained the urge to pull her close, kiss her, pick her up and carry her off somewhere where they could be alone. This was business, and business came first. He didn't even know if she wanted him anymore. Had she chosen this Greg as her mate while she was gone? He wanted to challenge Greg, wolf to wolf—he would be able to tear the other man apart easily, but then Dot would hate him.

She talked quietly to her friends, drawing arrows and erasing them, then drawing more. He had a hard time following their conversation, distracted by her nearness. Finally, they reached an agreement, and she turned to him. "We do the unexpected by doing the expected," she said with a bloodthirsty grin. "We attack the front gate. My appearance alone will be enough of a distraction to allow your people to get in somewhere else."

"Too dangerous," Gavin protested. "You're too tempting of a target."

"Which makes me the perfect distraction. They'll strip down their defenses everywhere else once they realize who I am, making your job easier."

"She'll be well protected," Greg added. "The Choates will never get near her. We'll make sure of that."

That's not the way it works, Gavin thought, in the middle of battle, unexpected things happen. And from the expression on Dot's face, she knew it too.

It was nearly midnight before they finished their planning. Gavin didn't like it, but from a warrior's perspective, the plan was a good one. Dot and her group would attack the front gate with enough fire power to do substantial damage, while he and his group would sneak in and rescue Tasha. Once Tasha was safe, Dot's forces could withdraw. The attack served two purposes, Dot explained, freeing Tasha and finding out which of the kin she brought with her would fold at the first sight of blood. Elder Fenner, who had joined them, agreed the plan was solid.

"I think we've done everything we can for the night," Gavin said. "Once we get your girl in here in the morning to see if anything on the map needs changed, we can finalize the details."

"I'll escort you to your beds," Elder Fenner said to Greg and Crystal. "Elder McKenzie, I had your things placed in the guest room of Elder Fairwood's house. I'm sure Gavin will be glad to escort you there."

"What did you call me?" Dot stared at him in astonishment.

The old wolf smiled. "Elder McKenzie. Even if free wolves don't use titles, you've earned the respect as far as the Fairwood pack is concerned. And although you may have planned to share your companions' lodgings, as leader of the group, you should stay with the leader of our pack." Looking at her lieutenants, he added, "She'll be guarded well there."

"It's okay, guys," Dot said. "I'll see you in the morning."

Henry waited until they were gone. "I'm going to bed as well. I'll see you in the morning, Elder McKenzie."

She nearly choked on the drink of water she had just taken. Gavin moved close to pound her on the back. When she'd recovered, he let his hand linger on the curve of her spine.

"Bad enough for Elder Fenner to say it, let alone you!" she protested.

"He was right. You may not have the age of the majority of the elders, but you have the wisdom." Henry smiled. "I'll encourage others to use it as well. It'll increase your status among the pack and perhaps among your friends also."

Gavin grinned as he heard her swearing under her breath. "If you're going to do it, at least use the correct last name. I go by Lapahie now. It was my grandmother's maiden name and I've chosen to honor her memory and the memory of my ancestors. I never legally became a McKenzie anyway."

Gavin checked the leather cord around her neck. At least it wasn't pink.

"I'll pass the word along." He nodded at the two of them, and headed home.

Gavin still didn't move his hand. Either she didn't notice it or she didn't mind. He hoped for the second. "That's not a Native American outfit, is it?" he teased.

Dot snorted. "I made the mistake of telling one of my friends in Orlando she could design a new look for me. She works in the costume department of one of the theme parks. This was all her idea. I had to talk her out of the pink boots with five inch heels."

"What were you doing in Orlando?"

"I worked a character actor. Which translates to wearing hot, bulky costumes for hours. It was a fun job and I added muscles in the process." She flexed one of her biceps. "See?"

"Nice. Still doesn't match mine," he grinned, showing his off. He hoped she would hit his arm like she had before so he would have an excuse to kiss her, but the ploy didn't work. "I think Greg was disappointed that you wouldn't be sleeping in the same place as everyone else."

Her hand flashed, there was a whir in the air, and he saw her catch a knife. "Greg thinks I should be sharing his bed, and I can't convince him otherwise." Another flash, and a second knife joined the first, taking turns rotating in the air and launching from her hand. "I keep hoping that as he and Crystal spend more time together, they'll fall for each other, but so far it hasn't worked. I'm afraid my matchmaking skills are non-existent." He stared in fascination as she smoothly returned both knives to her belt.

"That's new, isn't it?" he asked.

She looked startled, and then grinned. "Yes. Started learning so I could perform in one of the shows. I soon realized it had potential for other uses." A quick movement of her hand, and one of the blades was pressed lightly against his throat. He held his breath until she laughed and returned the knife to its holder. "It's a good stress reducer too."

He thought differently. He waited until his pulse had slowed back down before he answered. "Good for close-up work at least."

"Not bad for medium range work either." A knife glittered in the light, and he heard it whistle by his head and hit with a thunk, sticking in the bulletin board across the room. "Elder Fenner will be disappointed to hear that I still haven't learned to shoot a gun."

Gavin went over to retrieve the knife and examined it before handing it back to her. "Special steel?" he asked.

"Yes, chosen to hold its edge and point longer while still staying tough enough not to break under pressure."

"Like you."

The sudden rush of moisture in her eyes surprised him. "Is that how you see me, Gavin? If you knew how many times I've come close to breaking, you might think differently."

"Each time you learned and got stronger. Now you're as strong as the steel in your knives." He moved to put his arm around her waist, but she stepped away.

He wondered what he had done wrong as the silence grew. She walked over and stared at the whiteboard again. "This is dangerous, isn't it?"

"Yes."

She sighed. "Can I ask you a favor as a friend?"

"Of course." Gavin was puzzled but waited.

"Have you chosen a mate yet?"

She's standing right here, he thought, but she doesn't know it yet. "Not officially." Now that she was back, he needed to have that conversation with his pack leader soon.

"Oh," she said, "Never mind then."

"Why, Dot?"

She sighed. "I was going to ask you to have sex with me tonight," she said, and the knives spun in the air again. "But if you're spoken for, never mind." He waited again, sensing there was more she needed to say. "I realize there is a chance I'll get captured tomorrow night, and if I do, there's a better chance I'll be raped. Probably by more than one man as they either fight over me or share me as spoils. And I hoped my first experience would be a pleasant one." His fists were clenched as tightly as his teeth as she slid the knives back in place. "Can you believe that I'm still a virgin?" she asked, avoiding his eyes. "I've had a few offers, but decided I wasn't into the friends-with-benefits scene."

He cock grew hard instantly. He'd dreamt of holding her too many times for his body not to react. He had his arms around her and his mouth pressed against hers before she had a chance to move. "I can't have sex with you," he said as he backed her against the wall. "I told you in Atlanta I loved you and I heard you say it to me too."

"You heard that?"

He thrust his body against hers and kissed her again. "Yes, I heard that. And when I take you, it won't be just sex. I will make love to you, every part of you, and you will know that you are loved." His ran his hands up and down her back while his mouth wandered from her lips to her neck and back again. He raised his head and stared into her eyes. "Let me know now if that's not what you want while I still have the strength to walk away."

"Please..." She met his gaze and returned his stare, not blinking. The beating of his heart pounded in his ears as he waited for her to say more.

"Please make love to me."

He growled softly, and one hand moved to her breast. A soft moan escaped from her lips as he stroked it. He was surprised when she caught his hand and stopped the movement. "Not here," she whispered. "Take me to your bed, Gavin."

The house and his bed never seemed so far away. He laughed, and with a husky voice filled with desire, said "It won't matter. Neither one of us is going to get any sleep tonight."

She looks like a woman who has been thoroughly loved, Gavin thought as he studied Dot while she ate the eggs he had cooked for her. He hadn't been able to keep his promise about getting no sleep at all, but neither of them had gotten much. When his alarm went off, the temptation was to grab it and throw it against the wall, until he opened his eyes and saw her smiling at him, and a whole new temptation took over. Although he had indulged in the desire then, he was freshly tempted now, when she gazed up at him, chewing on her bottom lip. He wanted to kiss that lip and more. He chuckled instead. "You're thinking too hard. What's bothering you?"

"How do we handle this?"

"Handle what?"

She blushed. "Well, if everyone figures out we slept together, how will that affect things? Will people still take me seriously?"

He topped off his coffee cup and sat across from her. "From a pack's point of view, it can only help. The fact that the pack leader's son and heir has chosen a mate will strengthen the pack and give the members more reason to defend our territory. Now I'm off the market, I suspect you will find a lot more couples getting together in the next couple of weeks. As far as the kin you brought with you, I'm not sure. Obviously, Greg is going to be disappointed." He watched the shifting emotions on her face.

"Mate?" she said faintly.

"I told you I love you. Last night sealed our bond. You didn't think it was a one-night stand, did you?"

"I haven't thought much past tonight. Until I get through the raid, I can't plan for the future."

And I'm crazy, letting you go on the raid anyway, he thought, when I won't be around to protect you.

The sun warmed Dot's body as she sat crossed-legged in the small meadow, with two wolves pacing in circles in the woods nearby. The morning had been spent making final plans, now she needed to prepare her soul. Corn was a gift of the Creator, her aunt had taught her, both food and a prayer. But no one in the village grew any—the few gardeners in the pack raised flowers, not vegetables—and there was no corn pollen for her to offer. She hoped the tobacco she had burned was an acceptable substitute and its smoke would carry her plea to the heavens. Her mind and her heart were open to whatever messages the wind might carry to her.

A noise broke her meditation, and she opened her eyes to find a large crow sitting in front of her. It cocked its head, uttered a single caw, and flew away. One large black feather drifted down from the sky. Dot picked it up and stuck it into the scarf wrapped around her arm. In a mirror she had brought along, she painted four pink stripes on one cheek, symbolizing the wolf. On the other cheek, the design was a blue and green globe, in honor of the Earth Mother. On a whim, she added two arcs over the circle—the crow. She knew the painting was not traditional, but thought her ancestors would forgive her.

As she stood and stretched, the two wolves disappeared and Greg and Crystal stood in their places. Solemnly, she painted the mark of the wolf on each. They fell into formation behind her and the three of them walked back to where the others waited. By the time the sun set, each of her fifteen warriors bore four pink markings on their cheeks.

Gavin and his four companions joined them in front of the headquarters building. His was a covert operation, and needed only a few operatives. He resisted the urge to kiss her in front of the assembled troops. He bore his own markings. "The Marines do camouflage differently." He grinned as he examined her face.

"I think you need one more thing," she said. Crystal handed her the bag of paint and brushes.

He backed away and held up his hands.

"No pink for me," he protested. "I have to blend in with the trees."

"Not pink." He relented, and with a few swift strokes, he wore a green and blue globe like hers. She held up the mirror for him to see. "Works with your other markings."

He gazed into her eyes for a long moment. "I love you," he mouthed. She gave him a tremulous smile and nodded. "Are you ready to do this?" he asked.

"As ready as I'll ever be." She turned to Greg and Crystal. "Are we all set?"

"Just waiting for you."

Everyone knew their part, and silently loaded into their assigned vehicles for the short trip. Henry and the other elders stood on the steps of the building as they left.

A sound rang in the air, near yet not close enough to spot the cause. A deep tones throb, like a thump.

"Did you hear that?"

"I didn't hear anything." The sentry threw down his hand. "And unless you can beat a full house, I win again."

The thump repeated, resonating in the air.

"There it is again."

"I heard it that time." The first sentry grabbed his gun while the second man rapidly shifted into wolf form. *"I'll go investigate."* He trotted in the brush alongside the road until he came to the spot where the road curved, out of sight of the main gate. *"Well, I'll be darned. There's a chick sitting in the middle of the road playing a drum. You should come see this. She's kinda cute."* He didn't notice the second woman sneak up behind him and hit the side of his head with the butt of her rifle. He fell, nose first, into the dirt.

Dot smiled. "One."

The second one was almost as easy, but as more men and more wolves poured out of the gate area from the Choate village, Dot and her band had their hands full. Each time a rival went down, another replaced him. It would be easier to kill them, she thought, but tonight is not about death. Tonight is about rescuing Tasha.

Then a wolf, teeth bared, sprang at her from the woods. *"You're mine,"* he said.

Eighteen

A quick twirl put her out of his path.

"Think again." Dot sent back, pulling her knives. He paced around her, waiting for an opening.

When he stopped in mid-pace and leaped again, she was ready. One knife hissed through the air, and struck his chest while he was still in the air. It didn't stick, but drew blood.

"You'll pay for that, bitch." He landed awkwardly and with a twist and a step, attacked again. Her second knife found its home in the wolf's thigh and stayed. The wolf howled in pain, and rolled on the ground, knocking the knife out. *"You need to do better than that. Now you are out of weapons."* She smiled, and two more knives appeared in her hands.

"Give up while you can. Or didn't your mother ever tell you not to play with knives?" Before he had time to react, a knife stuck in his front paw. As he dashed for the woods, the fourth knife found its home in his rump.

Dot grinned, and searched for her next target.

Gavin and his band observed the movement as half of the sentries left their post. They had parked about a mile away, and crawled through the woods to this spot overlooking the selected entrance point. "That's our cue," he whispered.

Dmitri nodded. "Let's hope some of Tasha's guards have gone to help as well."

"You and I have been in worse situations," Gavin reminded him.

"I'm not worried." Dmitri bared his canines. "Let's do this."

It was easy work to avoid the last sentry in the woods, and the path towards the Choate village was empty as well. "It's too easy," Gavin growled. "Be watching for a trap."

Dmitri and the others nodded and as they came into sight of the first group of houses, they dropped to the ground. The street had a few residents, both human and wolf, on the sidewalk, but Gavin and his group would be taking the alley to the back door anyway. "Ready?" he asked the sound barely louder than a breath. He waited until each man nodded and he added, "Now!"

They worked their silent formation into the dark alleyway, and down to the target house. Brightly lit, it stood out from its neighbors. They paused in a dark corner of the yard, while two of the men shifted. Gavin sent the order, "*Go!*"

Dmitri took the lead and tested the back door. As

expected, it was locked, but when Dmitri rammed his shoulder into it, the door fell open. One wolf and one of the remaining men entered first. Their job was to secure the bottom floor. Gavin, Dmitri, and the other wolf headed up the stairs. Before they reached the top of the stairwell, they heard the sound of a battle behind them.

One sentry met them at the top of the stairs, but a quick blow from Gavin's rock hard fist laid him on the ground before he could react. Dmitri paused long enough to push the man out of the way while Gavin threw open the first door he came to. A glance inside showed it empty. But now in the hallway were two more men. The wolf sprang and knocked one over, while Dmitri engaged the second in hand-to-hand combat. Inside the next door Gavin opened he spotted two more men, and a third figure slumped over and tied to a chair.

Tasha.

The two men attacked him at the same time, and Gavin was able to deflect the blow from one, but not from the second. He stumbled, but didn't go down. Recovering, he kicked out and swept one off his feet. The second moved in for another strike and although Gavin was able to avoid it, he had no time to get in his own punch. He heard the sounds of more fighting in the hallway, but had to concentrate on what was happening in the small space around him.

The arm that wrapped around his neck staggered him for a moment, but he bent and threw the man over his shoulder and onto the floor. It went against his ethics, but a quick kick to the side of the man's head rendered the sentry unconscious. At least the kick wouldn't kill him.

Now he could concentrate on the second guard. The man had shifted to wolf form while Gavin was busy and was leaping, jaw open and teeth showing, towards Gavin's throat. Gavin threw up his left arm as a protective barrier, and felt teeth rip into his flesh.

Dr. Tracy is going to yell at me, he thought, and used his right hand to punch the wolf in the throat. A strangled growl and the wolf dropped to the floor.

From the corner of his eye, Gavin saw Dmitri kneeling by Tasha, a knife in his hand. Time to finish this. With one hand he grabbed the revolver tucked in his waistband while wrapping his other arm around the wolf's throat. "Tell your pack leader that we let you off easy this time," he growled. "We make no guarantees about the next time." Using the hand grip of the gun, he hit the wolf behind the ear and let him drop to the floor.

Dmitri was carrying Tasha out of the room. With a grin, Gavin pulled the pot of pink paint out of his pocket. Using his finger, he placed four stripes on the unconscious man's cheek and then followed Dmitri out of the room. The others waited for him at the bottom of the stairs. He took Tasha from Dmitri's arms.

"I think she's been drugged," Dmitri said. "And they used rope with silver running through it."

A deep rumble escaped Gavin's throat. "We'll get her back to Dr. Tracy." He ran down the alley flanked by two wolves and two men. Once they reached the relative safety of the woods, he added, "Someone radio Dot's group and tell them to withdraw. We'll meet up back at the village." At the sound of shouting behind them, he doubled his pace.

Dot was out of throwing knives, but she still had the wickedly sharp night stalker bowie knife Gavin had loaned her. The rival wolves quickly learned to avoid her, and when one shifted back to man form, she laughed and pointed the knife at his exposed genitals. He returned to wolf form, and paced around her, searching for another avenue of attack. A swift feint resulted in a nasty slice on his front leg, and a second saw a cut along his ribs. He wasn't about to give up, and as he bunched his muscles for a third attempt, one of Dot's companions rushed him from the side, knocking him over. While he was stunned, Dot wrapped a plastic zip tie around his muzzle, leaving enough of an opening that he could still pant, and two more ties went around his legs. "I should take lessons in calf roping," she joked to the wolf.

"That would be a unique battle technique." The mental voice identified him as Greg. *"I would like to see it."*

A series of shrill whistles echoed in the woods. "Time to go home," she said, and he nodded his head in agreement. With Greg loping by her side, she jogged back towards the vehicles. Surprisingly, no one followed them. A quick count showed all of her companions were accounted for, although more than one was bleeding or already bandaged.

"You fight good for a girl," Greg teased. He shifted back to human form and got dressed. "I'm proud to have fought by your side." The smile left his face. "You

need to get your leg examined."

She glanced down to see her pants leg torn and covered in blood. "I don't remember that happening," she said in amazement.

"Adrenalin," Greg told her. "You were so busy fighting your mind didn't process it."

"Shit." With the battle done, she was suddenly tired. "Gavin is going to be upset with me."

Dr. Tracy had her hands full, even with the help of the free wolves who had not gone on the mission. The minor scratches could be treated with topical antibiotics and butterfly bandages, but there were far too many wounds that required stitches, and those required her expertise. "Damn bloodthirsty wolves," she muttered as yet another of the free wolves climbed onto her examination table, assisted by Crystal. Crystal, at least, had come out of the fight with no more than a few cuts that would heal on their own within a few days. Dr. Tracy needed to conserve her strength, because Gavin and his group hadn't returned yet and she worried about what shape Tasha would be in.

Luckily, this girl needed few stitches, and the scar would be visible only when she wore a bikini. The scar wouldn't matter if she dated another wolf, every male wolf she knew would find it sexy. Dr. Tracy sighed. Her job had been easy until the past couple of months—the hardest part had been setting the occasional broken bone, but now she understood why the pack paid her so well for doing next to nothing. Times like these she earned her keep.

"Keep it dry, clean, covered, and use this ointment. If you see any redness developing come back and see me," she said as she put the finishing touches her handiwork. How many times had she said that already tonight? She stripped the gloves off her hands, and turned to Crystal. The girl had a nice touch with patients and she wondered if she had any medical training. She could use a helper. "How many more?"

"Just Maria. We need to check out her leg. But she is so worried about the other group, she won't sit long enough for anyone to take a look at it."

"Maria?"

"Dot. Elder Lapahie." Crystal smiled broadly. "She threatened to send us home if she hears us calling her that."

"Do me a favor and clean things up in here while I go and try to talk some sense into her." The doctor finished washing her hands, but left on her lab coat. Her supply was getting short and as bloody as it was, she would have to soak it in bleach to get it white again.

Dr. Tracy found Dot gripping a radio and staring down the road. "Any word from Gavin's group?" she asked although she already knew the answer.

"Not yet." Dot fiddled with the volume control. "The plan was to maintain radio silence until they got to the gates, but it doesn't make the waiting any easier."

"While you're waiting, why don't you come back to my office and let me check you over." She took Dot by the arm and turned her around. "Based on your pants, you saw some action."

Dot grimaced. "I'm not sure how much of this is my blood, and how much is the other guy's."

"Still, I want to check it." Dr. Tracy noticed Dot limped slightly, trying to avoid putting her weight on the injured leg. "Even a slight scratch can get dirt in it and result in an infection." Her tactic of keeping Dot talking as they walked worked, and they had reached the door to her office. "This will only take a minute."

Dot rolled her eyes, but went into the exam room. Seeing Crystal, she said "I suppose you ratted me out."

"Who, me?" Crystal grinned and grabbed a pair of scissors. "Now, pull those pants off or I'll have to cut them off."

Dot sighed. "That's going to go over real good when I walk out of here in my underwear."

"Is your underwear bright pink too?" teased Dr. Tracy. Dot suddenly realized she had lost both of her scarves and the crow feather sometime during the fight. "Don't worry, I have some scrubs here you can borrow. They don't make quite the same fashion statement as your current outfit, but I don't think anyone will mind."

The wound was not as bad as Dr. Tracy anticipated. "I'd say the pants got the worst of it," she said. "I don't think it's worth stitching if you promise me you'll take it easy for a few days."

"I'll try," said Dot as she slipped on the bottoms of the scrubs.

"I'll pass the word on to Gavin," Crystal said. "If anyone can make her behave, he can."

The radio crackled as Dot was putting her boots back on. "Gavin and crew just came in," the sentry broadcast. "They are in need of minor medical treatment. They have Tasha, and she needs the doctor immediately."

Dot pushed the button. "I'm here with Dr. Tracy," she said. "She's ready."

"I'm not sure what they used to keep her under," Dr. Tracy reported to the group assembled outside. "But it won't do her any harm to sleep it off. I already have several volunteers to sit with her through the night. She has sustained very little in the way of physical damage. She doesn't appear to have been sexual assaulted."

"There's a but in your voice," said Henry.

"Gavin says they kept her tied up with rope containing silver. Depending upon her level of sensitivity, and if she wasn't kept drugged the whole time, that would have been torture. I'm more worried about her mental state than her physical one."

Low growls rumbled from the group. Henry held up his hand. "From tonight's reports, we have already punished them for their actions. Until Tasha wakes up and we can get the whole story, we will take no further action." He studied the gathered crowd. "If anyone feels the need for action tonight, may I suggest you join the sentries on patrol? I doubt the Choates will retaliate tonight, but we must be prepared."

"I want to post sentries here at the medical clinic," Elder Fenner added. "Do we have any volunteers?"

Gavin grabbed Dot's arm before she could raise it. "We've done our share tonight," he whispered. "Let someone else have the glory."

The movement caught Dr. Tracy's attention. "Gavin, would you come see me before you go home?"

He sighed as he got up. "Foiled again," he muttered.

It was then Dot noticed the sleeve of his shirt was torn and bloody. "You're hurt!"

"It's just a scratch. Probably won't even leave a scar. I was just going to wash it and be done with it." He grinned. "But Dr. Tracy is going to want to put some ointment on it that will sting like the devil and I'll have to pretend it doesn't hurt at all."

"I'll go with you and hold your hand."

"And then maybe you can give me a kiss and make it better." He wrapped his good arm around her waist. He wasn't sure how she would react to being kissed in public, but he was tempted to find out.

"The doctor is waiting and she's had a long night." Dot winked and pulled away. "It's rude to keep her waiting."

It's been a long night for all of us, he thought as she took his hand, but I saved the energy for one more activity.

Her body was warm against his and Gavin strained to take it slow as he pulled Dot's t-shirt over her head. The pink bra against her deeply tanned skin had him moaning in anticipation as he moved his hands to her breasts. She was trembling as she carefully unbuttoned what remained of his shirt. Another one lost to the ongoing conflict.

He debated what he wanted to remove next—the bra or the pants? He loved the simple act of undressing her. She flinched as he reached to stroke her thigh, and he realized that she was not wearing the cargo pants anymore. He pulled back and his eyes asked the unspoken question...

"Just a scratch," she said, avoiding his eyes. "Didn't need stitches or anything. Dr. Tracy said to take it easy for a few days and it will be all right."

"Let me see," he growled, and pushed her down on the bed.

Carefully, Gavin worked the scrubs bottoms down her legs, making sure the waistband didn't drag along her skin. The wound was bound carefully in gauze and tape, but the length of it alone made him grind his teeth. "They will pay for this," he promised as he gently kissed the length of her leg, starting at her ankle and working his way up, avoiding the dressings.

"It looks worse than it is," she said, sitting up and catching his head between her hands, forcing it up so their eyes met. "I don't even know when it happened. Besides, you have your own." She ran her fingertips lightly down his bandaged arm.

He gently pushed her back down onto the bed, trapping her under his weight, intent on giving her something different to think about. She hadn't noticed his scars the previous night, and he didn't want to give her the chance to see them now.

NINETEEN

The next few days passed quietly as each of the packs took time to heal. While Gavin worked, Dot spent time with Elder Fenner. She had decided it was finally time for her to learn how to shoot a gun. He started her off with a Smith and Wesson. .22, and even that scared her the first few shots she fired. But by the end of the first day, she hit the target most of the time.

The second day he moved her up to a Colt .45. The strength of the kickback surprised her but she adjusted to it quickly and soon hit the target with regularity. Tasha joined her that day.

"I heard what you did for me."

"It was my fault." Dot aimed carefully and shot the target, but still couldn't get close to the bulls-eye. "I did what I had to do to fix it."

"And I thought I was such a hot shot, being your bodyguard." Tasha studied the target. "Let me try."

Dot handed her the gun and the ear muffs. Without taking more than a second to aim, Tasha fired off four quick rounds. Two of them hit dead center. She smiled as she handed the handgun back to Dot. "I haven't lost it. Elder Fenner seems to think I have. He wants me to go visit a pack in Maine for a while. He has cousins there. Give me time to recover, he said. I came to tell you thank you and goodbye."

"Don't stay gone too long." The two women hugged, and Dot was surprised at how frail Tasha felt. No wonder the Elders wanted her away from the action. "We need to go on another motorcycle trip one of these days."

The third day Elder Fenner handed her a 12 gauge shotgun, but no matter how hard she tried, Dot couldn't find the sweet spot to hold it against her shoulder. She ended up with a bruise the size of a small plate before he allowed her to give up, with a promise he would move her back to a handgun the next day.

The fourth day her shoulder hurt so she skipped the lessons. Instead, she spent the day with Greg and Crystal. They, and the uninjured volunteers, had been working with the sentries patrolling the pack's territory, both day and night. "Some of the girls are complaining they missed out on all the fun," Crystal told her.

"Fun? Do you have a pair of shorts I can borrow? I didn't bring any."

"I think I have a pair that will fit you." Crystal was puzzled, but soon returned with a pair of running shorts. Dot swapped them for the jeans she wore.

"Perhaps we should go visit the girls now," she said. Crystal nodded thoughtfully.

Dot had removed the bandages in the morning even though her wound was only half-healed. Although she religiously applied the lotion Dr. Tracy supplied, there were thick, ugly scabs covering the area where the cuts were the deepest. Bruises in various shades of purple and black covered her thigh around the wound. She never said a word about it, but as they stopped to visit with the free wolves on duty, she caught the glances sent her way. Hopefully, it was enough to remind them this was serious business.

The fifth day brought the first of the raids the Choates launched in retaliation. With the added strength the free wolves brought to the pack, the invaders were easily repulsed, but two of the free wolves received major injuries in the battle. She stood and held their hands while Dr. Tracy patched them up, but that night, in Gavin's arms, she cried.

"I understand they volunteered," she sobbed, as he tried to wipe the tears from her cheeks. "But I don't think they realized what they were getting themselves into."

"So tomorrow you make sure the word gets out that anyone who wants to go home can and nobody will think any less of them." He massaged her good shoulder. "If anyone without a vehicle wants to leave, the pack can arrange transportation."

She sniffed, and he felt the tension in her body easing. "Is this the way it's going to be from here on out?" she asked. "We raid them, they raid us back, and no one ever gains anything?"

He chuckled. "You do know the physical raids aren't the only way we have of undermining them, don't you?" He moved his attentions to her neck, and started working a knot out of a muscle at the base of her skull.

"Not sure I know what you mean."

"You realize the pack is an actual business? Dad is

the CEO. We sell custom software for businesses. The Choates own a similar business, and we are about to the point where we can buy them out. A hostile takeover in more ways than one."

"And then what?"

"We take over all the customers, keep the non-kin employees worth keeping, fire the rest. I suspect the pack will be forced to dissolve." He put a finger to his lips. "That's a secret of course, you can't tell anyone."

"What happens if the pack dissolves?"

"Most of the time, the members scatter to other packs here and there. A few of the older ones might stick around, and we will probably let them. And if any of the women, especially those with children, ask, we will consider letting them join our pack. We have enough unattached males that we can probably find them mates here if that's what they want."

"How long will this take?"

"Six months to a year, maybe even two years. We've been working on this plan for quite a while." His hand moved to the middle of her back, and he traced light circles just under her bra.

"And in the meantime, the raids continue?"

"It's the traditional way."

She sighed, and leaned against him. His hand moved to a much more interesting spot on the front of her body, and he felt her tense again. But with his lips on hers, his muscles were tightening as well.

Except for a few minor scratches, no one got hurt in the raid the pack launched on the eighth day. It had been devised for the sole reason of testing the enemy's defenses, and to give some of the free wolves battle experience. None of them had left, even after Dot made it clear they were free to go. A new tradition started that night based on what Gavin had done; each disabled foe was marked with four streaks of bright pink paint. Even the sentries guarding pack territory started carrying pink face paint with them, just in case.

Damyon Choate glared at the two young men in front of him. One of them would be his replacement, as soon as he could get his hands on his granddaughter. "What is this, some kind of weird breast cancer awareness gimmick?"

"The group that attacked the front gate last week was all painted this way," explained the largest of the men. His cheek bore four scars running lengthwise. "Although none of the group that infiltrated the village wore the mark."

"One of the men guarding the bitch we captured muttered something about pink when he reported to us." The second man was not as tall as the first, but more muscular. Arnold and Lucius. It amused Damyon to make them work together, as they were rivals for his position and hated each other.

"So we have two different packs working together? I don't know of any pack that uses pink in their logo."

"The sentries reported the girl playing the drum had pink hair and a pink scarf on one arm." The muscle in Arnold's marked cheek twitched and Damyon knew he was nervous. Arnold would never make a poker player, the twitch was a dead giveaway.

"She was too far down the road for the security cameras to get a picture. But the others were protecting her, and most of them were females."

"So the men got beat up by a bunch of girls? Maybe you two need to step up the training."

Lucius reached into his pocket and pulled out a knife, the blade wrapped in cloth. Handle first, he set it down on the desk in front of Damyon. "She used these as weapons. She was good with them too. Have no idea how many she had, but we found three of them. Then she switched to a big combat knife of some sort. My men said she never shifted the whole time."

He said my men, noted Damyon, not the men or your men. I need to keep a closer eye on him. "What do your spies have to say about her?" Each man had his own spy network, and he already knew what they knew, because he had his own spy attached to each.

Lucius cleared his throat. "Well, if you ignore the rumors going around that she's an Indian spirit come back to wreak vengeance on us, that leaves us with her being some sort of leader of the free wolves."

"Which doesn't make any sense either," interrupted Arnold, snarling. "We all know the free wolves don't have leaders. The information I have is that she is the girlfriend of the pack leader's son."

This was news to Damyon, but he hid his excitement. He would have to find out why his spy hadn't reported this to him. "You realize what that means don't you?" he asked casually.

Both of the men stared at him blankly, and he did not try to hide his sigh. Perhaps he should be trying to find his replacement elsewhere. These two were strong physically, but he often wondered how smart they were. "My granddaughter has finally resurfaced."

The picture was hidden away in a locked drawer of his desk. When the younger men had left, Damyon unlocked the drawer and pulled the picture out. His granddaughter reminded him of his long-dead mate. Something about the set of her mouth and the spark in her eyes. Whoever replaced him would have their hands full trying to control the girl. He hoped they would have more luck than he did. Even the beatings had not tamed the defiance of his chosen. If only she would have learned to obey him, maybe they would have had other sons and he wouldn't need the girl. Instead, she chose to run, and he had made sure she would never leave him again.

Like every other time he looked at the picture, he was tempted to tear it up and throw it away. Instead, he tossed it back in its hiding place, slammed the drawer closed, and locked it.

Dot lay on her stomach, her arms in front of her, holding the Colt, shooting at a target fifty yards away and only hitting it about half the time. She could probably hit it more often with her knives. She didn't understand why Elder Fenner was so determined to make a marksman out of her, but she was giving it her best effort. At least he hadn't asked her to try the shotgun again, although he talked about having her try a small rifle. For now, she was happy sticking to the handgun. She clicked on the safety, and sat up. The clip was empty and she needed to stretch anyway. As she slipped off the ear guards, she saw Crystal coming her way.

She tried to hide her smile. A few days earlier, Crystal had come to her and asked to be relieved of her lieutenant duties, suggesting Daphne take them over. Dr. Tracy had asked her to be a permanent assistant, and Henry had agreed to have the pack pay for her to take classes to become a LPN. And only this morning, Dot heard a rumor that Crystal and Dmitri were seen together at the pizza place. Crystal seemed happy, and that made Dot happy too.

"I thought I would find you here." Crystal must have been running, because she was out of breath. The range was in a remote corner of the pack's territory. "Elder Fairwood requests you come to the conference room for a meeting. I don't know what the meeting is about."

Dot checked the chamber of the gun one more time before holstering it. The way the gun laid on her hip gave her the feeling of being in control, like an old-time sheriff. She knew it was just an illusion. "Did he say how soon?"

"He said to hurry, but not to run, whatever that means."

"I think it means not to change clothes first." Dot brushed the dirt off her shirt and jeans. To her amazement, Gavin had stored all the clothes she left behind in the hotel in Atlanta. He'd also retrieved her mother's journals, and Dot spent a little time each day reading them. "Am I decent?"

"You make me jealous." Crystal grinned, as she reached out to pluck a strand of dead grass from Dot's hair. "There you were, lying in the dirt, and you look better than I do after spending hours getting ready. It's not fair."

"That's not what Dmitri thinks, from what I hear." She laughed as she watched her friend's face turn deep red.

"It's your fault, you know," Crystal said as they walked back. "Well, yours and Gavin's, anyway. Dmitri called it the spillover affect when the pack leader mates. And Gavin is as good as the pack leader."

That's what scares me, Dot thought, I love him but I don't know if I am any good for him. All I am is trouble.

"Elder Lapahie, thank you for coming." Henry was seated at his traditional spot at the head of the conference table, and Dot noticed the large screen was displaying an empty room. He was the only one in the room.

"Elder Fairwood," Dot said, nodding towards him. If he wanted formality, she could give it to him. "I hope I didn't keep you waiting too long. I came as quickly as I could." Some instinct kept her from mentioning where she had been. She wondered why Gavin hadn't been invited, but she could handle this on her own.

"Counselor Carlson will be joining us in a minute."

She carefully kept her expression blank. She was not eager to see the man again, after the way their last meeting had gone. She poured herself a glass of water from the pitcher on the table, took a sip, and waited quietly. She watched the screen as the council chairman entered the room and sat in the vacant chair.

"Is she there, Elder Fairwood?" He adjusted the screen in front of him. "You have changed your appearance, Ms. McKenzie."

"I also changed my name, Counselor. I go by Lapahie now, in honor of my grandmother and my ancestors."

"No wonder the Choates didn't find you." Dot was relieved to see him smile. "I hope that sometime you and I can sit down and you will tell me how you did it."

She smiled back. "Only if you promise not to tell anyone else."

He leaned back in his chair. "You're too good for the Choates." He quickly sat back up and glared into the webcam. "And if you ever tell anyone else I said that, Ms. Lapahie, I will deny it. Understood?"

"Yes, Counselor," she said demurely, suppressing a smile.

"Now, on to the real business at hand. Elder Fairwood, Elder Choate called me demanding the Council take action against your pack. He says you are defying a Council order by giving Ms. Lapahie your hospitality."

Henry stared steadfastly at the screen. "I would remind you, Counselor, that Elder Lapahie does not acknowledge the Council's authority over her."

"You called her Elder?"

"Yes." Henry nodded at Dot. "It is honorary, but she should have some recognition as a leader among the free wolves."

"She's the one who organized the free wolves? Ms. Lapahie, I mean Elder Lapahie." The chairman grinned, "Do you know how many of the council representatives you have upset? We didn't mind when they were just scattered here and there, but when the delegates heard someone was actually getting them to band together, some of our members feared it threatened their power." He shook his head. "Henry, do you think you can stand another visitor? I really want to come and spend some time with the young lady."

"I would love for you to visit, but perhaps you should delay the trip. The pack would be unable to guarantee your safety during the current state of hostilities."

"That bad, Elder Fairwood?" The counselor switched back to his formal mode.

"Yes, and that was before Elder Lapahie joined us. Now the Choates have found out she's here, I suspect things will only get worse." Henry stared at the screen and avoided Dot's eyes.

TWENTY

Dot knew things with the Choates could get worse, of course. But it didn't make it any easier to hear Henry say it. Even if she left now, the Choates wouldn't stop hurting her friends. She tried that before, and it didn't work. But what else could she do? Give herself up?

She had burnt tobacco and cleared her mind but the wind brought no answers to her troubled spirit. Even the crows had no message for her. Greg and Daphne circled around her, out of her peripheral vision, and she sensed their concern for her. When Gavin came and sat in the grass beside her, she kept her gaze on the ants crawling in the grass near her feet.

"I thought I did the right thing," she said. "Coming to help rescue Tasha. But now I don't know. It seems like I only made things worse. You don't know how much I regret that."

He sat silent for a long moment. "Do you regret us?"

She took too long considering her answer. "No. You are the best thing that has ever happened to me. Do I worry about you getting hurt because of me?" She touched his arm lightly. Though mostly healed, one spot of his wound was taking longer to get better. She'd put a fresh bandage on the sore after he showered that morning. "Yes. But I remember you told me once that you can protect yourself and I trust you."

"I talked to Dad earlier. Asked if there was any way to move up the takeover. He said it's too risky, too big of a chance of failure."

"I guess I don't understand how the pack functions. The whole pack as a business thing confuses me."

"It's really pretty basic. Packs used to share hunting rights, food sources, childcare, that sort of thing. We still do, but now pack members have shares in the business, and the business pays for the school, medical care, and other shared expenses. Any profits go back to the members."

"And you and your father each have a share like everyone else?"

To her surprise, he blushed. "No. Dad holds a controlling interest of fifty-one percent that he will pass to me when I take over. I have one share, and so does Raven. So no one can ever take over the pack by buying shares. They can't be sold outside the pack anyway. They are tied up nice and legal. The Choate setup is similar—that's why we have to destroy their business before we can buy them out."

Dot stood up suddenly and walked away. He waited a minute to give her time to come back, but when she didn't, he got up and followed her. He noted with approval Greg and Daphne fell in not far behind. He caught up to her, but she didn't look at him and kept walking. "Did I say something wrong?" he asked, putting his hand in her shoulder.

She stopped abruptly and he nearly stumbled trying to stop with her. "Every now and then I get reminded of who you are, and I get scared," she said. "When will you stop fooling yourself, and realize I'm not good enough for you? This is all a joke the spirits are playing on me and one of these days you will find your true mate and realize I was a mistake."

He had his arms around her and his mouth crushed to hers before she could react. When she tried to push away, he just pulled her closer. "I'm not letting you go," he whispered, his voice rough with emotion. "I've let you go too many times, and I can't do it any more. You are my mate, and you know it as well as I do. Nothing else matters." Then his lips found hers again, quieting her soft sobs.

Dawn giggled as she tried to put a ribbon in Dot's hair. "Won work," she finally decided, and stuck it in her own hair instead, then settled in Gavin's lap. Dot was amazed at how much she had grown up in the past few months. The TV was tuned to a sitcom no one watched while they let the fried chicken Raven had cooked settle in their stomachs. Raven had invited Greg and Daphne as well, so they wouldn't feel obligated to prowl around outside the house while Dot was inside eating. With the Choates aware of her presence in the village, Elder Fenner had tightened her security measures.

Raven pushed herself out of her chair. "I better go take care of the dishes or they will sit there all night."

Dot jumped off the loveseat she shared with Gavin

and Dawn. "Let me help." As she followed her hostess into the kitchen, she grabbed a few dishes off the table, stacking them four deep.

"You've done that a few times," Raven said, taking them from Dot and putting them in the sink.

"I worked as a waitress for a long time," Dot said, opening the dishwasher. As Raven handed the rinsed dishes to Dot, she loaded the machine. "It was one of the few jobs I could get without references. Half the time the restaurants paid me under the table, which made it even better." Raven handed her some silverware, and Dot felt a tingle in her hand. She put the pieces in one by one, and realized the tingling went away after placing a serving spoon in the tray. She lifted it back out and felt the tingling again. Raven noticed what she was doing.

"Sorry, that's a piece I got as a gift. I don't use it very often. It's silver-plate, not stainless."

"What's that got to do with anything?"

"You don't wear silver jewelry, do you?"

"No, it bothers me. Feels like I'm allergic to it or something."

Raven nodded. "I suppose no one ever told you. Most shifters have a similar reaction. That's why we were so upset to hear the Choates used a rope with silver threads to tie up Tasha. It also can prevent us from shifting."

Dot rubbed the medicine bag dangling under her shirt, put the spoon in the dishwasher, and went to get more dirty dishes from the table.

Gavin wore only a towel around his waist when he came out of the bathroom and saw Dot sitting on his bed. She had on a red bra and matching bikini bottom, held her medicine bag in one hand and stared at something lying on the bed. Something about the expression on her face stopped him from making the first comment that sprang to his lips.

"I figured it out," she said.

"Figured what out?" he asked, sitting beside her and putting his hand on her thigh.

She stood up, put the bag on the bed, and stripped off her underwear. As always, the sight of her naked stirred the beast in him, but he waited to see what she was doing. In the blink of an eye, the air shimmered and she switched to her wolf form.

"Didn't hurt," she said.

A growl rumbled in his throat. "I think you are just as sexy as a wolf. Maybe I should shift too."

"No." She shifted back and reached for her bag, put the object on the bed back in it and put the bag back around her neck. The sight of her naked and bent over the bed had his inner wolf howling, and he reached for her. "Just like a man," she muttered but smiled before she shifted again. *"Hurt that time."*

Quickly, he shifted too. The space was crowded with two large wolves in it. *"To do this right, we need to go outside,"* he said, *"So we can run first and mate afterword."* He put his nose to hers and licked her. *"What is different?"*

He was disappointed when she shifted back. She rubbed her nose where he had licked her and reached into the medicine bag. "My mother's ring." She held it up to the light. "She got it from my grandmother. No telling how long the ring has been in the family. It's traditional Navajo jewelry—silver and turquoise."

He shifted as well, and pressed against her, his front to her back, put his arm around her and looked over her shoulder at the ring. His hand rested just under her breasts, but he didn't allow it to move any higher—not yet, anyway. "How long have you had it?"

"Since she died. After the accident, the sheriff gave it to me, and I decided not to bury it with her. I wore it for a while, but it's too big for my finger and I didn't want lose it, so I put it on a chain. When I started my medicine bag, the ring was the first thing I put in it. That was before I started to shift."

He had given up resisting, and his mouth wandered around her neck, kissing and nipping. She didn't stop him, and he took that as encouragement. "So what are you going to do about it?" he asked as he finally moved his hand higher.

She tossed the bag on the nearby dresser, reached behind her and stroked his upper thigh, then allowed her fingers to wander towards his inner thigh, drawing a moan from him. "I guess I'll have to figure that out later, won't I?"

"You worked as a paralegal in Florida, didn't you, Daphne?" Dot and her newest lieutenant were reviewing the free wolves' accommodations. Penny had called, more volunteers were on their way, and they needed to figure out where to put them. It was going to be tight quarters for a few days but a couple of the women would be leaving soon—their vacation time was used up and they needed to get back to work.

"More of a secretary, but I was training as one. Why?"

"What do you remember about the legal structure of the Choate pack?"

"They didn't let women participate in much of anything—that's one reason I left. The males controlled everything. If there were only girls in a family, the share went to the mate of the oldest, she didn't get to control it herself. It was like living in the 1800's or something. My grandmother says things didn't used to be that way, before Damyon Choate claimed pack leadership."

"But doesn't the pack share everything like they do here?"

"On paper, yes, but the males always got first choice of everything. Unless you have a good mate, the females get what's leftover. I don't know if you saw, but the night we fought at the gate—all the guards were males. Not a female in the bunch. They know they aren't wanted as fighters, and most of them won't fight against another pack anyway."

"How hard would it be to get your hands on the paperwork showing the setup?"

Daphne stopped with her hand on the doorknob. "Why do you need to know?"

"I'm curious. Wondered if there would be anything in them that would be helpful to me."

"I can get a friend at the firm to pull the documents and send them to me. It might take a few days."

"Thanks, Daphne, I appreciate it."

"Whatever happened to my bike, Gavin?" she asked, out of nowhere. "I miss it."

"You know you can't go for a ride, Dot."

"Not even if you go with me?" They sat on the swing on the porch, half-shaded from the streetlight by the rose vine growing on the trellis. He'd plucked a rose earlier, and given it to her after tearing off all the thorns, and she was rocking slightly, clutching the flower in her hands. He had an arm around her shoulders as they were watched the moon rise above the horizon. At the edge of the yard, she could see the shadows of the sentries. She knew the surveillance was for her own good, but the loss of her freedom grated on her nerves.

"Not even if I go with you. Especially not after the raid last night." His AK-47 leaned against the wall of the house, within arm's reach. She still didn't feel confident enough in her abilities to carry a handgun, but her replacement throwing knives had arrived earlier in the day, and her belt was fully loaded.

She shivered. "It was a bad one, wasn't it?"

"Yes." Two members of the pack had been seriously injured in the attack, and Gavin saw the lights of the medical center were still on. Either Dr. Tracy or Crystal must be spending the night there, keeping an eye on their patients. Privately, Gavin thought the goal of the Choates had been to inflict as much damage as possible without actually killing anyone. They were changing the rules in the middle of the game. Previously, the aim had been to disable temporarily. "Maybe tomorrow at lunch you can take it for a quick spin around the village. Dmitri wants to show you what he's done with it."

"What do you mean?"

"He adopted your motorcycle as a hobby. He's been fiddling with it for months now. You'll just have to wait to see it."

TWENTY~ONE

Dmitri had his hands over Dot's eyes. "Now three steps down." He chuckled. "And Gavin is walking in front of you, so if you miss a step he'll catch you." Privately, Dot thought the whole process silly, but Dmitri was enjoying himself so she played along. After all, how much could he have changed on her bike? Washed it, put on new tires, but the possibilities were limited. "A few more steps—you're on the sidewalk now, and voila!" He moved his hands. "You can open your eyes now."

Dot blinked to adjust her eyes to the bright light of the sun at noon, and then blinked again. "So where's my bike?" she asked.

She swirled to face Dmitri, her hands on her hips. "This isn't it." Behind her, Gavin laughed, and Dmitri got a huge grin on his face.

"Actually, it is your bike. I started by replacing your seat—I figured the tears got uncomfortable on long trips. Then I realized you needed new tires. Next I figured I would take the dents and scratches out of your fenders. While I was working on those, I got the idea to completely redo the paint job. Of course, once I got that done, I figured the chrome work needed redone too. I couldn't do that myself, I had to send the parts away. I overhauled the engine while I waited for those parts to come back. Start her up and see how she sounds."

She didn't sit yet. She was still studying the pictures decorating the bike. On the front fender, there was a painting of a wolf's head, staring back at the observer. The rear fender was painted with a picture of a flower-filled meadow. Each side of the gas tank had a large gray wolf running through a forest. The top of the gas tank bore the likeness of another wolf's head, and its eyes seemed to stare directly at her no matter where she stood. Each of the wolves bore pink markings on their cheeks.

"Well, what do you think?"

She avoided his eyes, and settled into the seat. The keys were in the ignition, and she made sure the gearshift was in first, held the clutch lever in, twisted the throttle to feed the motor a little gas, and fired it up. The engine caught first try, and she gave it some extra fuel. The twin mufflers purred with a sweet rumble. She eased off the accelerator, and listened to the steady tone of the idle. With a sigh, she turned the key to shut the bike down.

"It's beautiful, Dmitri. I can't believe you did this." She slowly ran her hand over the curve of the gas tank.

"Ready to take her for a ride?"

"I didn't think I could," she said sadly.

Dmitri and Gavin both smiled. "We decided if we trailed you in the jeep, it would be okay," Gavin said. "Not too far, but far enough that you can get a feel for the way she handles." Dot realized the Jeep was parked not far away, and Gavin walked over and pulled something from behind the passenger seat. "You need your helmet if you're going to take her on the road." She suspected their guns were behind the seat as well, tucked out of sight.

She pretended to move an imaginary strand of hair away from her eyes so she could wipe away the tears that were forming in them. Dmitri had painted her helmet with a design to match the bike, with a wolf running through the woods. It, too, had pink markings on one cheek. With one finger, she traced the pink design.

"I added those last week," admitted Dmitri. "Only took a couple of minutes."

She planted a quick kiss on his cheek before slipping the helmet over her head and fastening the chin strap. "Think you guys can keep up with me?" she said, grinning, before she clicked the face shield down.

Despite the threat, Dot behaved herself and didn't try to lose the Jeep. She stuck to the main roads and stayed within the speed limit, and even stopped at orange lights instead of proceeding through them when she knew Gavin and Dmitri would get a red. Not until they had returned to pack territory did she gun the engine, pop a wheelie, and leave them far behind.

She was waiting for them in the parking lot when they pulled up, the engine turned off, the kickstand down, and the helmet balanced carefully on the seat. She casually strolled over to them as they climbed out of the Jeep. "That was fun, guys," she said. "Can we do it again tomorrow?"

"Probably not." Gavin shook his head. "As soon as it becomes a routine, it also becomes a security risk."

She sighed. "Never hurts to try." She gave Dmitri another kiss. "It really is amazing. I can't wait until I can ride her whenever I feel like it." She handed him the key. "Now do me a favor, and put her in the garage. It's supposed to rain." She kept her helmet, and didn't tell them about the spare key in her medicine bag.

Dot's dream of riding free again seemed a little closer when Daphne got the paperwork detailing the business operations of the Choate firm. "The setup seems pretty straightforward," said Daphne. "At least according to Paul. He's the one who pulled the documents for me. But he spotted a few things that made him curious, so he dug deeper. That's when he found this." She shoved a single piece of paper at Dot.

"What's this?" Dot skimmed the sheet, but all the legal terms made her head spin.

"I remember my mother going on about how things would be different if Merikh was pack leader. I guess he was for a few weeks before his death. He was your father, right? Anyway, after he got killed in a bar fight Elder Choate took back the position. That happened before I was born, but I got the feeling nobody outside the pack ever found out the transfer had been made. Some of the younger men were upset the leadership didn't get opened up to a pack challenge back then, but since Elder Choate wasn't that old, nobody made a big deal out of it. He could still beat most of them in a fight anyway."

Dot's head spun even more because Daphne talked

so fast, but the information was good for her to know, so she tried to stay focused.

"I don't know why the younger men haven't challenged him in the last few years because any of them could take him now," Daphne said.

Dot remembered the way the Elder had appeared in Atlanta. Even she could win a one-on-one fight against him, in either human or wolf form. Everything led back to her—what made her so important?

Daphne was still talking. "Anyway, Paul highlighted a few parts he figured were pertinent. I barely glanced at them before I brought these to you." She handed an overstuffed manila envelope to Dot. "I'm no lawyer, but if you have any questions, we can try to figure things out together."

Dot added the single piece of paper to the others in the envelope and set off to find a quiet place to read them. She nodded at the girl that followed her, today's shadow. A new addition to the free wolves' forces, Dot had a hard time remembering her name. Sabrina? Samantha? Something like that. She didn't talk much, but Dot understood she had earned a black belt in mixed martial arts. A good skill to have. In a fight, the two of them would make quite a team.

The girl seemed bored. Rumor was the task of being Dot's personal security guard was no longer considered an honor, but a chore. She had been behaving herself for too long. It was time to shake things up.

In the meantime, she needed to read these papers. The thought gave her a headache, and she found a bench under a tree to sit on. The other girl stood a few feet away. "You know, I wouldn't care if you sat down," Dot said. "You can guard me just as well sitting on the bench as you can from over there."

"If you don't mind," the girl said hesitantly.

"I'm sorry, but what is your name?"

"Samantha."

"I don't bite, Samantha, not my friends anyway." Dot grinned as Samantha sat on the edge of the seat. "You're a free wolf, right?"

"Yes, Elder Lapahie."

Before Samantha could blink, a knife quivered in the bench between them. "You are a free wolf. To you I am Maria or Dot, whichever works better for you. I'll answer to either. But I want none of this elder stuff coming from you or any of the other free wolves. If the Fairwood pack members insist on calling me Elder, I'll put up with it, but not from you. Pass the word to the others." Dot pried the knife from the seat and examined the tip. Satisfied she had not damaged it, she slipped the knife back in her belt. She picked up the manila envelope and pulled out the stack of papers. When Samantha started chuckling, Dot looked up, startled.

"So much for the story that you are just the spoiled plaything of the leader's son."

"Is that what they are saying about me?" Dot asked, putting the papers down.

"Well, you don't run night patrols like the rest of us, you're staying in the fanciest house in the place instead of bunking in the school, you don't have to do any of the drills that Greg and Daphne put the rest of us through, so yeah, some of us figure you are spoiled."

"How long have you been here, Samantha? And how many times have you gone to the pub or into town?"

"I've been here a week, and I've only been to the

pub twice," Samantha said defensively. "I don't go every night like some of the girls do."

"I've been here almost a month now, and do you know how many times I've been to the pub? Zero. Zip. Nada." A knife glittered in the air. "No, you can't go, Dot, it's too risky. Go for a ride on your motorcycle? Too big of a security risk, Elder Lapahie. Spoiled? I don't think so. More like a prisoner." The knife went back in her belt. "Sorry, I'm having a bad day. I would like be running night patrols alongside everyone else. I never wanted to be just a figurehead."

"So why do you let them tell you what to do?" The question startled Dot, but she didn't have a chance to answer before Samantha continued. "Sounds like you need a girl's night out."

"Like that's going to happen." Dot surprised herself. She didn't normally allow herself to be so negative. The lack of freedom was getting to her.

"You have any plans for tonight?"

"No. What do you have in mind?"

"No one will get upset if you spend the night with us, will they?"

Gavin might, Dot thought, but it sounds like a plan to me. "I think I can do that."

"Good. We'll get some movies and popcorn and beer and we'll have a girls' night in."

Dot smiled, but a plot started taking shape as she picked up the legal paperwork again.

Dot ducked as several handfuls of popcorn kernels headed her direction. "Your roots are showing, Maria.

Time to dye your hair again!"

She managed to avoid most of the missiles. "I think I should just dye it brown and go back to my natural color for a while. What do you guys think?"

"Brown is boring."

"Maybe red."

"Purple."

"But the pink made it easier to keep track of her. We always know where she is"

Precisely, Dot thought. Exactly why I want to go back to brown. "How about black," she suggested. "It would cover the pink better."

Hands rang over the top of her head, and she forced herself to sit still. "Black would work, but no matter what color you choose you need to trim it."

"Everyone get dressed, we'll go into town and get supplies. The drugstore there is open twenty-four hours."

Dot sat unmoving as the other girls scrambled to find their clothes. She wore an oversized T-shirt of Gavin's as a nightie. Her jeans and t-shirt were neatly stacked nearby, but she made no move to retrieve them. She noticed Daphne didn't move either.

"Come on, Maria, you have to pick the color," one of the girls said.

Samantha stopped in the process of zipping up her jeans. "You can't go, can you?"

"No." Dot managed to get the word out without sounding too bitter.

"Cool it, everyone." Samantha scrunched her face. "Who has a car? Okay, Joy, you and me will go into town. The rest of you stay here and keep the party going. We won't be gone very long." She finished getting dressed. "Final vote, everyone, black?"

Daphne came and sat beside her. "I didn't realize how hard this is for you. When Elder Fenner made me promise to keep an eye on you, I think he knew this might happen." Dot nodded but didn't answer, afraid of the emotions bubbling inside. "You can't live like this forever, we need to do something about it." Daphne gave her a quick hug and whispered in her ear, "Remember, we are your friends too."

She'd passed a test, Dot decided, as she stood in the mirror and fluffed what was left of her hair. The other girls had managed a cut that evened out the appearance without sacrificing too much of the length, and the color Samantha picked out for her not only hid the pink, but worked with her skin tone. Gavin wasn't sure he liked the new style, but Dot thought it made her look more like her native ancestors.

Gavin also hadn't been happy about Elder Fenner deciding to ease up on the guards trailing her all day. As long as she stayed in the pack's territory, the security chief decided she didn't need to have someone with her. She promised both of them that she would always get someone to go with her when she went to the meadow to meditate or to the firing range, when she wouldn't be paying attention to her surroundings. One step at a time.

Why did she let Gavin and Henry order her around, Dot wondered, not for the first time since her conversation with Samantha. Was it guilt that she had put them in this situation? Or was it just easier to go along with what they wanted? As she poured herself a cup of coffee, she pushed the thought aside.

She needed to tackle the legal documents this morning. Her gut told her the paperwork contained something she needed, if she could find the information. Maybe she would give up reading each page and check out only at the highlighted portions. She settled into the porch swing with her coffee, waved at one of the neighbors going to work, and picked up the manila envelope. The only thing needed was a white picket fence, and she would be living someone's dream. Not hers. She didn't allow herself to dream anymore. She needed to remember that.

Twenty minutes later she was standing in the office of Henry's assistant. "Is Elder Fairwood available?" Dot asked. Henry was a smart man, he should be able to explain the legalese in the document she held. If it meant what she thought it implied, she'd found her answer.

"Sorry, he's out," said the lady. "But he should be back in fifteen minutes or so. Do you want to wait for him in his office?"

"Sure." As she sat in one of the comfortable leather chairs, she realized she'd never seen Henry in his role as CEO. He was always the pack leader or Gavin's father. From the appearance of the office, he ran a successful business as well. It didn't take her long to get bored and she got up to gaze out the large window. The branches of an old tree hung close by, and on one of them, a crow perched. It cocked its head at Dot, and opened its mouth. Although she could not hear the bird through the heavy glass, she imagined it cawed at her before flying away.

She ran her hand over the desk as she walked back to the chair. The manila file on the top of his inbox was labeled with her name. Curious, she picked it up to see what was inside. The first few sheets were list of the guards assigned to her. Dot flipped through them without paying them much attention. A few more sheets seemed to be correspondence between Henry and Counselor Carlson, and they didn't appear to hold any information Dot didn't already know. But the next document brought a surge of anger that almost made Dot shift. Except for the notes scribbled in the margins, it was a match to the one in her manila envelope. And the notes confirmed her suspicions.

She was shaking as she went to the doorway of the office. "Elder Fairwood is on his way now," said his secretary, glancing up.

"Would you call Gavin and ask him to come too?" Dot asked. She marveled at how steady her voice sounded. The wall was back. She was still staring at the title of the document when Henry came into the room. The Last Will and Testament of Merikh Choate.

"So how long have you known?" she asked a snarl in her voice.

TWENTY~TWO

"Known what?" Henry asked, before spotting the file in Dot's hand. He maintained his composure and went to sit in his chair.

"This." She slammed the file down in front of him. "And don't try to tell me you don't know what I'm talking about."

"I started researching it after we left Atlanta." He put his elbows on his desktop and leaned forward. "Took me a month or so to get my hands on the paperwork to confirm my suspicions."

"So you've been using me. Did your plan to get me officially mated to your son and then take over my share of the business? I should have listened to my grandfather in Atlanta, because you're no better than he is."

"Gavin has no part in this, Dot. I never told him. I knew he would try to stop me."

"You never told me what?" Gavin's deep voice rumbled from the doorway.

"That I am heir to fifty-one percent of the Choate pack's business." Dot didn't take her eyes off Henry. "That the shares were signed over to my father when he claimed pack leadership. That he knew about me, and named me as the beneficiary in his will. That my grandfather has been running the pack and the business by holding the shares in guardianship for me. That's the reason I'm so important. Because he expects me to sign over my shares to my mate—whoever he picks for me. And your father has known this for months." She turned to face Gavin. "And that he expects me to believe he told you—his heir and the next pack leader—none of this."

The thunder in Gavin's face should have scared her, but she was past caring. "So what was the plan, to string me along long enough to get your hands on my shares and then ditch me? You had me fooled, Gavin, I really thought you loved me. I should have known I couldn't trust you. I haven't been able to trust anyone most of my life, why did I think things had changed now?"

"He didn't know, Dot." Henry placed his hand on her shoulder.

"Don't call me that," she hissed, jerking away. "I am Maria Lapahie now. Dot is dead, and you killed her." She reached over, picked up her manila envelope, and tried to leave the office, but Gavin blocked her way.

"Don't leave, Dot. We'll straighten this out right here." He tried to put an arm around her, but she ducked under it and got by him.

"And to think I actually loved you," she said, before running out of the office.

Gavin started after her. "Let her go," Henry ordered in his best leader-of-the-pack voice.

"What?"

"Let her go. She'll come to her senses in a few

minutes. You're an alpha wolf, and second in command in this pack. You can't go chasing her."

"I believe that is the worst piece of advice you have ever given me," Gavin said. "And I will ignore it, Elder." And I don't think I will take advice from you ever again, he thought, as he went in search of her.

Dot found Daphne and Samantha at the school. "Get the free wolves back here," Dot said. "We're leaving. If anyone wants to stay, it's up to them, but I'm out of here."

"What happened?" Daphne asked, grabbing her arm. "And where are your things?"

"I'll explain later. I don't want to take anything the Fairwoods have given me. Besides, I can't take them on my bike. I don't know where my saddlebags are, and we don't have time to hunt for them."

Samantha grabbed her other arm. "You need clothes. You can put a suitcase in one of the cars."

Several more of the girls came into the room, attracted by the conversation. "Who's going where?"

"Get packed, and let everyone else know. We leave in half an hour," Daphne ordered. "We'll have a conference once we're on the road. We're getting Maria out of here."

"She's going nowhere. Not until we've talked." Gavin said from the doorway.

"I have nothing to say to you," Dot said.

"But I have plenty to say to you." Gavin took a step towards her, and was stopped by the free wolves placing themselves between the two of them, weapons drawn. Dot glanced around, and almost smiled as she slowly turned to face him.

"Whatever you want to say, say it now. My friends deserve to hear it too. You and your father have betrayed them as much as you have betrayed me."

He needed to touch her, but there wasn't a way to get to her. He felt helpless for the first time since the night in the desert when his sense of immortality had disappeared. The night the IED exploded under his lieutenant's tank.

He had to convince her to stay. "Please don't leave me, Dot. I love you. I will make this right, somehow. I had no idea what my father was up to, I had no part in it. But I will fix it if you give me the chance."

"Pretty words. I'm sure Dot would fall for them. But like I told your father, Dot is dead, and your words mean nothing to me. Now I suggest you leave, before my friends make you go. Unless you want an all-out battle. It would be interesting to see just where everyone's loyalties are when they hear my story."

More of the free wolves pushed into the room, their bodies filled the space between Dot and Gavin, forcing him to back up. He couldn't reach her without hurting some of them and getting hurt himself. "Dot," he called out, trying to put all his love into that one short word before they pushed him out of the room. She stood there and watched, not blinking.

The scarf on Dot's arm was black, not pink, and the one tied to her pants leg was the same. The wolf marking on her cheek was also black, and the circle representing Mother Earth had been replaced by a stylized crow's feather. She nodded with satisfaction at the group gathered around her—almost all the free wolves had joined her and many of the other volunteers as well. Each of them bore the same face markings, four black streaks. She nodded at Daphne and Greg, and they gave the order for everyone to climb into their assigned vehicles.

She waited until the engines were rumbling, and slipped on her helmet. Repainting it would have to wait. With a smooth movement, she slung her leg over the seat, and knocked the kickstand up. A quick pull of the clutch, a kick to put the bike into first, and a turn of the key. With the comforting vibration of the motor between her legs, she slid the face shield into position. A fast release of the clutch, and her front tire found air. She held it there for a few seconds, then leaned forward and lowered it to the ground. Her tires squealed, and the bike sped off, followed by six cars. She closed her mind to the message echoing in her head as she passed the spot where Gavin stood, watching. Once she could no longer see him in her mirrors she allowed the tears to fall.

Twenty-Three

The group held a meeting in a clearing outside pack boundaries. After hearing Dot's story, they had narrowed the options down to three choices: go home and do nothing and try to pick up their lives where they had left off; go home and wait for Dot get a lawyer and called them; or invade the Choate town and have Dot challenge Damyon Choate face to face.

Dot had vetoed the suggestion of one hothead to raid the Fairwood village, they all had friends there and she was not seeking payback at their expense. She was surprised to find out over half the free wolves in the group had ties to the Choate pack, and were thirsty to take part in what they didn't see as revenge, but justice.

She let Daphne and Greg lead the discussion, content to follow whichever choice the group picked. She found her own thoughts too incoherent to be reliable. She kept seeing the expression on Gavin's face as she drove away—was it heartbreak or anger?

She tried to force her attention back to the

discussion. Greg and Daphne made a good team. She wondered if they would be willing to stay and work with her no matter what the group decided. She hoped they would even get together personally—she wondered from the glances they exchanged if they already had mated. She wasn't sure why she was so anxious to see Greg mated with someone. Maybe so he wouldn't keep trying to get with her? She already had a mate. The thought almost made her physically sick. No, she didn't have a mate, she never had, and she doubted she ever would. She should be paying attention—they were taking a vote.

A cheer arose. "So we take over the Choate pack business today," Daphne announced with pride.

"Anyone who doesn't want to take the risk, this is your chance to leave," Greg added. "See me or Daphne in private."

"Speech. Speech. Speech." The chant started somewhere in the back of the group, and Dot could not identify who started it. She held up one hand to stop it.

"I appreciate your trust in me," she said, her voice shaking. "You do realize, I have absolutely no experience in running a business. I don't even know what kind of software the pack sells."

"There are enough of us here that do to help you out," called out a skinny man. Dot knew if she'd passed him on the street, she would not have suspected him as kin. He didn't have the typical muscular build of most men who shifted. She wondered what form he took. Perhaps he was a rabbit, like Penny. "And I have friends who would love to get involved. They are tired of being stuck in the jobs they have."

"All right then." Dot nodded. "Let's figure out how we do this."

She knew this was a bad idea. Even as Dot mounted her motorcycle to start the convoy, the human portion of her instinct screamed at her to stop. But the feral grin on her face was that of the wolf, and the wolf was in charge.

The sentries at the entrance of the Choate territory didn't stand a chance of stopping her as she blew through the swinging gate, followed by the caravan of six vehicles. She pulled to the side a short distance down the road to let the cars pass—they knew where they were going. A place she'd never been.

Just before they reached the parking lot of the Choates' office building, they re-formed into a procession going two-by-two with Dot riding in the middle. Naturally, all the parking spots nearest to the entrance of the building had vehicles in them, but that didn't bother her. She gunned her bike up over the curb and onto the sidewalk skidding to a sideways stop at the bottom of the stairs. The tires left a black tread mark on the concrete. The mark of a very angry wolf, she thought. She pulled off her helmet and handed it to Daphne who was now at her side, ran her fingers through her hair, and stalked up the stairs to the front doors.

Greg and Daphne strode inches behind her as she stormed by the receptionist's desk, with Daphne whispering soft instructions. They veered to the right, climbed two sets of stairs, and took a left. People were standing at the doors of their offices, watching, but no one tried to interfere. On the floors below, more of the free wolves spread out and entered key offices, turning off computers and yanking phone cords from the walls.

In the outer office of her grandfather, a young man tried to stop them. "Elder Choate is not in his office," he started, but with a snarl Dot pushed right by him. Soon this would be hers.

Dark drapes covered the windows and she resisted the urge to tear them down; instead she pulled them aside to let the sunlight in for now. Over the protests of her grandfather's secretary, Greg and Daphne were opening the file cabinets in the outer office. She picked up the file folder in the middle of the desk and scanned the first few sheets of paper—it seemed like a list of companies that had recently stopped using the company's product. A soft growl—that was a sore she would need heal. All the chairs in the office were old, dark leather. That would need to change too, and soon. The place had the feel of a funeral home, and she wouldn't be able to work in it. She had just picked up a second file from the desk when she heard a commotion in the outer office. Then her grandfather stepped into the office. He paused, but when he finally recognized her, a slow smile that wasn't reflected by his eyes spread across his face.

"So which of my men finally brought you here?"

Dot laughed, a short harsh, laugh. "None of them. If you can't tell by the state of your offices, me and about twenty-five of my closest friends brought ourselves here. Seeing as how I am the majority shareholder in this operation, I figured it was about time I take charge. I'm giving you two choices—either get your lawyer in here and sign everything over to me, or we can take this outside to the parking lot, where all your staff and the entire pack can watch you get beat to a pulp by a female. Your choice, grandfather."

"You can't do this."

"According to my father's will, I can. Do you want a copy? I can make you one. I think you also owe me about eight years of company profits. Let me remind you, you acknowledged me in Atlanta—claimed me might be a better word, and I don't think I will have a problem getting a lawyer to take you for every penny you have." The sound of fighting came from the outer office. "And don't think your security people will be able to save you." A knife flew through the air and landed solidly in the door inches from his head. "What's it going to be, grandfather?"

"You cannot be pack leader," he said, moving threateningly towards her. She stood her ground.

"I am a free wolf, and free wolves don't have a pack, they have friends. I have no desire to be pack leader. I think I can get Counselor Carlson to declare pack leadership open and have the issue resolved the old-fashioned way without a problem."

"And you will mate with whoever wins?"

She casually walked over and pulled her knife from the door. Before he could react, she grabbed her grandfather's head and pulled it back, exposing his neck, and had the knife pressed against it. "I am packless and mateless," she hissed. "And will remain that way." She released him and walked back over to the desk, noting with satisfaction she had left only one small cut in his throat. It was enough for now. "You've delayed long enough," she said. "Make your choice. Get your lawyer in here or take this outside."

"You cannot beat me," he growled.

"Daphne, Greg," she called and waited until they entered the room. "The old man has unwisely chosen to meet me in combat. Please escort him outside and get a couple of the others to prepare a suitable spot for the confrontation. We do this now."

"No. We wait until tonight when everyone can be here."

"You think you are still calling the shots? You think the outcome will be any different? Or are you hoping your pets will get here and save you?" Dot shook her head. "Take him outside, free wolves. But be careful, I don't want him harmed before our fight." She saw more of her companions in the outer office. "You all can bear witness to his shame. And get as many members of the pack and the employees of this place as you can to watch."

"Do you know what you're doing, Maria?" Daphne asked as they waited outside for a space to be cleared. Picnic tables were being moved from the side lawn to open up a space. "Rumor has it you've have never fought as a wolf."

"That's one rumor that's true." Dot grinned. "And go ahead and spread it. Think how much worse it will be for my grandfather—beaten by an untested female. Do me a favor. Have a blanket available to cover me when I shift back. I don't want any of these men to get any ideas in their heads about my availability."

They stood at opposite ends of a large circle

bordered by the spectators. To whistles from the gathered group, Dot stripped down to her underwear, slipped her medicine bag over her head and handed it to Daphne. "Get an eyeful now," she called out, not letting the catcalls upset her. "Because none of you will ever see it again." She stared at her grandfather at the other end. "Ready, old man?"

In the blink of an eye, he shifted and was dashing at her. He was bigger in wolf form than she expected, but a quick glance and she decided there was very little muscle left. She met his first strike without changing herself, but moved out of his path at the last moment. The miss made him tumble. While he picked himself up, she switched. She reached inside herself to find the sense of *other*, and released the beast that was her. With her medicine bag in Daphne's care, there was no pain, only a brief moment of disorientation, and then a sudden rush of total focus. *"One,"* she said.

She waited as he snarled his displeasure and bunched his muscles for another attempt. When he leaped, she misjudged his path, didn't move fast enough to get totally out of the way, and one of his paws caught her side, scratching it. *"One for you,"* she sent. *"And that's all you're going to get."* Then she pounced on top of him, with her mouth snapping at his forequarters, drawing blood. *"Two."*

She stepped away, and he sprang at her, but with one quick jump, she met him in mid-stride, and knocked him to the ground. *"Three. You sure you want to keep this up?"* He leaped at her again, and she maneuvered out of his way. He was panting heavily now. He sprang again, and she dove underneath him. There was a hiss from the spectators, thinking he had overpowered her, but she pushed off with her powerful front legs and tossed him on his side on the ground. *"You need to do better than that, grandfather,"* she sent as she paced away. *"That made four. Haven't you learned your lesson yet?"*

With a growl, he rushed her again. This time she met him square on, snarling and biting, but he maneuvered into a spot where he drew blood from her tender nose, and forced her back towards the edge of the ring. Dot didn't listen to the murmurs of the crowd as she focused all her attention on the wolf in front of her. He'd proven tougher than she'd expected. She backed off a few feet to give herself room to maneuver. He paced on the other side of the circle. She moved the opposite direction, keeping her distance. Desperate, he rushed her again, and she easily got out of his way. *"I'm getting tired of this game, Grandfather. I will give you one more chance to stop now."*

For the first time, he responded. *"Never,"* he said. *"This pack is mine until I say so."*

She was almost sad as she shook her head. *"Your choice."*

He sprang again, and she was waiting. When he rushed her, she stepped out of his way, twisted, and grabbed his throat firmly in her jaws, while knocking him over with the weight of her body. He landed on his back, and she tightened her grip on his throat as she placed her front paws on his breast, holding him down. *"New choice. Choose to live and leave, or to stay injured and helpless."* When he didn't answer right away, she clenched her teeth, not quite tearing the skin of his throat.

"It's enough, Maria. You win." Greg's voice filtered through the sound of the blood pouring through her veins.

"Not until he says it," she snarled.

"I will sign over the business to you and I will leave, but this pack will never survive without me."

She knew it was as much of a concession as she would get. *"Heard and witnessed?"* she asked.

The crowd was chanting. "Heard and witnessed! Heard and witnessed!"

She slowly let loose of her hold and backed away. Dot didn't change until she watched her grandfather shift back into human form. Someone wrapped him in a blanket and led him away. She paced over to where Daphne and a few of the other free wolves waited for her. They used another blanket to give her some privacy as she shifted and got dressed.

"You need to get that wound checked out, Maria," Greg said in her ear.

"Later. Can't show any sign of weakness now." She gratefully took a swig of water from the bottle he handed her. "Anyone keeping an eye on my grandfather?"

"Yes," Greg told her. "He went back to his house. We assigned a pair of our people to keep an eye on the place."

"Good thinking. Are you finding a place for us to spend the night?"

"We thought we would occupy the headquarters building. Give us time to check out financial files and the like. The executive floor even has a kitchen and a shower. We don't have a key yet, but Samantha thinks she can pick the lock."

"Check if security has the keys first. Someone needs to remind them they work for us now."

"Consider it done. I suppose you will take over your grandfather's office?"

She snorted. "Not to stay in. Place feels like a coffin and smells like old people. I'll sleep with everyone else, on the floor if that's what it comes down to."

They rode the elevator to the third floor this time, and the same man met them at the outer office. "Miss? I served as Elder Choate's secretary, and I hope you'll let me stay." His attitude had done a complete turnaround. "I really need this job."

Dot studied him, and didn't trust him immediately due to something in his eyes—or the lack of something. They were hard to see through his oversized glasses. Short and heavy set, his skin was pale, like he never spent any time in the sun. "You're not kin, are you?"

"No miss. That's why Elder Choate hired me. Said he knew I wouldn't be able to listen through the walls. I thought he was joking at first."

"What's your name?"

"Jim." He swallowed nervously and she caught herself gazing at the movement of his protruding adam's apple. "Jim Bonds." He blushed as Dot and Greg stared. "My father thought it was funny to name me that."

Dot controlled her urge to laugh. "Tell you what, Jim, you help me out for a few weeks and then I'll make a decision about your future. I assume you know where all the paperwork I need is kept, who runs what, who is overpaid and who is underpaid, and all the dirt on everyone."

"Yes, miss, I can help you with that."

"Good. And for now, you can call me Ms. Lapahie. First thing, Jim, does this company have its own lawyer on retainer?"

He had the phone in his hand, but it had no dial tone. He gulped again. "I'll go get him."

"No need. I'm here." A quick glance and Dot guessed he wasn't kin either, but at least he appeared as if he could hold his own in court. She bet he had been a surfer in his younger days, with his light blond hair and lean body. She wondered how hard he worked to maintain the look. "They told me you were in the building, so I got some paperwork together. If we can step into your office?"

She led the way, with Greg and Daphne not far behind. "I'm Alan Kirk," he said extending his hand. "No, I'm not a shifter. And before you ask, I didn't exactly work for your grandfather—I work for the company."

Dot shook his hand. "Legally I am Maria Winters, so I hope that's how the paperwork is made out. Otherwise you have to start over, Mr. Kirk." She took the seat behind the desk. It felt strange. She would have to either move offices or redecorate right away.

"I'll change it." He sighed. "But may I ask what your plans are for this company first? My contract is up shortly, and I need to know if I should start checking around for a different job."

"If you don't want to work hard, I'll see about getting you released from your contract early. But if you want to be part of a growing organization, stick around. My plan is to make myself a place to call home, something my grandfather denied me all these years, and to make sure that the Fairwoods can't take this company over." Her eyes narrowed as she leaned back in the chair. "It's revenge, pure and simple."

Twenty~Four

He'd avoided his father for several weeks, but now Gavin paced in the conference room, waiting. He didn't anticipate this being easy, and he needed to do it in neutral territory. He glanced on the clock on the wall one more time—his father was late. All part of the game. After many years of watching, he knew how his father played it. In the next few minutes, he needed to play it better. Under other circumstance, his father would be proud of him for taking this step.

He went to the window and stared outside, his hands clasped behind his back. From here, he could see the porch of the house where he and Dot sat and rocked so many wonderful evenings. The house he had moved out of after she left. He shook his head and forced himself to relax. For now, he wouldn't think about her. He didn't move when he heard his father's footsteps enter the room. The game had begun.

"What's going on, Gavin? Why did you want to meet here, instead of my office?"

He took his time turning. "Elder Fairwood," he said, nodding his head once. "It is time, Elder."

His father understood immediately. "What makes

you think you are ready? Just because she's gone doesn't give you cause to challenge me. You would be better picking a mate from the pack. This just shows you aren't ready."

"I acknowledge it hurt me deeply when she left, but that is not why I challenge you now." Gavin held his voice steady. He noted his father didn't use her name, so he didn't either. "Her leaving not only hurt me, but the pack as well. Your overwhelming obsession to damage the Choate pack and Damyon Choate has lost us many allies, not solely among the free wolves, but from other packs as well. I cannot second-guess your decision to withhold the knowledge of Elder Lapahie's inheritance from her and from me; I can only hope to remedy the damage you have done. It is time for you to retire. You can either pass leadership of the pack and the business to me now, or I will call challenge in front of the pack and we can fight for it. The decision is yours." He had practiced the speech many times in his head, and thought it came out well.

Henry laughed and said, "This is foolishness on your part." Still, Gavin detected a note of desperation in the sound. "You really think you can pull this off?"

"For the good of the pack, I have to." Gavin examined his father closely, and realized how old he was. "I've not been in a hurry to take over your position, but perhaps I've waited too long." He stared at his father, and hoped the coldness of his heart would chill his father's spirit. Henry blinked first.

"The Elders will never back you up. The pack will never accept you."

"Empty threats. As always, the Elders will do what is best for the pack as a whole, even if they are your friends. That is their responsibility. A growing faction of the pack has urged me to do this for several years. No, your time is past. It's my time now."

"And what happens if I decide to fight?"

"Do you think you can beat me in a one-on-one battle? It's not going to happen. I'm too strong, and have fought many battles recently. You haven't fought one for years." Gavin tensed so the muscles in his arms and chest rippled in a subtle threat. "You still hold a good reputation with most packs. If you fight, you damage the pack and I'll be forced to hurt you more than I already have. Retire now, keep your reputation, and let me keep my love for you."

Henry slumped into the nearest chair and glanced up at his son. "You don't give me much of a choice, do you?"

Dot would say there is always a choice, Gavin thought sourly, but I won't tell you that.

Henry sat silently for a long time and Gavin stood, not moving, waiting. Finally, with a deep breath, the older man said, "You know, maybe it is time I retire. I've never had the time to go out to see the redwoods. Do you think two weeks is enough time to make the transition?"

I've won, thought Gavin, but the victory tasted bitter. If he had done this a few weeks earlier, she might be there to share the moment with him.

Dot was tired, so tired her bones seemed to hurt. Even back in her waitressing days, she had never been this tired after work, and all she had done today was sit behind a desk and spend hours on the phone. At least the small amount of redecorating she had finished helped—the heavy drapes had been replaced with pale gold ones of lighter material, and the dark brown walls repainted a lighter tone of gold that reminded her of the color of the evening sun.

She was calling every customer of the company to find out what worked right and what needed fixed. At first, she didn't understand much of what they told her, but she was learning fast. She didn't understand programming, but she was slowly finding a good staff to take care of that. Customer relations, on the other hand, had a lot in common with the skills learned as a waitress.

Some customers were beyond saving, others on the edge, some so pleased with the new CEO reaching out to them personally that they had renewed their accounts immediately. The ones on the edge would be tackled by the second part of Dot's scheme; a personal visit from her, accompanied by one of the company's veteran programmers to see if they could fix what needed to be fixed and save the account. There would be no salespeople involved as the last thing the company needed was for someone to make promises that couldn't be kept. She had scheduled the first trip for the Monday after the challenge which was in two days.

Dot really didn't want to be around for it, but the elders had requested her attendance as the sole direct relative of the Choate family line. There were lots of cousins and almost nieces and nephews—she enjoying meeting her relatives and she crossed her fingers that one of the men might win pack leadership—but she was trying to establish some kind of relationship with the pack elders as well.

She knew they hoped she would choose to mate with the winner, and hadn't been able to convince any of them she had no interest in any such thing. For the time being, her single interest was the business. She found small consolation in the early indications that the Fairwood business had backed off its takeover efforts. Absentmindedly, she reached for a knife, but she hadn't worn her belt today. Today she wore a loose fitting dress with a floral pattern. Quite a change from her old camo's.

A reminder shot up on the computer monitor, time to make an unscheduled visit to one of the offices. Dot did this once a day, every day, at random times to get a better feel for the employees of the company. Her employees, Daphne kept reminding her. Who had Jim scheduled for her to meet today? She sighed. Another of the managers. She wasn't in the mood for more brown-nosing. Today might be a good day to wander down to the basement and meet with the housekeeping staff. The manager could wait. She wondered if any of them were pack members—so many of the employees were not kin—just another thing her grandfather messed up and she needed to fix.

Thanks to Alan, there were a few things her grandfather hadn't been able to mess up. Alan froze the company bank account and her grandfather's personal account within minutes of her winning control of the company and within days he switched them to her name.

She made sure her grandfather had access to enough money to leave pack territory. Dot didn't know where he'd went and didn't care, but she arranged to send him a monthly stipend to live on once he notified the other Elders where he settled. The house he lived in was part of the company assets, and Dot and several others of the free wolves lived there now. She'd claimed the smallest bedroom so that Daphne and Greg could share the master bedroom. They were a couple now, and the thought made her smile. Two of the free wolves who sometimes acted as bodyguards for her shared the third bedroom. She didn't need them very often anymore, and certainly didn't need them here at work.

She took a whiff of the flowers by the office door before she left. Flowers arrived for her on a regular basis from other local business people congratulating her on her new position—hoping for favors later on, she assumed—but Counselor Carlson sent this particular arrangement.

Gavin sent a bouquet on a weekly basis as well, but they ended up going home with one of the secretaries. His phone calls went directly to voice mail and were then deleted without being played. It still hurt to think of him, but sometimes she couldn't help it. She had never stopped thinking about him those long months in Orlando, so what made her think a mere two months would be enough time to get over him?

Lost in her thoughts, and busy reviewing the files on the housekeepers she'd retrieved from her file cabinet, Dot wasn't paying attention as she walked into the outer office. She stopped to tell Jim where she was going, and was puzzled by the smirk on his face and the matching expressions on two other men sitting in the office. She had no time to react when they sprang out of their chairs and grabbed her, shoved a cloth into her mouth, and wrapped a silver-coated rope around her chest. Another rope tied her wrists together. One man reached out when he finished tying the knots and grabbed one of her breasts "Damyon Choate promised you to us for years, and now you are ours," he grunted. She wanted to scream as the rope burned into her arms and wrists, but couldn't.

The other reached over and fondled her other breast. "Your grandfather was always after us to work as a team, and now we are. He would be proud of us."

Dot was helpless as a black cloth was wrapped around her head, covering her eyes, but she felt the prick of a needle and the burn of a liquid pushed into her arm, and she heard the harsh laughter of all three men as she collapsed on the floor.

Twenty~Five

"The one named Arnold tossed her over his shoulder and carried her out," Daphne sobbed. "At least that's what the witnesses told us."

"Where were her bodyguards?" It took every ounce of self-control Gavin had to keep from shifting into wolf form and run, howling, all the way to the Choate holdings.

"She doesn't use guards anymore," Greg explained over the speaker phone. "She said there was no need with her grandfather gone."

"Didn't anyone try to stop them?"

"Yes." Gavin heard Greg's quick intake of air, and Daphne's renewed sobs in the background. "The company lawyer ended up with several broken ribs, one man got shot in the arm, and they pushed an old woman who is one of the secretaries against the wall. She is bruised, but will be all right." The notepad on his desk was already covered with a list of people and supplies Gavin wanted to take. "The sentries didn't think anything was wrong with letting them in because they are pack members, and they didn't want to stop them when they left

240

because they were worried about Maria getting hurt."

"They left pack territory?"

"All we know is they headed east. They could be anywhere."

"They'll be back tomorrow." Daphne sniffed. "Tomorrow night is the scheduled challenge for pack leadership. If there's anything these two guys want more than they want her, it is the title of pack leader."

"Is it an open challenge?"

"Only to pack members. Maria had requested they open it to mated males as well, as she has no intention of mating with the winner, and the Elders agreed," Greg told him. "Problem is, these two guys are the strongest males left. A lot of others left the pack because they didn't agree with Elder Choate's policies. We are trying to get in touch with them, but only one or two have said they will be able to make it back."

"They can't have gone too far then." Where was that file his father had finally shared with him? The one with all the contacts he had built up over the years. Gavin needed a few favors, and he needed them now. "Can you get me in?"

"You can't challenge. You're not a pack member."

He growled. "No, but if they bring her along, I can get to her. I can take both of those guys by myself if they are unarmed, and they will need to be unarmed for the challenge. Will the rest of the pack back them up?"

He heard Greg and Daphne conferring in low voices. "Some might, but we don't know how many," Greg said finally. "You know how it is. We're brought up to believe the pack comes first. Even though Maria has been trying to make things better here, it's a long process and we can't guess how many people will take her side in a fight. It's too risky. The free wolves will back you, of course, but that still leaves us outnumbered."

"It won't be just me. Dot has lots of friends here."

"They will kill her, Gavin. Once one of them is pack leader, they won't need her anymore. Her shares will pass to them. At least that's what the lawyer thinks."

"I need whatever information you can get me on these guys. Full names, dates of birth, social security numbers—if they drew a paycheck from the company, all that should be in their files. Find out if they had access to a company credit card. And if you can get it to me two hours ago, it would be good. I've got work to do now. Call me back as soon as you can." Gavin stared blankly at his notepad after he hung up. I've failed you Dot, he thought. I promised to protect you and I failed you. He buried his face in his hands, and for the first time in his adult life, he wept.

Her wrists and ankles burned, but Dot stifled the scream rising in her throat and stayed motionless. If they didn't realize she had woken, they wouldn't give her more of the goddamn drug they used to knock her out. She needed to stay awake to make plans for her escape. She wondered how shifting would affect the ropes around her wrists. She always hurt when she changed forms, how much worse would this time be?

She tried to hear what the men were talking about but their voices were too faint to understand. Tentatively, she reached out with her *other* sense, but it did her no good. Perhaps the silver blocked the effort, or it might be the drug inhibiting her mental abilities. She lay quietly, and tried to ease the pressure on her wrists with the barest of movement, hoping it would go unnoticed.

A loud burst of laughter from outside stilled her. "Leave my beer alone," one of the men said, opening the door of the cabin. "This will only take a second." She quieted her breathing, and concentrated on seeming to be asleep when footsteps approached. Then, the all too familiar poke in her arm and the cold burn of the liquid shot into her muscles. In the moment before the blackness closed in again—it seemed to take longer this time—she wondered if she should give up and let them have her. She had nothing left to fight for anyway.

Every road leading to the eastern entrance of the Choate territory was staked out. Gavin had wanted to cover the northern and southern routes as well, but he didn't have the manpower. Samantha had gotten a description of the car they left in, so as long as they didn't have a second vehicle, chances were good they would be spotted.

As a "favor" to the Choate pack, the free wolves volunteered to take guard duty at the remaining entry points so at least Gavin would find out when they entered the pack's area and hopefully, if Dot was with them or not. Greg assured him they were covered if they smuggled her in the trunk because one of the free wolves knew how to break into almost any car. It would take her only a minute or so to pop the locks.

Gavin checked his cell phone one more time to make sure he hadn't missed any calls. So far, none of his contacts had been able to detect the use of credit cards by any of the three men. But he knew sometimes small places processed their cards at close of business, so it might take an extra day for them to show up. He slammed the phone closed—they didn't have an extra day. As an added precaution, a trace had also been put on Damyon Choate's cards. They were being used, but in Arizona—too far away to be of any concern.

He checked over the lists covering his desk trying to see if they had missed anything. The only unknown was if they brought Dot to the challenge and kept her under guard during the fights. Not knowing how the pack would react if he and the others attempted to free her worried him. He wanted to avoid an all-out battle that could destroy both packs as well as the free wolves.

"The limo is on its way to the airport," said Dmitri, entering the office. "And all the teams are on their way out to their positions. It will be a long day for them, but I wanted to get the roads covered early."

"Good call. We can't be sure when those goons will make their appearance." Gavin shoved the papers he had been studying across the desk. The desk was one of the few pieces of furniture he had retained when he had redone his father's office to make it his own. He vaguely remembered his grandfather using it, and saw no reason to break tradition. "Take another look at the plans and make sure I haven't missed anything."

"I've been over them, Elder Fenner has been over them, and they are as good as we can get them." Dmitri put his hand on Gavin's shoulder. "If she's anywhere within 100 miles of Choate territory, we'll find her. Don't forget, we have the state police in two states watching out for her too. You need to relax, you're so tense it will be easier for you to make a mistake."

Gavin wished he had one of her knives to throw at the dartboard he requested be installed in hopes he could convince her to return someday. "I can't relax—not until I am holding her in my arms again."

Gavin's cell phone was in his lap and the ringer turned up as loud as it could go. Over his objections, Dmitri drove the Jeep. They had switched spots a few miles back when Dmitri noticed how many times he was taking his eyes off the road to check the display of his phone. "Can't you go any faster?" he asked.

"I'm already breaking the speed limit, and we're ahead of schedule. Until we get more information, we don't know our final destination anyway. So let me drive. You just keep watching the phone. All right?"

Gavin banged his fist on the dashboard. "No, it's not all right," he muttered, but Dmitri ignored him and kept talking.

"These guys are going to show up eventually, right? Until then, you need to keep your cool. Dude, I've never seen you keyed up like this, not even when we were on patrol in the desert, and our chances of a successful mission are better tonight then they were back then."

"I've got more at stake on this one." He was staring out the windshield, and jumped when the phone rang. He punched the button hard before holding it to his ear. "It's Gavin. What do you have for me?"

"The north entrance? Shit...No sign of her?

Damn...All three of them? They brought along the non-kin? I wonder what he's hoping to get out of this...Following them? Good. Tell the scout to keep his distance and not make any moves...Her distance?" Gavin almost smiled. "I love the free wolves. Remind me to tell them so. Keep me posted."

He turned to Dmitri. "We need to change our destination."

"Already done. The north entrance it is."

The new destination would add a half hour to the trip, and Gavin was second guessing himself. Maybe he should have gone straight to the Choate village. He had told his people to go ahead and move in to their second posts within pack territory, but perhaps he should have them sweeping the area north of it instead. It didn't make sense—why were all three men in the car if Dot wasn't with them? Surely one of them needed to stay behind to guard her, unless she was already dead. No, she couldn't be. They wanted her alive. She always said they needed her alive. Hopefully, nothing had changed.

His phone went off again. "It's Gavin...She was in the trunk?...Old cabin where?...How many?...Tell her to keep an eye on things. We'll be there as soon as possible."

He slapped the phone closed. "They've got her in an old cabin a few miles from the entrance. Hasn't been used for years except for young men wanting a place to get together away from their parents. They were met there by several other males. The scout says she appeared unconscious when they carried her in—all tied up and gagged. They left the non-kin behind with her, as well as the other men. Just two of them left to go to the challenge."

"Can the scout get us there?"

"She can and she will. They made their mistake and now we have the advantage."

Another free wolf was waiting for them as they entered Choate pack territory and flagged down the Jeep. "I'm Lori," she said as she jumped in the back. "And I'll be your guide for the day." She reached in her pocket and pulled out a small container. Dmitri watched in the rearview mirror as she marked four pink streaks across one cheek. She grinned and tapped Gavin on the shoulder, handing him the jar when he turned around. "Care to join me?"

He didn't hesitate, but with one finger, quickly made similar markings on his cheek.

"Save enough for me," Dmitri said. "Once we get stopped, I'll want to use that. Whose idea was this?"

"Greg's. All the free wolves are carrying this stuff tonight. The plan is to show up at the challenge unmarked, and put it on during the competition. We'll also share it with pack members that we know will support Maria."

"How many free wolves are expected to show up?"

She smiled. "Twenty or so. We're getting all kinds of additional bodies here. And if they think that any of us are going to stay on sentry duty, they're wrong. Not like the Fairwoods are going to mount a raid tonight anyway." She laughed, and it was not an easy laugh, but a threatening one. Gavin was glad they were on the same side.

A few minutes later she patted Dmitri on the

shoulder. "Pull over here," she said. A wolf came out of the woods and stared at her. She nodded. "We walk the rest of the way." With an easy movement, she sprang out of the Jeep. "There are four pack members and the traitor at the cabin. We should be able to handle them." She smiled broadly, and Gavin could see her canines. "They ought to have one or two more men to make things even."

Dmitri and he exchanged glances before they followed her into the woods, Dmitri drawing pink streaks on his cheek.

They lay on their stomachs, peering through the underbrush at the cabin. "So what's the plan," asked Lori. "Would you like me to stroll up to the front door, knock and pretend I'm lost in the woods?" She fluttered her eyelashes at them and twisted a lock of her long blond hair. "I'm Goldilocks, and I'm hungry. Can I have some of your porridge?"

Gavin grinned in spite of himself. She would be quite a challenge for some lucky man. "I'd like to see that," he said. "But we are better off kicking in the door and keeping the element of surprise. As old as the cabin is, I can't imagine the door is going to be very strong."

She sighed. "One of these days I'll get to try it. But we'll do it your way this time."

"Remember, the goal here is to disable these guys, not kill them or permanently maim them." The reminder was as much to himself as it was to his companions. "We only want to get her out and to safety."

"Can we use silver rope on them like they did on Maria?" Lori snarled.

"No. I brought along zip ties if we need them."

"Time to stop talking and start moving," Dmitri said. "The longer we're out here the longer she's in there."

Silently, they crawled through the brush until they were within a few yards of the cabin. A nod from Gavin and they rose as one, and rushed the door. Gavin threw the full weight of his body against the door and almost stumbled when it collapsed under the blow. He barely had time to glance around the single room before one of the occupants jumped him.

A raised arm deflected the first blow, but a second man moved in on him at the same time. Gavin needed to eliminate one as quickly as possible. A hard kick to the knee staggered the first, but the other got an arm around Gavin's neck. Off balance, Gavin took a sideways step backwards and fell to the floor, dragging his attacker with him. He maneuvered so he was on top, and landed a solid punch to his opponent's midsection. But now the first rushed him, and was on top of him before he could get up. Gavin was unable to avoid a blow to his chin, but returned the favor by landing several hits on the man's chest. Both men scrambled to stand, and Gavin was able to deliver a series of blows to the man's head, knocking him back to the floor. The second man was still trying to struggle to his feet, and Gavin, with a carefully aimed kick, swept his legs out from under him. Another kick ensured he would stay down.

Dmitri and Lori seemed to be handling their solo opponents with ease, so Gavin glanced around the cabin. An overweight and under-muscled man hovered near a small bed, in the process of punching buttons on his cell phone. "Hell, no," Gavin growled, and in four long strides reached the man, stripped the phone from his hand, and smashed it on the floor. It took only one blow to the chin to knock down the non-kin.

A blanket covered the figure on the bed, but Gavin could see the arms stretched above the head and the wrists tied to the bed frame with silver rope. He cut the ropes and knelt beside the bed, pulling the cover down away from the head. Dot drew a ragged breath, and her eyes fluttered, but she did not open them.

A purple bruise covered one side of her face, and Gavin pulled the cover down the rest of the way, fearful of what he would find. She was clad only in her bra and panties, and there were other bruises on her torso. He ran his hands over her body, but didn't feel any broken bones. He wrapped the blanket back around her, laid a very tender kiss on her lips, blinked to clear away a suspicious moisture forming in his eyes, and gathered her into his arms.

Dmitri and Lori were busy binding the last of the enemy. "Sure you don't want to kill 'em?" Lori asked, seeing the expression on his face.

"Don't tempt me," Gavin said, but he did plant one swift kick on the face of the nearest one. He hoped the bruise would be as bad as the one Dot wore. "We need to get her home and to Dr. Tracy."

He ran as quickly through the woods as he could while trying not to jostle Dot too much, with Dmitri and Lori bringing up the rear. As he ran, he plotted a new course of action. When they reached the jeep, the other scout, back in human form and dressed, waited for them. Gavin laid Dot tenderly in the back, and tucked a blanket they had brought under her head as a pillow, and then kissed her forehead. "Take her back," he said to Dmitri. "I have business to take care of here." He turned to Lori. "Go with him. She may need a woman with her if she wakes up."

She clenched her fists. "You think she's been raped?"

TWENTY~SIX

Gavin couldn't voice the words but Lori read the deep concern in his face. "I'm going with you. Tilly here can go with her back to your place. She's better at hand-holding than I am. Besides," and she grinned that bloodthirsty grin again, "I feel like ripping out a few throats."

"All right." His hands gripping the Jeep's door, Gavin stared deeply into Dmitri's eyes. "Don't let anything happen to her. I'm counting on you."

"Get back safely or I'll never forgive myself for leaving you."

Gavin nodded, and watched until the taillights of the Jeep disappeared in the distance. "What's the quickest way to the village?" he asked Lori. "Do we run?"

"Another time, maybe." She rattled the set of keys she held. "But tonight we take Tilly's car."

They parked away from the village center. No one was on the road and Gavin knew everyone had gathered to see who would become their new leader. They heard a roar in the distance. "We missed it," he said, and swore.

She paused and listened. "No, that must have been a preliminary bout. We have time." Still, they ran the rest of the way. Everyone was so busy watching the ongoing battle no one noticed them slipping into the back of the audience. Lori nudged him in the ribs and pointed out two men standing apart from the group. "That's Lucious and Arnold. Arnold's the one with the scars on his cheek. Maria gave them to him."

Gavin stood hunched over so he was not as visible. "Which one wants the leadership job?" he whispered.

"They both do. I assume they worked out a deal so they don't have to fight each other."

He studied the crowd. There were a few faces already bearing pink stripes scattered around, and the jar was being passed from hand to hand. He edged slowly to the far side of the enclosure, and saw more pink stripes and more jars. He felt a flash of hope for the first time since hearing about Dot's abduction.

A gray haired man Gavin assumed was one of the elders stepped into the opening. "Are there any other challengers?" he called out, his voice surprisingly strong.

The two men that Lori had pointed out conferred, smiling. The elder waited, and raised his hand. "In that case..." he started.

"I challenge," Arnold called and pushed his way through the crowd. "Is anyone here who denies my claim to leadership? I have beaten most of you in the past."

The murmurs from the crowd grew louder, but no one volunteered. Finally, a man with pink stripes on his cheek stepped forward. "I challenge," he said. "You have never beaten me."

"You are no pack member," Arnold said scornfully.

"You renounced your membership two years ago. You are ineligible."

The elders huddled together. "Unfortunately, Arnold is correct," they decided. "Are there no other challengers?"

"I will challenge." A young man, not yet at full growth, pushed into the center. His face, too, wore pink markings. Gavin admired his courage, but doubted he had a chance.

Arnold laughed. "Go home to your mother, cub."

The young man's face reddened, but he held his ground. "Do you accept my challenge?"

"Accept it? I will even give you the first blow."

Both men stripped, and shifted. The young man's wolf form was smaller and lighter than Arnold's, and Gavin knew from experience the disadvantage that gave him. He paced warily around the bigger wolf, trying to find a weakness. Arnold-wolf yawned. The young man sprang, and with one swipe, Arnold knocked him over and grabbed his throat in his jaws. *"So I lied,"* he broadcast. With one paw he cruelly scored the younger man's chest. *"Anyone else care to play?"*

No other man presented himself, but Gavin saw more pink markings in the crowd. Almost every woman bore them. "Then I am pack leader!" Arnold roared after changing back to man form. "Acknowledge me."

There were scattered cheers and applause, but most of the audience remained silent. Gavin decided his turn had come, and elbowed his way to the cleared space. "You stand accused of assault, kidnapping and torture," he said so quietly the people at the back had to strain to hear him. "Therefore, you cannot hold leadership. I request the Council declare this challenge invalid. As there seem to be no worthy contenders, I also request the Council dissolve the pack."

"You have no say in this," Arnold snarled. "Go back to your own pack."

There was a rustle, and the crowd parted. Counselor Carlson, surrounded by four large men, stood calmly at the edge of the ring. "By Council rules, the leader of any pack has the right to petition for the dissolution of another pack if circumstances warrant. I have seen evidence and taken testimony from others regarding the charges Elder Fairwood has brought against you. Unless you can convince me otherwise, I am inclined to agree to his petition, pending full Council agreement." Gavin smiled. At least one favor he had requested paid off. "Besides, based on what I see in front of me, you do not have enough females to sustain a mating pack. Where is Elder Lapahie, anyway?"

"The bitch is mine, and you will never have her," sneered Arnold.

"Elder Lapahie is on her way to the doctor, if she hasn't already arrived," Gavin said. "Her guards are tied up in the cabin where they kept her captive." He pulled a piece of rope out of his pocket, and held it up so it glittered in the street lights. "Here's a piece of rope they used to bind her. As you can see, it is woven with silver." He tossed the rope at Arnold's feet. The crowd surrounding him murmured their protest. They knew what a rope like that would do to a shifter.

"Also by Council rules, I can challenge my accuser, isn't that correct, Counselor?" Arnold asked.

"Yes, those are the rules."

"Then I challenge you, Fairwood."

"That's why I'm here," Gavin said as he stripped off his clothes and shifted.

He had an advantage in size, Gavin decided, as he sized up his competition. Another slight advantage because he had seen Arnold move in wolf form earlier. If he could force Arnold to come to him, he could win this challenge. He heard a commotion behind him, but he didn't turn around. *"We've secured the other one,"* Lori said in his head. *"These two don't play fair. He had a dart gun. The fight is all yours now, Fairwood. Good hunting."*

He barely nodded in acknowledgment as he circled the other wolf. Arnold wasn't nervous yet, and he should be. *"The bitch has nice boobs, I enjoyed playing with them,"* Arnold broadcast. The crowd fell silent.

The blood in his veins turned to lava, then to ice. He had to stay calm. *"If your performance in bed matches your ability in battle, I'm surprised you ever get hard,"* he sent back. When the audience tittered with nervous laughter, Arnold broke, snarled, and rushed Gavin. Gavin anticipated the move, and with open jaws, met him head on, snapping at his face. Neither did any real damage to the other, but Gavin quickly twisted, got a hold on one of Arnold's ears and bit it. Arnold snarled and tore free. They both backed off and circled again.

"Is the bitch worth dying for?" Arnold growled.

"I have no plans to die tonight," Gavin said. *"You might ask yourself the same question."* He made a move to the left, then switched and rushed from the right. Arnold tried to side step, but Gavin got a

mouthful of flesh from his loin, breaking the skin. Gavin tried to push the moment, but he couldn't reach Arnold's underbelly. He moved away, and circled again.

Arnold paced opposite him, limping slightly. *"Do you want to hear what I'm going to do to the bitch when you are dead?"*

"Is that all you can do? Talk? Why don't you shut up and fight? Talking hasn't done you much good so far."

Arnold growled and attacked. Again, they sparred with their mouths and except for a few minor scratches, neither scored the other. Both backed away and circled, Arnold limping. Gavin was tempted to try for the same spot, but decided Arnold might anticipate the tactic, so he waited. When Arnold came at him again, he didn't move until the last moment, when he twisted his body and grabbed at the side of Arnold's neck. He got a mouthful of fur for his effort, but nothing more. He swiveled, placing him side by side with the other wolf, and he leaned against Arnold with his full body weight. Arnold staggered, and as he tried to regain his balance Gavin bit his front left leg, and tore out a small hunk of flesh.

"You'll pay for that!"

In most fights, Gavin offered his opponents the opportunity to give up when he knew he could defeat them. Not this time. No surrender would be given. Total defeat was the only outcome. He made no reply, but pushed in and attacked Arnold's right rear hock. He scratched it, but not deep enough for a disabling injury.

Arnold moved slowly, his eyes wild as he waited for an opening. He sprang, but the damage to his leg threw off his balance. Gavin met him full-on, and knocked him to the ground, sprang, and raked a wound in his opponent's withers.

As he positioned himself for another strike, a piece of his mind finally processed the chant from the crowd. "Lapahie! Lapahie! Lapahie!" Time to end this fight.

Gavin circled, waiting for his chance. If Arnold was smart, he would give up. Gavin doubted he was that smart. "It is enough," Counselor Carlson said.

"My apologies, Counselor, but not yet," he sent. He moved quickly, feinted for the withers again, and when Arnold tried to avoid the rush, grabbed for the throat instead. Arnold fell, and Gavin stayed on top of him, not loosening his hold on the neck of his opponent. He placed one paw on the underbelly, and waited. Arnold whimpered and lay still. *"Admit defeat, fool."*

"It's done. You win. The challenge has been fought. The Choate pack is no more." Counselor Carlson put a hand on Gavin's head. "Let him go. We'll take charge."

The crowd chanted. "Heard and witnessed! Heard and witnessed!"

Gavin shook his mouth, almost tearing through the soft tissues of his opponent's throat. *"This is for the young man you marked earlier,"* he said, and drew his paw down Arnold's belly, leaving a deep scratch. *"And this is for me. You already wear Dot's scar."* Another quick swipe left four marks on the previously unmarked cheek. He backed away, and shifted back to man form. Someone handed him a blanket, and he wrapped it around his waist. The crowd was chanting again. "Lapahie! Lapahie! Lapahie!" He walked away, sat down with his back against the trunk of an old tree, and lowered his head. He needed to rest a minute and then get back to her. He would close his eyes for just a second to gather his strength.

The rush of cold water over his head jerked him back to attention. Lori handed him a bottle of water, and squatted down beside him. "Let me take a look at your face," she demanded, and he obediently turned it towards her. She wiped it with a rubbing alcohol pad, but he didn't flinch. "A few minor scratches," she said. "Nothing that will leave a scar. You have any other wounds?"

He swallowed half of the water before dumping the rest over his head. "No. I didn't want to give Dot a reason to yell at me."

She snorted. "We're in touch with your people and arranging transportation to get you home. Counselor Carlson has agreed to stay for a few days until we can get things sorted out here. Lucky how he showed up, isn't it?" She tossed him his clothes. "Get dressed, and someone will come and get you in a few minutes."

Gavin sat by her bedside, watching her chest rise and fall. Dr. Tracy assured him Dot was only sleeping and would wake up when the drugs they'd injected her with wore off, but he wouldn't leave, so she and Crystal had gone to get some rest. He wanted to wrap his arms around Dot and hold her close, but the small, hospital-type bed couldn't hold both of them. So he sat beside her and held her hand and waited.

Without additional equipment, Dr. Tracy had been unable to figure out exactly what they'd given her.

"But I drew blood for the state police," she told him. "They'll be able to figure it out." Her preliminary exam hadn't shown any signs of rape to Gavin's great relief. They'd have to wait for Dot to wake up to find out how she got all the bruises.

She twitched and moaned, and he reached out to gently stroke her cheek until she settled back down. "You're home now, Dot," he said. "You're home and you're safe." She sighed, and grimaced as she tried to roll on her side. He moved his hand to her shoulder and laid it there until she gave up trying. Eventually, he propped his arms on her bed, put his head down on them, and fell asleep.

He dreamt of a warm, soft hand running over his scalp, and tried not to wince when it found one of the scratches he'd acquired in last night's combat. In his dream he smiled as a soft voice murmured his name. "Gavin."

"I love you, Dot," he said, still dreaming. But the sudden withdrawal of the hand and quiet sob woke him and when he raised his head he was staring into a pair of brown eyes with yellow-gold streaks.

"Do you?" she asked.

TWENTY~SEVEN

He lost her question in the shift between sleep and wakefulness. "You're awake!" Gavin said, and wondered about the frown that hovered on Dot's face for a moment to be replaced by a vague smile. Then she sat upright, panicked. "Where are we?"

"Dr. Tracy's clinic. You're safe, Dot." She tried to swing her legs around to slip of the bed, and he grabbed her. "You're not getting out of bed until Dr. Tracy says so." He pulled his phone out of his pocket. "She told me to call her when you woke up."

"No need, I'm here." The doctor entered the room, yawning and stretching, and held Dot's wrist to check her pulse. "Elder Fairwood, if you would please leave, I need to examine my patient. Besides, you need to go home and take a shower and change clothes."

"I'll be back later." He leaned over and kissed Dot's forehead. "Don't go anywhere."

Dot waited until he had left. "Elder Fairwood?" she asked.

"No one told you? He's pack leader now." Dr. Tracy listened to her heart. "Deep breaths." Dot obediently drew several and remained silent while the doctor checked her blood pressure. "He took over shortly after you left. So far, so good," she continued as she removed the blood pressure cuff. "Where do you hurt?"

Dot moved carefully. "I'm sore all over, but I don't really hurt," she decided.

"You have a lot of bruises. Do you remember how you got them?"

"I remember fighting. I think they didn't give me enough of whatever drug they shot into me the first time. I recovered faster than they expected. When they tried to move me into the cabin, I ran away." She laughed bitterly. "I didn't make it very far."

"What was it, three against one? You can't blame yourself."

"I don't remember how I got here."

"The pack collaborated with the free wolves to rescue you. Elder Fairwood led the effort. But that's his story. You'll have to ask him about it."

"What day is it?"

"Saturday."

Dot tried again to get off the bed but Dr. Tracy stopped her with a gentle hand on Dot's shoulder. "I have to go. I need to be in Chicago on Monday."

"You're in no shape to travel. Besides, the state police want to interview you. I told them I'd contact them when you regained consciousness. Promise to behave yourself and I'll find you some clothes so you can shower and get dressed."

"I suppose if I try to leave someone will try to stop me. Do I have to deal with bodyguards following me again?"

"No, no bodyguards. At least, I haven't been informed of any." Dr. Tracy smiled. "But I think you'll have a hard time shaking Elder Fairwood. I'm surprised he left without arguing."

"I'm back." Water droplets still clung to Gavin's hair, but he had changed into his typical khakis and green polo shirt. "I brought along some clothes for you, Dot. Are you hungry? Would you like some breakfast?"

"Slow down," Dr. Tracy laughed. "She needs to take things easy today, and I want her on a bland diet. We'll let her shower and change, and I'll write out some instructions. If you will follow me."

The hot water felt good digging into her bare skin, but it couldn't wash away the memories of the men pinching her nipples and rubbing their bodies against her. Had they raped her? She didn't remember. With tentative fingers, she explored the area between her legs. Nothing seemed to be more tender than normal. Before getting dressed, she examined herself in the full length mirror. So many bruises. The one on her cheek was her reward for biting Lucius when he tried to kiss her. She had drawn blood, and had no regrets.

She slipped on the clothes Gavin brought, and examined herself again. The jeans and T-shirt would have to do, but she was missing something. "Dr. Tracy," she called out. "Where's my medicine bag?"

"Your what?" the doctor asked, opening the door slightly. Dot opened it the rest of the way.

"My medicine bag. Where is it?"

"You weren't wearing it when we found you," Gavin said. "Did they take it from you?"

"I don't recall." She studied the floor. "There's a lot I don't remember."

"We'll find the bag for you," he promised.

Dot slept too much. Gavin was unhappy she'd chosen to sleep in the guest room, but it bothered him even more that Dot seemed to sleep all the time. She wasn't awake when he went to work in the morning, and when he got home he'd find her sitting in front of the TV, dozing. Dr. Tracy warned him it might take several days for the drugs to get out of her system, but four days had gone by. She wasn't eating right either, and he thought she was losing weight. He longed to touch her, to hold her, but every time he got close she moved away. He put down the report he was reading. It was almost lunchtime. He decided to skip the scheduled meeting and head home to check on her.

In no mood to stop and chat in the hallway, he chose the back steps from his office to get outside. It was a quick stroll in the warm summer air. No matter how much sky he could see from his windows, there was nothing like being out in the fresh air. "Dot?" he called as he opened the back door.

He didn't get an answer. Was she still asleep? He needed to talk to Dr. Tracy again because this didn't feel right. He paused in the doorway while his eyes adjusted to the darkness of her room. Not only were the curtains closed, she'd thrown a blanket over the rod as well. But she was gone.

He quieted the momentary sense of fear by reaching for his cell phone. He'd kept his promise and not assigned bodyguards to her, but someone was keeping an eye on her. At his request, Elder Fenner had someone discretely following her movements. He'd know where Dot went.

Only a few wildflowers bloomed in the meadow, with the spring blossoms mostly done for the year, and it was too early for the late summer buds. Gavin plucked a few daisies before he sat beside her. Dot's eyes were closed and she sat crossed-legged with her hands resting on her knees, palms up and open. The chatter of the birds that had stilled at his entrance resumed and he examined the clouds floating overhead. One resembled a crow, he decided, except it was white.

"They won, you know," she said suddenly, startling him.

"Why do you say that?" He laid the flowers in one of her outstretched palms, and she closed her hand around them.

"Because they ruined everything I worked for. I was making progress, getting the business in the black and giving the women of the pack back what is rightfully theirs and all that's gone now. Your father won, too."

"I don't understand." He reached out and stroked her back, and, for once, she didn't pull away.

"He separated us, didn't he? Do you know how bad it hurt to lose you again, to think you were part of your father's scheme? And with the pack dissolved, what hope can I hold for the business? I might as well let it fold right now." She wiped away the tears running down her cheeks with the back of her hand. "I thought I finally had a place I could call home."

He knew how much it hurt to lose her. His heart had been ripped out the day she left with the free wolves. Twice he had lost her and he never wanted to go through that again. He wanted to show her how much he'd missed her. He wanted her to know how much he loved her. "I was hoping you'd make this your home, Dot."

She let out a deep sigh, almost a sob. "I still wasn't convinced you really loved me, even though you helped rescue me. How could I be sure you weren't picking up where your father left off? Even if the Fairwood business backed off trying to raid my customers, how could I be sure it wasn't a temporary thing? Another ploy to throw me off the scent?"

She raised her head and watched a flock of birds wing their way north. He wanted to do more than rub her back. He ached to take her into his arms and hold her close, but he didn't want to rush her. "Then I found out about the fight you had the night of the challenge. You didn't tell me that part of the story. I had to find out from Daphne. I wish I'd been there to see you in action. On the other hand, it might be a good thing I wasn't there. I might have ended up killing one of them." She absentmindedly pulled the petals off one of the daisies. Gavin kept track—she loves me, she loves me not. The last petal pulled off on a she loves me.

"I needed to figure out me before I could really understand what love is. I couldn't do that running from place to place, always checking over my shoulder. Just when I thought I finally had found love, it was snatched away from me."

His heart lurched and he reached to hug her when she laughed "By the way, tell Elder Fenner his shadows need more practice. I've known I'm being followed for two days now."

He put his arm around her and she leaned against him, straightening out her legs, and shaking out the tautness in her muscles. "I thought," she said, "Once I proved myself capable of running the Choate business, your father would see I was good enough for you, even after he took me away from you. I know he thought you should pick a different mate."

With a swift movement, he flipped her so she lay flat on the ground, trapped under his body. He raised himself so he could study her face. "He could never take me away from you. You have always been the one for me," he growled. "And I don't need or want his approval." He lowered himself so his lips were just inches from hers. "I love you, Maria Dot McKenzie Lapahie Winters, or whatever your name is this week, and I claim you as my mate. Maybe one of these days, you will say those words back to me."

"I've told you I love you," she said with crooked smile on her lips. Was she teasing him, even now? "What else do you want?"

"Say the other," he pleaded.

She raised her head and touched her lips to his. He savored their softness, but he wanted more. With each breath he drew, her sweet scent filled his nose, driving him crazy. The wolf begged to be set free. Too many days had passed since he had held her, made love to her, and what little control he had was close to breaking.

"Tell my shadow to go away, Gavin."

He laughed and raised his head slightly. "Go away, shadow."

After a rustling in the underbrush, a young man's

face peeked out. "You'll cover me with Elder Fenner, right?"

"Yes. Now leave."

"Geesh. Consider me out of here."

Gavin used his *other* hearing and listened until the footsteps faded away. "He's gone," he said. "Now tell me, please." He lowered his lips to hers and kissed her. "I'm waiting." The yellow-gold streaks in her eyes seemed to spin as he watched. His pulse pounded in his ears as he waited for her to say the words he wanted to hear.

"I claim you as my mate, Gavin Fairwood," she said as she pulled him back down.

Gavin set a cup of coffee on the nightstand and stared at her for a moment. His mate. Finally. He moved a stray lock of hair away from her face and kissed her forehead. He had a mission, and if he allowed himself anything more, he would never accomplish anything. "Wake up, beautiful, we're going on a field trip today."

Dot opened her eyes, smiled and stretched, exposing one soft breast. "I'd rather stay in bed." Her hand reached out from under the sheet and moved to his bare chest, playing with his hair and promising more. He grabbed her hand and kissed it. "Not now, Dot," he said regretfully. "Take a shower and get dressed, there's something I need to show you."

"Are you going to take a shower too? We could take one together."

"Don't make this so hard on me." If he avoided her eyes, maybe he could maintain his composure.

She glanced down. "That's not the only thing I'm making hard." Her hand followed her eyes, stroking his stomach on the way.

He shivered at her touch. "I give up," he groaned, but smiled as he pounced on her.

They were snuggling afterword, and he was trying not to go back to sleep, when she wiggled out of his grasp. "So where are you going to take me?" she asked, flipping over and kissing his nose.

"I'm not going to tell you. I don't want to ruin the surprise." He grinned as he sat up. "Go jump in the shower in the guest room, I'll shower in here, and by the time you are done I will have picked out some clothes for you to wear."

The Jeep sat outside the house, fully gassed up and ready to go. The forecast called for rain, so the mechanics had thoughtfully put the softcover roof on. Dot adjusted the skirt he'd picked for her and pulled it almost to her knees. The fit was a little loose—she'd lost some weight since the last time she'd worn it.

"A business suit?" she asked when she realized how he was dressed. She hadn't seen him in a suit since Atlanta. She shivered at the thought, and then realized that his blue shirt picked up the same tone as the blouse he had picked out for her. She hid her smile. "Where are we going?"

"You'll find out when we get there." He adjusted the mirrors and put on his seat belt, checking to make sure she'd fastened hers before he started the engine. "It's a long ride, but it's a beautiful day, so let's enjoy ourselves."

They drove on back roads that Dot wasn't familiar with, and she wondered where they were going. She didn't figure it out until they reached the edge of Choate territory.

"What are we doing here?" she asked, her voice strained.

He smiled. "A few people are waiting to see you. Your lawyer has some paperwork for you to sign."

She slid down in the seat. "He could have sent it by mail."

"He thought it important enough for you to come here."

"You tricked me, Gavin." The smirk on his face made Dot suspect she hadn't seen the end of the surprise yet.

The parking lot to the business office was almost full when they drove up, but Gavin found an empty spot right up front to pull the Jeep into. Hardly anyone was on the street, and Dot wondered if everyone had already left pack grounds to find new homes. "It's so quiet," she said as he held the front door open for her. "I don't like it this way."

As she stepped inside, the receptionist glanced up and smiled. "Welcome back, Ms. Lapahie. They're waiting for you in the executive suite." Dot noticed the four pink markings on her cheek and wondered, but before she had a chance to say anything, another woman emerged from one of the offices. She too, had pink markings.

Gavin grinned as he punched the button for the elevator. When the door opened, two employees stepped off. They smiled at Dot, murmuring "Good morning," before they hurried off. They, too, bore four pink stripes. "What's going on, Gavin?" she asked as the elevator doors closed.

His grin got bigger. "You'll find out in a minute."

When the doors opened on the third floor, the hallway was lined with people. Many she recognized as employees, other as free wolves. They all wore pink stripes on their cheeks. As she made her way down to her office, they clapped and cheered, and started a chant. "Lapahie, Lapahie, Lapahie." She was trembling and glad for Gavin's strong arm around her waist.

"I think we're supposed to go to the conference room," Gavin whispered in her ear, and steered her that direction.

"We've been waiting for you." Counselor Carlson stood in the doorway. His cheek bore four pink stripes.

TWENTY~EIGHT

Dot sank into the chair that was pushed under her.

"We thought you would be here earlier," the counselor said.

"We got delayed," Gavin explained. Dot blushed, and the counselor smiled broadly.

"Not to worry, it gave us time to hammer out a few last minute changes. Elder Lapahie, you don't know how glad I am to see you again. I was worried about you."

"Thank you, Counselor," Dot managed to say. She looked around the room. Alan was there, as well as Greg and Daphne and several other free wolves. "What's going on?"

Counselor Carlson sat beside her. "Normally when a pack dissolves," he said, "the Council takes responsibility for dividing its resources and making sure the remaining members find places to live. But this case has proved an exception to our standards."

Alan cleared his throat, and Dot noticed he was moving stiffly. "The Choate business is doing well. It has a long way to go, but it seemed a shame to sell off the assets. Especially when the shareholders want to keep it alive."

"As I have said before," the Council head grinned, "You have an inherent ability to inspire others. Most of the women of the former Choate pack decided to join the free wolves rather than align themselves with another pack. Their shares of the business go with them."

"We figure eighty percent of the shares are held by women who chose to be free wolves." Daphne said. "Including yours, of course."

"What does this all mean?"

Alan smiled. "It means the free wolves are taking over the business."

"We're going to change its focus," Greg said. "Move away from strictly software development to Web based support and training."

"Turns out a lot of us are closet geeks," Daphne grinned. "Maybe that's part of the reason we didn't fit in with our packs. We're going to set up a program at the school here for kin who want to learn advanced computer related skills." She tucked her arm around Greg and gave him a little squeeze. "There are currently very few school-aged children here, so there are lots of extra rooms in the school building we can upgrade to our meet our needs."

"There's more," Counselor Carlson said. "The Council has been watching with growing concern the number of wolves who do not seem to fit into the traditional pack structure, the whole reason the free wolf movement started in the first place. And your case made us realize how hard it is for a wolf with no support."

"We're going to be a sanctuary," Daphne interrupted. "We'll have Council protection, but won't fall under Council rules. That way any of us who want to stay here can. We will be open to any shifter who needs a place to stay, not just wolves. It will be a non-profit organization funded by the company."

"I've got a stack of paperwork to make it happen," Alan said. "Requiring the signatures of both you and Counselor Carlson, but the Council lawyers already approved the concept. Of course, I, as the company's lawyer, have already evaluated the contract and negotiated the necessary changes."

"What's the catch? There's always a catch. Are you trying to turn me into a do-nothing figurehead again?" Dot gazed at the occupants of the room suspiciously and then glanced at Gavin. As he casually leaned against the wall, he reminded her of a kid who had opened his Christmas presents and got everything on his list.

"No catch, Elder Lapahie," Counselor Carlson assured her. "You will remain CEO and the company will operate under your direction with the help of a very active board of directors."

"But I can't do this." Dot pushed away from the table. "I can't stay here. I can't be in two places at once."

"What's wrong?" asked Daphne.

"I believe Dot is concerned about a personal commitment she made," Gavin said.

"You mean you and her? We thought about that." Greg grinned. "We need to add some equipment here, but we figure she can attend meetings by the web. She'll only need to come here once or twice a week. A lot of what she needs to do can be done through email and phone calls."

"We all want you to be happy, Maria. You deserve it." Daphne gave her a hug. "Now go ahead and sign those papers and make it happen for all of us."

In a daze, Dot scrawled her signature where Alan indicated, and watched as Counselor Carlson signed in his spots for the Council. She smiled and posed for pictures until her face hurt. Just when she thought she was done, Alan stuck another piece of paper in front of her.

"What's this one?" she asked, rubbing her wrist. It hurt from all the writing she had done. She hoped the long-sleeve blouse Gavin had chosen for her covered the sores the ropes had left on her skin.

"This one has nothing to do with the Council," the lawyer said. "I prepared it at the direction of your temporary board of directors. They think the name of the business should no longer carry the name of the Choate clan. They want to convey a more positive vision for the future so they voted to change the name to Lapahie Industries. Sign here and I will be able to file the needed paperwork with the state."

Daphne started the chant. "Lapahie, Lapahie, Lapahie," and the others joined in. With tear filled eyes, Dot wrote on the line, Maria Dorothy Lapahie Winters.

Gavin beamed, watching as she hugged everyone in the room. He heard a hiss from the hallway. "Hey, Fairwood."

"What's up, Lori?" he asked, slipping out the door.

"I found it," she said. "Near the first cabin they held her at. She must have lost it when she tried to run away from them. Darnedest thing, a big old crow was standing guard over it. He made so much noise that I had to check it out, then flew away when I got there."

"You want to give it to her?"

"Naw," She handed it to him. "You do it. She'll probably start crying, and I'm no good at that kinda stuff. Besides, I don't want to be in the room with all those bigwigs. I mean, I know you're a bigwig too, but I fought with you. That makes you different."

"Thanks, I think."

She grinned and walked away.

They stayed for supper, and drove home at sunset. Dot was quiet, but Gavin figured she was worn out after the long day. The rain had finally let up, so they were driving into a rainbow. The perfect ending for a great day, he thought.

"You know we have another problem," she said suddenly.

"What would that be?"

"Isn't the pack leader's mate normally the alpha female for the pack as well? How is that going to work if I need to remain a free wolf?"

He mulled the question over in his mind as they drove down the road. "Dual citizenship," he said finally.

"Huh?"

"Like a person with parents from two different countries. You will be able to claim status as both a free wolf and a member of the Fairwood pack. I don't know if it's ever been done before, but why not?" He smiled. "Or in your case, triple citizenship, since you aren't one to play by the rules. Free wolf, Fairwood pack and Navajo." He took one hand off the steering wheel and reached into his pocket. "Speaking of which, I have something for you."

"Now what?"

"Close your eyes and hold out your hands."

"I think I've had enough surprises for one day," she complained, but closed her eyes anyway.

He slipped the bag into her outstretched hands and waited. She kept her eyes closed, and ran her fingers over the familiar texture and shape. "You'll need a new leather strap," he said. "That one's broke. Are you going to get a pink one?"

Her eyes flew open and she laughed. "If you only knew how much I used to hate pink."

Two large gray wolves stood at the top of a hill watching the orange moon rise from the horizon. A meadow ran the length of the hill, leading into an old-growth forest. The bigger one nuzzled his companion tenderly. *I have waited too long for this,* Gavin said.

"Do we hunt first?" Dot asked. A beat-up leather bag was hanging from her neck.

"Not tonight. Tonight we run." He licked one of her ears. *"And then we mate."*

She raised her head and howled. *"If you can catch me."* She sprang down the hill with him following close behind. He would let her run, and she would let him catch her, and they would be together. Then, finally, she would be home.

The End